Gift of Virginia T. Ripley
to the School of American Research
July 1980

N Of Fiction

# Throw His Saddle Out

*yours truely*

*Charlie Newcomb*

# THROW His Saddle Out

## by Charles Newcomb

WITH ILLUSTRATIONS BY ROBERT JACOBSON

NORTHLAND PRESS / FLAGSTAFF, ARIZONA

LIBRARY OF CONGRESS CATALOG NUMBER 70-132697

SBN 87358-063-0

*To a much loved lady who has been my good wife*
*for 57 years and to our three daughters, Norene,*
*Doris, and Shirley, who are also greatly loved.*

# CHAPTER 1

WESTBOUND NUMBER NINE pulled in on the siding at Pino, New Mexico, giving the right of way to the Eastbound Limited. A young man jumped down from between the engine tender and the mail car and ran across the tracks toward some stacks of lumber. The fireman, climbing down from the engine cab, picked up a couple of rocks and heaved them after the fleeing figure.

"Dang hobo, wonder how long he was on there?"

"Probably slipped on at Albuquerque," guessed the engineer. "Well, he's that pumper's problem now." He motioned toward the tall red-haired man standing in front of the pump house.

The pumper shaded his eyes against the brilliant September sun as he watched the scene. Behind him the pumps throbbed, working their usual twelve-hour shift filling the two big tanks which supplied water for the thirsty locomotives.

"No chance for that hobo to get back on Number Nine, that fireman will see to that," the pumper announced to no one in particular. A moment later the Limited showed in the distance and, as soon as she had whizzed by, Number Nine pulled out.

The pumper strolled down toward the lumber piles. "Well, what breed of hobo has been ditched in my front yard this time?" he said in a loud stage voice.

The hobo emerged from his retreat and came forward. He was young, in his teens, and was dressed in a decent looking — although dusty — dark colored suit, a blue shirt, and heavy black shoes. He wore no hat over his wavy brown hair. Narrow hips and a good set of shoulders indicated a future strong build. His brown eyes looked straight and unashamed at the pumper.

"Tough luck, kid, they're taking siding here, otherwise you could have ridden right to town. Where're you heading for?"

"Anywhere, just so it's west," the boy answered, as he tried to dust himself off.

"Well," the pumper said, "this is the West — Southwest at least. See the Indians," and he pointed to three Navajos riding by.

"Yeah, I saw Indians in Albuquerque," the boy said.

"Sure, but those were likely housebroke, these are the genuine, long hair and no English spoken. Well, come over to the pump house if you want to wash up. I'd kinda like to see what you look like. What you got in the package, grub?"

"Underwear and socks," the boy answered, as he took the paper-wrapped bundle from under his arm.

"You're better outfitted than most of our visitors, I'll say that, and I've entertained a heap of travelers since I first landed here — 1902, that was. Four years ago! My, my, time sure flies. Well, come along."

The pump house had a hard, clean-swept dirt floor and the glistening, fast-moving machinery showed that the pumper was a man who loved his work and his machines.

2

"Now, young fellow, me lad, let's us sit down and do a spell of talking, after which you can help yourself to a good hot bath. My name's Mike Branagan, what's yours?"

"Nick Norton."

"Where're you from?" Mike asked.

"Wisconsin."

"How old are you?"

"Seventeen."

"Kinda young to be riding the blind baggage, aren't you? Get too tough for the old man so he had to kick you out?"

"My father and I got along all right. It was my stepmother who finally got my goat," Nick told him.

"So you think it's better to be a hobo, eh?"

"No, I don't, and I'm not a hobo and I'm not going to be one either. I'm going to find a job and I'm going to keep it too. But where am I now? What's the name of this siding and where did all the lumber come from? I don't see many trees around here."

"Well, sir," said Mike with a grin, "you are now in Pino, a thriving little community inventorying a Swede, a Dutchman, a German, five Americans, numerous Long Hairs and a fair quantity, but poor quality Mexican teamsters. There's an Indian trading store over there beyond that long sheet-iron shed which is a planing mill and ten miles back this way in the mountains is a small sawmill, which accounts for the planing mill and the lumber piles."

"Maybe I could find a job around here," Nick said hopefully.

"Could be," agreed Mike. "Suppose you're broke?"

"Wrong suppose," Nick told him. "I've two dollars and forty cents in my pocket."

"Not bad, but not good," said Mike, "but let's go fill that wash tub. Fill her with cold water first and then I'll turn steam into it until you say when. There's soap on that box and I'll go to my humble shack and rustle you

3

up a towel. Don't forget your face, maybe back of your ears too," Mike grinned as he left.

He soon returned with a towel and a whisk broom. "Thought you might like to brush your suit," he said.

When Nick finished and came out, Mike was sitting on a bench in the shade. "Well, well," Mike exclaimed, "am I surprised. Quite a likely looking young snapper. And look at the nose, somewhat of an Irish tilt to it, and freckles and everything. My, my, you don't look like a hobo now."

"I never was," stated Nick. "I said I was coming west and I did. That's all."

"Well, I'll tell you what we'll do," Mike said. "I'll take on this job-getting for you. Did you ever work in a store? Not that it matters much."

"I worked in a grocery store last summer."

"Then you'd at least know what size sack to use for three pounds of sugar. I'm not going to ask if you're honest because I believe I know an honest face when I see one."

"Thank you," Nick replied, "the only stealing I've ever done was to steal a ride."

"I shouldn't call that really stealing," Mike assured him. "The trains were coming this way anyhow and I guess your extra weight didn't cause them much expense. Now you sit down here and take it easy for a little while and when I come back I might have some good news for you."

Nick felt that he had made a friend and how well he already liked this tall lean-waisted man with the twinkling blue eyes and the heavy moustache. Maybe all Westerners were helpful and friendly. Perhaps it was a good thing Number Nine had taken siding and he had had to get off. And if he did get a job here, then he would write his father so he would know where he was and not worry.

In a half hour Mike came back. Nick got up and walked over to meet him. Mike had a couple of paper bags under his arm.

4

"Well, my young buck, you've got a job, I think. At least, we're going over to the store tonight and Mr. Olson will talk to you. I knew several days ago they were going to hire another clerk as soon as they could find one. The bookkeeper has been having to help trade, which forces him to work nights on the books, and he isn't at all happy about that. I think we'll land the job all right."

"I sure do thank you, Mr. Branagan," Nick said.

"Mike's the name, so no more of that 'Mister' stuff. We're friends, you know. Now there's one thing more I'd like to know — when did you eat last?"

"This morning," Nick answered, "but I'm getting used to not eating very regular."

"Just as I thought, so here we have some bread, butter, bacon and eggs. Let's go, I'm kinda hungry myself," and Mike headed for his house.

He quickly made a fire in the little stove and soon the bacon was done and then the eggs. "I generally eat at the cook shack with the rest of the bunch," Mike told Nick, "but not always. Say, I left out one of the population, the cook. He's an Irishman too. You'll like him, he's been cooking for forty years and I'm still betting he'll learn how to cook before he dies."

Nick laughed, "Pretty bad, huh?"

"Oh, there's always plenty of it," Mike assured him. "Let's wash these eggy dishes up and get them out of the way, so they'll be ready for the next time."

Then they went out and sat on the bench until seven when Mike went and shut off the pump. "Now we'll go over to the store and meet the bunch," he announced.

The store was a stone building, forty feet wide by eighty feet long. The large double doors were open and Nick followed his new friend in. The store was well lighted by an acetylene lighting system. There were four or five men sitting on the counter. Later on Nick would know by this that the boss was away. He allowed no counter sitting.

He was introduced to these men: first, the bookkeeper; then, the butcher, a middle-aged man with a red beard; the station agent, the clerk, and the section foreman. They all had beards or big moustaches, except Roy, the clerk, who didn't look much older than Nick, not more than two or three years older, Nick was sure.

The trading store sure looked different from any store Nick had ever seen. Seemed to him they had everything a person could think of. The showcases and shelves were full and from the ceiling hung a great assortment of frying pans, pots, kettles, ropes, bridles, saddles, lanterns, and hardware.

Nick stood listening and answering a few questions until Roy came over and said in a low voice, "Guess you're going to be my side-kick, at least I hope so, as I can sure use some help around here. Let's go in the office and see Mr. Olson. Mike has told him about you."

In front of the store on the east side was the post office, back of this a door led into the office. Roy introduced Nick to Mr. Olson, a very large, good-natured Swede. He asked Nick a number of questions, pausing occasionally to tell some funny story about the Indians, then finally said to Roy, "I seem to feel satisfied with this young man so, as you are the one who will have to teach him this business, we'll leave it up to you."

Nick already knew he liked Roy and hoped Roy felt the same toward him, so he was not greatly surprised when Roy said, "I'll sure take a chance on him and I'll do my best to make a Trader of him."

"Fine," said Mr. Olson, then to Nick, "Your salary will be seventy-five dollars a month with room and board. You'll get more when you earn it."

"Thank you, Mr. Olson," stammered Nick. Seventy-five dollars a month clear! My gosh, he thought, back home twenty-five with room and board would have been big wages for a boy.

6

Out in the store again Nick asked where all the Indians were. Roy told him they generally left before night — good Navajos should be home before dark, any out at night were quite likely to be up to some mischief — but that he would see plenty of them in the morning. He locked the big front door of the store and then showed Nick the dry goods room. Here, stacked high on long tables, were piles of manta, calico, gingham, sateen and velvet. The trading business had been good ever since the store had opened in 1900 and merchandise was bought in large quantities.

Roy and Nick were to room together so Roy took him back to show him where the room was. Running the full width of the store and about twelve feet across was a room with a large fireplace at one end. On two sides of this room were great piles of Navajo rugs. As Nick had never seen a Navajo rug he had to ask what they were. He was surprised at the number and wondered where they got so many and if they ever sold any. Adjoining this room were two large bedooms, one of which he was to share with Roy.

Roy asked Nick if he played pitch. Nick told him he did — but he soon found out that he didn't. Seems they had a big pitch game two or three nights a week. They played high, low, jick, jack, and the game. Ladies and children were barred from the room. Nick soon caught on. If he had two points in his hand, he'd bid at least four on them. It was a nice way to get acquainted and when they quit soon after eleven, Nick was calling the other players by their first names.

The next morning after sweeping the store, Nick was shown where the canned goods were kept so he could bring them in and fill the shelves. The Boss demanded that the shelves be kept filled.

Before long Navajos began drifting in. The men were dressed in overalls and shirts, and some of them wore shoes. No hats, just a fancy cotton or silk handkerchief tied around their heads, after being folded into a band with a point sticking up in front. Roy said they probably all had good hats but did not wear them every day. Nick noticed several men who had, what looked to him, pretty swell looking silver buckles on their belts. The men also wore turquoise in their ears, some just rough pieces tied through with string and some rimmed with silver.

The women had velvet shirts and calico skirts. They all seemed to wear moccasins attached to buckskin leggings which reached to their knees, protection against rattle-snakes. Most of them, when they found Nick could not understand them, would wait to trade with Roy. But one old lady was in a hurry. She wanted a sack of salt. She kept repeating it, raising her voice higher each time she told him. If the salt had been in sight so she could have pointed it out to him, Nick would have made his first sale unaided. Roy had to tell him what she wanted and Nick gave it to her. She put down a small, tinny looking chip, which he refused, telling her to come across with a dime. Roy came to the rescue again and told him it was all right. It was a ten-cent piece and he had forgotten to tell him they used *seco* — tin money with the store name stamped on it — and showed him a money drawer with lots of it.

Roy then explained that all trading stores off the Reservation had their own trade money. On the Reservation, Traders were supposed to pay the Indians cash for their wares, but he never knew of many who did. This trade money enabled the Traders to pay the Indians more for their produce as they had to trade it out with the store that issued it. This was better for the Traders, as Nick could see later on when he had learned the cost mark (the code mark the store used which showed what each article cost) and helped mark goods for sale before putting them out on the shelves. It was better for the Indians too.

Nick's second sale that morning was a bottle of furniture polish. A good-natured Navajo man pointed to it, indicating very plainly that was what he wanted. As the price was clearly marked, Nick sold it to him. Later on he asked Roy if the Navajos bought much furniture polish. Roy said he had never known them, nor anyone else, to ever buy any. The furniture polish had arrived by mistake in a shipment of goods from St. Louis. Nick then told him he had sold a bottle to a Navajo. Roy was of the opinion that the Navajo had bought it for cough syrup as that was about the only medicine they ever bought.

"It might poison him," Nick said.

"No danger, I doubt if you could poison a Navvy," Roy told him.

The Navajo, who worked in the lumber yard, came in the next day, so Nick had Roy ask him if the furniture polish had helped him. He said yes, very good medicine, but very strong, so he had only taken two drinks of it, which had completely stopped the cough.

"Here's a word for you, Nick — *Chischilly*. That's 'curly hair,' and also that's you. I was sure that was going to be your name."

"What do they call you?" Nick asked.

"They just call me Loy. Not many of them can make the *R* or *P* sound. Well, I must get busy. You can dump a sack of sugar in the bin."

"Do you think I can ever learn Navajo?" Nick asked Roy as they were walking up to the cook shack at noon. This was about two hundred yards from the store.

"Sure you can," Roy assured him. "Bet you know one word already — salt."

"I think so, because that old woman kept repeating *'ashen, ashen.'* "

"All right," Roy said, "now we'll add sweet to it and you'll know their word for sugar. *Ashen-la-kon*, salt sweet. You'll learn fast enough. I'll write out a good list tonight for you to study and when the Navvies get acquainted and know you're going to be here right along, they'll sure help you and you'll learn to speak it correctly too."

9

The real Boss came down from the sawmill the next day after Nick started to work. Nick liked him right away. He was a slightly heavy-set man of medium height. He wore a light-colored Stetson hat with a low crown and a three-inch brim. He had thick-lensed glasses, a clear complexion and, of course, a good-sized black moustache. Roy said he smoked cigars all the time and, when he said 'all the time,' that's just what he meant. When he awoke in the morning, before starting to dress, he lit a cigar. He laid his cigar down while eating and as soon as he finished, he lit it again. He was a very nervous man, perhaps from so much smoking, and one seldom saw him sit still unless he was reading. He had been educated in Germany and spoke seven languages fluently. He allowed no loafing in the store when he was there, neither Indians nor clerks.

When an Indian came in, he would ask him what he wanted and, if the Indian didn't want anything, the Boss would tell him to loaf outside as he didn't have time to watch him. Occasionally, an Indian from some other locality, where the store rules were not so strict, would come in and climb up on the counter to rest. If the Boss was not there, no one paid any attention to him; but, if the Boss was there, everyone would pretend to be too busy to notice this infraction of rules. The Boss was never too busy to notice. He would stroll down back of the counter until he was behind the unsuspecting Indian. Then, with a mighty push, he would land him in the middle of the floor and pleasantly explain that the counters were put there to sell goods on and not for seats or beds.

Roy said the Boss had the best, but meanest, pair of horses he ever helped hitch to a buckboard. It always took two men to harness them, and three, if they hadn't been driven for a week. They were chunky, wild-eyed broncos of about nine hundred pounds each. The front end of the bay was the most dangerous because, if he could help it, he didn't allow anyone to touch his ears. Somebody had evidently mistreated those ears when they were trying to tame him and he certainly hadn't forgotten it. It generally took two good men about five minutes to get a bridle on him. What took time with the sorrel was getting the crouper under his tail. This was a cautious and dangerous operation.

When they were harnessed and hitched to the buckboard, the Boss would get in and take the lines. One man would stand in front with a grip on each bridle while the other ran and swung open the twelve-foot gate. The man at their heads would then jump to one side and away they would go on a high lope, which they would maintain for the first two or three miles. Roy couldn't see what anyone wanted with mean horses like they were except he knew the Boss wanted speed.

Nick had a good memory and by the time he had been there a week he was surprised and pleased at the jumble of Navajo words he knew.

"You're going to learn fast," Roy told him. "You pick it up as easy as a Mormon. Learning any Mex?"

"Yeah, but that's easy compared to Navajo," Nick answered. The section crew was from Mexico and none of them spoke English. While most of the Mexican lumber freighters could speak some English, most of their wives could not, so it was necessary for Nick to learn Spanish also.

While they were talking, a Navajo woman came up to the counter and pulled out a blanket from under her shawl. Roy took it, weighed it, and spread it on the counter. Then he reached back to the drawer and threw down seven dollars — *seco*. Nick could see plain enough that she didn't want this, although he couldn't understand the fast chatter she turned loose on Roy. When she wound up Nick asked what it was all about.

"She says she wants cash this time," explained Roy, "and I've told her we don't want the blanket bad enough to give her money."

11

Just then her husband, Red Shirt, came up and gave Roy quite a talk.

"What does he say?" Nick asked again.

"He says they must have the cash because lately their daughter has been having dreams about a bear and, as their good friend — meaning me — knows, this is very bad. Yesterday they sent for a Medicine Man to come and remove the evil spirit that has been causing the trouble. He says the Medicine Man has done this. After chanting all night, along about sunrise he sucked a little stone bear from the back of the girl's neck. And for this valuable service, the Medicine Man wants four silver dollars, no *seco*. I've told him to give the Medicine Man *seco* and let him come to the store and buy goods to take home to his family. He claims this has been suggested to the Medicine Man; no go, he wants silver. I'll ask Mr. Olson if he cares to do it."

Roy came back a minute later saying Mr. Olson said to go ahead and give it to him. That night about eight o'clock a very excited Navajo came pounding at the door and, when Roy let him in, he said there had been a big fight at Red Shirt's hogan (home) and that they were all drunk and Red Shirt had been hit on the head with an axe and his brains were sticking out. Roy asked him if he saw the fight, because Navajos exaggerated a great deal. He said he didn't, although his sister-in-law did and she came over and told him to come get help.

"Want to go over, Nick?" Roy asked. "It's not far, less than a mile."

"Sure," Nick said, "a walk will do us good."

When they arrived they found things not quite as bad as reported. Red Shirt's father-in-law had missed with the axe, but hadn't with a good-sized rock that he had whammed on the side of Red Shirt's head, cutting quite a gash which was still bleeding freely. The father-in-law wasn't in sight when Roy and Nick arrived. He had staggered off somewhere. The wallop on the head had likely sobered Red Shirt some as he didn't seem too drunk.

Red Shirt then admitted there had been no Medicine Man and he had only been joking about that, but there had been a Mexican along with some very strong whiskey. He had paid the four silver dollars for that and then invited his father-in-law to come help him drink it. But the father-in-law, when drinking, proved to be a very disagreeable person whose chief desire was to knock someone in the head with an axe or a rock.

"Let's go back," Roy said, after he had told Nick what Red Shirt had said. "Nothing for us to do. They know how to take care of a cracked skull better than you or I do anway."

The next afternoon Roy, who was standing outdoors in front of the store, yelled, "Here they come again!"

Nick ran to the door to see what was coming. Quite a sight it was too — a big three-seated carryall with a top. This was filled with officers from the Fort and pulled by four big-eared mules. The Fort was twelve miles from the store. The driver, a buck private, pulled the mules to a quick stop, amid a great cloud of dust, in front of the store.

"Come on inside," Roy said, "and we'll tell Mr. Olson he has company. Those swell-headed lieutenants wouldn't speak to us common trash, anyway."

But one of them did. He came striding in and said in a commanding voice to Roy, "Boy, get out there and open the corral gate so we can put the mules inside."

"You aren't talking to any of your buck privates now, Lieutenant, and can't you see I'm busy," Roy told him.

Mr. Olson and the other officers were in the store by now and, having heard the conversation, Mr. Olson said, "Nick, please skip and open the corral gate so the driver can put the mules away."

When Nick came back Roy said, "All that lieutenant had to do was put that little word 'please' in his request, but I guess 'please' isn't in the *Officers' Manual*. Anyway, I don't like lieutenants. Now that old colonel is a fine man. He'll speak to common scrubs like us and he's interested in Indian craft and wants to see what we have new and extra nice that the Navvies have brought in. He'll include us too when he's mixing drinks, which is a darn sight more than any of the lieutenants will do. Do you drink?"

"My father, on certain occasions, has given me drinks, so I know what whiskey is," Nick said.

"I like a drink or two at times," Roy said, "although I don't believe in too many. Well, we won't get much sleep tonight because they're a loud bunch and will play cards and drink two-thirds of the night and the blanket room is darned close to ours."

Soon Navajos began to drift in. They had seen the big *sin-a-bas* (wagon) and came over to see what the *selah* (soldiers) were doing there.

Later on, Roy came to Nick and said, "See those two girls over in the corner?"

Nick looked over to where the two girls stood. He knew them. Mr. Olson had thought them cute and made a fuss over them. He had told one he was going to call her Gracie and had her repeat it after him, but she had spoken it "Glacie" so he told her to let it go at that. She could be Glacie and her sister, Gracie.

Traders generally named some of their customers because the majority of them refused to tell their names, thinking it brought them bad luck.

Roy went on, "Their bucks have gone back to the saw-mill, won't be home until tomorrow so the girls are at, what you might call, liberty. It's all fixed for us to visit them tonight; that is, if you want to go. Me, I'm going anway. They're the nicest, prettiest, cleanest girls around here and if you ask me, we're darn lucky."

Nick thought a moment before answering. His experience with girls was very limited and he didn't know how

14

far this might go. But why not? He was on his own and could do as he pleased, so why not have some fun. He said, "Sure, I'll go. Which one is mine?"

"To show you how I feel about those two kids, you can have your choice," Roy answered.

"I'll take Glacie then," Nick told him. "I feel I'm a little better acquainted with her." Glacie was eighteen, a year younger than her sister, and Nick thought her the cutest little trick ever.

"Suits me just right," laughed Roy. "You fix up a good sack of candy and slip it to her; then she'll know. As I said, we wouldn't get much sleep anyway. When we do come back, maybe we'll be plenty sleepy."

Just then Mr. Olson came from the office and spoke to Nick. "Will you please slip over to the cook shack and tell Slick there'll be five extra for supper and breakfast. That'll burn him down."

"Sure I will and sure it will," Nick said with a big grin. He knew Slick plenty well by now, liked the little shriveled-up Irishman too. Hard to tell how old he was, anywhere from fifty to sixty-five would be Nick's guess. Slick was a fairly good common cook. One thing you could be sure of and that was that any piece of meat he cooked was tender. Nick knew the answer to that though, because one day the butcher had cut off a great chunk of chuck and shoulder and sent it over with Nick. Slick took one look at it, snorted like a surprised bronc, and said, "You lug that hunk of boloney meat right back to that half-baked Dutchman. He knows I haven't any dog. Also tell him if he can't cut me meat from the hindquarter, there'll be sowbelly for supper. Damn a lunk-headed Dutchman anyway."

Now as Nick stepped into the little kitchen, he found Slick laboring over two canned peach pies.

"Bad news, Slick," announced Nick, "five extra for supper." He waited for the explosion.

15

"Well, now, isn't that just ducky?" roared Slick. "Five extra for supper, he says. Officers, I'll bet, and each and every one of them can eat more than a Norwegian lumberjack, and here I have the roast, which is enough for us, but which would look like a nickel's worth of dog meat by the time it passed the fourth cockeyed officer; and besides it's after four and how in the hell does Olson think I can roast another chunk of beef and have it done by six in that four-dollar tin stove? Have to make another pie too," he went on. "Well, go out and bring that meat in and and I'll cut some steaks. I can get them cooked and likely I'll give this juicy roast to some Navvy. Why can't those bastards stay at the Fort where they belong?"

Nick brought the meat in and put it on the table; then stood and watched Slick put pie crust lids on the pies and tamp down the edges. Slick was good on the common food and served a nice variety, but when it came to desserts, he sure sank to the bottom. Generally, he served canned fruit for dessert, but about twice a week he made pies. Pies and a gooey rice pudding were his limit. The pies were bad, but everyone ate them, regardless, because it was known by all that if anyone insulted him, or made him mad by not eating thereof, that very night he'd slip out, catch a freight to town, get drunk, and stay drunk until the Boss went and brought him back. The Boss was the only one who could refuse pie, but he didn't eat there much anyway as he stayed up at the sawmill most of the time. The Boss had sized the situation up correctly the first time Slick served pie. He had firmly stated that he never ate pie. The pies did look suspicious. The crust had a firm flint-like appearance with great smoothness and lustre. If he had finished them off with varnish, they couldn't have had a finer glaze. Over this high polish was sprinkled a liberal amount of granulated sugar, which must have been applied after he set the pies on the table, for, at the slightest movement of the pies, sugar would shoot around like bird-shot on a glass counter. At seven, twelve, and six Slick put the grub on the table, and if you wanted to enjoy it while it was hot, you'd better be there.

When Nick got back to the store, Roy said, "I suppose Slick was pleased and happy with the news you brought him."

"From what he said, I judged he doesn't care too much for officers," Nick laughed, "but they'll get supper all right."

"Sure they will, and Slick will be pleased, too, because the colonel never fails to tell him what a swell meal he served. Also, the colonel will manage to slip him a drink."

After supper Besher, the butcher, and Mike drifted in. Mike always seemed very pleased with his part in getting Nick a good job and that he was doing so well and liked it and was liked by all. Nick had not forgotten either and had spent many pleasant evenings in Mike's little shack. Also every Sunday morning, he went to the pump house for a good scrub in Mike's big tub.

"Guess you can talk to the Long Hairs fairly well by now, can't you?" Mike asked. He didn't like Navvies and always called them "Long Hairs" or "Dirty Necks."

"Oh, I'm learning," Nick told him.

"He sure is," Roy said. "He certainly learns fast."

"Too much for me," admitted Besher. "I've been here two years and I don't know a dozen words. The Navvies are good about helping me though, except when too many of them get to crowding around when I'm slitting open a beef. They understand me all right when I start swinging that bloody knife and yell, 'Get the hell out of here!' They can hardly wait to get to the nice warm insides."

"Made me fairly sick the first time I saw those naked kids milling around with a loop of intestines around their necks, all greedily chawing on an end," Mike said. "Anyhow there is quite a bit of fat on them and that's what those poor little devils need."

"They sure don't leave much for the coyotes," laughed Besher.

"Everyone to their taste," Roy said.

The Boss had the contract to supply beef to the soldiers at the Fort, so three times a week there was butchering — and full Navajo bellies. Sometimes cattle didn't arrive when they should, so Besher, who was a resourceful man, would mount his horse and by night he'd be back with cattle, never bothering to notice whose brand was on them. Little extra profit for him. He and the Boss were partners on the deal, although Roy said the Boss knew nothing about that part of it as he wouldn't stand for any crooked business.

About nine Mike and Besher left, so Nick locked the doors. "Thought they'd never go," said Roy. "Now, let's us go; the girls will think we aren't coming."

It was about a mile to the two hogans where the girls lived. When they arrived, there was much embarrassment and giggling from the girls and laughing and joking from the boys.

"What if your husbands should come in now?" Roy asked.

"We should send them away," Gracie answered.

"Would they go?"

"They would for two dollars each, I think."

"Well, I hope they don't come," he said, "because the way I feel now I just know it would cost me two dollars."

"How do you feel now?" Glacie asked, and they all laughed heartily. She went on, "Maybe my Chischilly feels the same way, so now I am going to my hogan."

Nick could not understand all that had been said, but he did know the meaning of her last words. He got up and immediately followed her.

"She'll bite you," Gracie warned Nick.

"Let her bite," Nick said, as he pushed the door open and stepped out.

18

Time must have passed pleasantly and fast because it was almost two when Roy stepped out of Gracie's hogan and called to Nick, "Don't you think we should be going now? We ought to catch a little sleep."

"Just a minute and I'll be out," he answered.

"Have a good time?" Roy asked when Nick appeared.

"Best time I've ever had in my life," Nick answered. "She's the nicest and cutest little thing, and it's only her face and hands that are brown. The rest of her skin is about as white as ours. She taught me a lot of Navajo too."

"Probably all bad," laughed Roy, "I've heard that sleeping dictionaries are a great help."

"Too bad she's married to a Navajo, she's too nice for that."

"Whoa now, kid," said Roy seriously, "none of that chatter. Don't you ever get any funny notions in your bean about getting serious with Navajo girls. Do you know what a white man who marries an Indian woman is called? 'Squaw Man.' And that's not a pretty name. I've been around the Navvies quite a while and I've seen some pretty good-looking Navajo women married to white men, but you ought to see them after six or seven years of three hearty meals a day — mostly wobbly fat, and good looks absolutely gone. It's fair enough to spend a pleasant evening like we did tonight — and we'll do it again without a doubt — but it all ends when we leave the hogan and if it don't I'll punch your nose for you."

"I understand, and I don't want my nose punched," laughed Nick. "I guess I was so dazed when I left her, I didn't know what I was saying. My head is clear now."

"Good," Roy said, "I thought you were a sensible kid."

# CHAPTER 2

WINTER HAD PASSED, as well as the windy spring, and June, with its lovely, calm, sunny days had come. Nick could hardly realize he had been studying and striving to learn an outlandish language for eight months. But he was succeeding, he knew, because now Mr. Olson frequently called him into the office to interpret when he was filling out a claim for some Navajo whose pony had been hit by a train. Of course, Mr. Olson knew a smattering of Navajo, but not enough to get a detailed account and description of the deceased pony. The right-of-way wasn't fenced and lots of ponies wandered onto the tracks while others, without a doubt, were driven on. The dumb brutes would stand there and watch the train come, with the whistle screeching. When it was almost on them, they would make an effort to get off, but they were generally a bit tardy. It was mostly the worthless broomtails that were killed, but if one heard the Navajo's description of the slain pony, one must believe it to have been one of the fanciest riding horses in the territory. Some turned out to be race horses and very valuable. If it happened to be a woman whose horse had been killed, so much the worse for Mr. Olson. While trying to get the brand and description, he would listen to a woman who could hardly think about this fine dead and mangled pony — that she probably had not laid eyes on for six months — without bursting into tears and heavy sobs.

Mr. Olson, through Roy or Nick, would be informed that the dead pony had been one of the two she used to pull the wagon, also for plowing. Now what could she do with only one live pony left and how could she bring the wool to the store when one fine pony was dead? And Ram's Neck — as Mr. Olson was named by the Navajos on account of his thick, heavy neck — must know that a pony one could hitch to a wagon was worth much more than just a riding pony, although this dead pony could be ridden too and was very strong and could take one to the houses of the *Natgoho* (Lagunas) in a single day and the dead pony had been very gentle too and Mr. Olson must know this also, as he had surely seen her little boy ride him to the store.

So, after this had all been dished out to Mr. Olson, he would inform her that eight dollars was about the top price the railroad people would pay for a dead Navajo pony, that she better get a move on and give him the description and brand, or he wouldn't make out the paper and then all she would get out of it would be the horsemeat.

Once a day, at a little after five, someone had to take the mail pouch down the tracks a couple of hundred yards and hang it on the mail crane. The mail clerk on Number Three, the California Limited, would hook this pouch and throw another off. The leather pouches were fastened top and bottom to the crane arms by hooks. These hooks were supposed to let go when the mail car hook struck the pouch, but sometimes things did not work out quite right and that iron hook, traveling at eighty miles an hour, would cut the pouch in two. The contents would drop beside the track and immediately be picked up by the suction from the train. Then all hands, including Navajos, would search the right-of-way for letters.

Roy took the mail the day Number Three hit the Indian's team. An old Zuñi man and his wife attempted to drive across the tracks just below the hay house. They had three heavy sacks of wool in the wagon and it was about all the two ponies could pull. The old man whipped them up and got them over the side track, but the main line was ballasted higher, a much harder pull. The ponies were up on the main line track and stopped there with the wagon between it and the side track. The old man was using the whip and did not see the train until it was about two hundred yards from him. Probably he and his wife were too frightened to move, because they didn't. The engine smashed both horses and took the harness, neck yoke, and wagon tongue along with it leaving the old man sitting there with a short piece of rein in each hand. The old couple were simply paralyzed and finally had to be helped from the wagon seat. The train did not stop; engineers were used to hitting horses and cows.

*     *     *

One afternoon when Nick was in the back of the store, Roy called to him. Nick went over to where he and a Reservation Navajo stood talking.

"This fellow has just told me a queer yarn," Roy said. "An eight-year-old Navajo girl, who herded her folks' small flock of goats and sheep, was killed four days ago. She herded on a gentle old pony and had a small dog that always went with her. Four days ago in the late afternoon, the pony came back to the hogan, with the little dog — dead — dangling by a short length of rope from the saddle horn and dragging along the ground behind the pony, was the strangled body of the little girl. He says the parents

22

thought it was murder and the father started right out to backtrack the pony and trail the murderer. He came to the place where the pony had started to run, dragging the girl. Backtracking farther, he saw tracks where the girl had gotten down from the saddle and evidently tied the rope around the dog's neck, which the dog didn't like as the father could see by the dog's tracks that he had been pulling back. Then, she had evidently decided, as the dog didn't like his part, she'd play being the dog, so she dismounted, tied one end of the rope around her neck, the other to the saddle horn and, with the short length of rope tied around the dog's neck, sat him in the saddle with his rope also tied to the saddle horn. They had only gone a short distance when the dog must have slipped from the saddle, the rope tightening and choking him. His frantic scratching had hurt and frightened the pony so he had run away, dragging and choking the little girl to death."

"Well, I'll be darned," exclaimed Nick. "Navvies are real trackers though, aren't they?"

"They read tracks like we read books," Roy answered, as he handed the Navajo a sack of Bull Durham. Roy wasn't being free with store property; he and Nick probably gave away as much tobacco as they sold, but it was an order from the Boss. Every Navajo kid who came into the store got a stick of candy. Navajo parents are very fond of their children and the Boss said he figured if the Trader remembered the children, the parents would remember the Trader. Looked like he was right because the store did a big business. A can of pears, with plenty of unsalted crackers — Navajos don't care for the salted ones — generally went with a blanket purchase. Quite a number of Zuñi Indians brought their wool to the store. When any of them came they were given a big feed while Mr. Olson phoned to the sawmill for the Boss, as he was the only one connected with the store who spoke Zuñi. The telephone line was just a private one from the store to the sawmill, strung mostly on trees, and at times things happened to it. If the line happened to be down, Mr. Olson would dispatch a Navajo with a note.

The Zuñis didn't seem to Nick to be as jolly a tribe as the Navajos. A half-dozen Navajo women, seated comfortably on the floor of the store, would outdo, for gossip and belly laughs, any sewing circle in the country, although if a strange white person entered, they'd close up like a zipper.

"Fifty watermelons over in the freight house," announced Mr. Olson one morning early in June. "Any Navvies around to bring them over?'

"Oh, I suppose so," Roy answered, "but if not, Nick and I'll get them over."

Nick went out to see if he could find anyone. Seeing two young bucks lying against the warehouse sunning themselves, he hollered for them to come over. Even before Nick opened the freight house door, one Navajo said, "I smell watermelon."

"You knew they were in here," Nick told him.

"No," Notah, the other boy, said, "he didn't know. Neither did I, but I could smell them plainly too."

"Well, I can't," Nick said as he opened the door, "but anyway carry them to the store." It wouldn't take long as the boys took a melon under each arm.

"I could eat a whole one right now," Notah said after some seven or eight trips had been made.

"You mean by yourself?" Nick asked.

"By myself," stated Notah firmly.

"All right, I'd like to see you do it," Nick told him. "I'll buy the melon and if you eat it, fine, but if you don't, you'll have to come work for a day unloading oats or hay."

Notah readily agreed to this so they went on carrying melons. On the last trip Nick went with them. He told Roy about the deal.

"Well, sport," laughed Roy, "you're stuck before he cuts the melon."

"They're big melons," Nick said.

"Sure," agreed Roy, "but pick it out, give him a knife, and watch it go down the hatch."

"I'll let Notah select the melon, maybe he'll take a small one which won't cost me so much."

But he lost on that too, because Notah walked straight to the largest in the bunch. In less than fifteen minutes all that was left of the melon was a quantity of seeds and some strips of very thin rind.

"Want to buy him another?" grinned Roy.

"Could he eat another?" asked Nick.

"Oh, maybe a small one," Roy answered. "It's a good idea not to bet on how much a Navvy can eat or on how little he can get along on. They aren't fussy either about what they eat, as you know, and I guess you couldn't poison one of them. I never heard of any dying of poison. How about canned tomatoes and such that say on the can to empty contents as soon as opened? If a Navvy has something left in a can that he can't eat — which probably isn't very often — it sits right there in the can until the next meal and no harm done as far as I ever knew."

"About like a pig — hard to poison a pig," Nick said. "Guess the Indians do have upset stomachs though, once in a while, because they do buy some sardines."

The Navajos didn't eat fish except at certain times when they felt sick; then they would buy a small flat can of sardines and go over by the hay barn with the opened can. Nick had been in the hay house doorway one afternoon and had watched Old Short Leg try to take his medicine. First there was a great hawking and spitting and clearing of throat; then Short Leg selected an oily fish with his dirty forefinger and thumb and, with closed eyes and a shudder, plopped it into his mouth. He shuddered like a drunkard with his first drink of the morning. This passed

25

and he reached for another and got it down with the same effect as the first one. The third one was barely down when up came the three little fishes with a lot of other stuff right behind them. Nick ducked back. He had seen enough. Sardines were good medicine.

"No, I guess they're tough," Roy said, "and look at the water they drink. Water is water to a Navajo. He isn't fussy where he gets it or where he keeps it. He'll drink out of a cow track. He drinks it hot in summer and cold in winter. If he has a wagon, he'll get hold of a barrel — any kind will do. An oil barrel is all right, because in a year or two it will begin to lose the oil flavor. It sets out in the sun and the water is hot but who cares, it's wet. If we had ice here, we sure wouldn't waste it cooling soda pop for them. They like it better warm the way they're used to it. Great people, aren't they, Nick?"

"I like most of them," Nick answered, "although most of the old ones are pretty dirty."

"But the dirty ones don't stink as bad as you'd expect, do they?"

"Because they don't wear underwear and all their velvet shirts have big air holes under the arms," Nick answered.

"Must be it, air gets at all of their body," agreed Roy. "The younger ones buy plenty of soap and, of course, use plenty of soapweed on their hair. Yucca root is sure fine for hair. Doesn't Glacie's hair always smell nice?"

"Hair and all the rest of her," Nick answered, "but those two sisters are always neat and clean. They're exceptions though, you've got to admit."

"You know what I'd like to do, Nick?" Roy said, "I'd like to see those two girls dressed up in American clothes. I'll bet they'd look darned cute. They've sure got the forms — right now — and the features. Oh, well."

"Too bad they're married, especially to men twice their ages," Nick said, "but it's none of my business. Are they exempt from having babies?"

"The Navajos know of a certain herb and those two little devils seem to have a plentiful supply on hand," Roy answered with a grin.

"Well, anyway," said Nick, "let's go rabbit hunting tomorrow. Tomorrow is Sunday, isn't it?"

"That's right. Half the time I don't know what day it is. You mean get ponies and go with the Indians or go with rifles?"

"Rifles, I like that better," answered Nick.

The country around was thick with sage and cottontail, and jack rabbits were very plentiful. Nick and Roy would take 30:30 rifles from the store and go for jack rabbits. They were big fellows and made a nice target, although they generally, when scared up, ran quite a distance before they stopped and sat up. The Navajo young men went hunting almost every Sunday but they hunted in a different way. They rode horseback and carried rabbit sticks — a stick about two feet long with a curve on the end like a hockey stick, only a longer end curve. A jack rabbit practically always runs in a circle, so when one was started, a Navajo on horseback would take out after him. He'd run the rabbit fast for perhaps a quarter of a mile, and then another rider would cut across and take up the chase. Perhaps three or four would do this before the rabbit began to tire. When the waiting bunch of riders saw the rabbit was really slowing up, they would gallop over and surround him; then the yowling fun started. The rabbit, although pretty well played out, would duck and dodge among the sagebrush and weeds, the Navajos whooping and yelling, pushing and jostling, leaning down pony sides to get a crack at him. It was great sport and they would keep it up until dark.

Once or twice during the summer the Boss would arrange a Chicken Pull. With three days notice, he could figure on five or six hundred Navajos being there. On horseback and in wagons they came, generally arriving the night before. The majority came from the Reservation.

Umbrellas were the fashion and practically every woman, on horseback or in wagons, carried one over her head. The Boss bought them by the gross. Good, heavy-ribbed, substantial umbrellas they were too. He had found that the Navajo is always ready to buy a good article at a higher price, rather than something inferior, although cheaper.

The Chicken Pull wasn't a very expensive affair. About half a carload of melons to be distributed free and about twenty-five dollars for prizes, and, of course, a half-dozen or so live chickens.

The store did a rushing business while the Navajos were there. Hundreds of goat and sheep pelts were bought. And they would bring blankets, nice ones. The women on the Reservation were much better weavers than those living along the railroad.

The Chicken Pull was staged in the afternoon. A live chicken was buried in the loose sand with the head and neck sticking out. The riders then lined up about a hundred yards away and, at a signal, raced for the chicken. As they galloped by, they leaned over and tried to grab the chicken's head and pull it out of the sand. A chicken's head is a rather small thing to grab from a galloping horse, but before long someone would be successful and pull the chicken out. That wasn't all there was to it. In order to win, the rider had to bring the chicken back to the starting point. Whoever brought it in was the winner.

The rest of the riders flocked around him, barring the way, trying to take the chicken from him. Sometimes it changed hands three or four times before the battle was over. Needless to say, there wasn't much left of the chickens. Generally, the head was all that was brought in and, if the chicken was buried too firmly, the head was all there was to start with.

About two weeks before the Fourth of July the Navajos

would begin asking how many days until *Nah-ho-hi* (which means chicken, but Chicken Pull is understood), although they kept track and knew as well as anyone, Roy said. Gallup generally had a celebration; they put on some good ones and arranged plenty of sports to attract the Indians. Nick didn't get to see much of the celebration the first year he was at Pino. Everyone who could left the night before except Dale, the bookkeeper, and Nick. Mike didn't go because the Santa Fe engines were as thirsty on the Fourth of July as any other day. Slick didn't go because he claimed there would be just too damn many soldiers lined up at the bars and a quiet law-abiding citizen would stand a slim chance of getting up to buy a drink. He preferred to do his drinking when conditions were normal. The Boss told Nick that he and Dale could catch a freight to town in the afternoon.

Dale was some fifteen years older than Nick and had T.B. He was not strong and never walked any farther than to the cook shack and back. He seldom went anywhere, so Nick was quite surprised when he said he was going to the celebration.

"I've never seen a Wild West Fourth of July celebration either," he told Nick, "and probably this is my last chance so I'm going."

"Good for you," agreed Nick. "Let's get ready and when a freight takes siding, we'll be there to climb on."

But it turned out to be one afternoon when no freights stopped.

"There were freights stopped this morning. We could just as well have gone; there hasn't been a customer here all day," growled Dale.

They thought they had a chance at five-fifteen when the California Limited pulled in and took siding for an east-bound passenger. There was a Pullman door open and the step was down when they rushed over and went into the vestibule. The conductor, an old man, met them and said they would have to get off. Nick told him they only wanted to ride into Gallup — just twenty-two miles — and expected to pay their fares. The conductor knew the Boss well, but that made no difference, they couldn't ride that train. They tried to work on his sympathy. It was their first Fourth of July in New Mexico and they had never seen a Wild West celebration, might not ever have another chance and that if he didn't let them ride that train, they wouldn't be able to get there. They would stand in the vestibule all the way. But he had no heart and made them get off.

The broncs were there so Dale suggested hitching them up and going. With the aid of the cook they got them hitched, and away they went. Of course, they got there after the afternoon sports were over, but they hung around watching the gambling — everything was wide open — and some fights between the town boys and the soldiers.

They ran across the Boss and he was feeling fine, as he had won quite a bit on the Zuñi racers. He always claimed that a good Zuñi runner could beat anybody in a twenty-five mile race. He would bet a hundred dollars, or a thousand, that he could get a Zuñi runner who would put a twenty-four pound sack of flour on his shoulder and run fifty miles between sunrise and sunset. That would be in the summer time. He said he had seen it done. In a long race, most any healthy Zuñi could outrun a horse. It was nothing to see them race twenty-five miles kicking a short stick or stone the entire distance.

Nick told him they would start back about two o'clock in the morning. The Boss said he would stay over because they had some matched races between Hopi and Zuñi runners and he might win some more money on the Zuñi boys.

*     *     *

In the fall of 1907, after working in the store for a year, Nick was sent to the sawmill to run the commissary which

30

was ten miles up in the mountains. Made of rough lumber the store building and houses were hot in summer and cold in winter. The store building was not large — a room in front, a warehouse at the back, and a bedroom. The walls were lined with red building paper to cover the cracks.

There were six or seven white men, ten or twelve Mexicans and a few Navajos working in the mill and woods. It was a small mill, cutting about ten thousand feet of lumber a day, and not a very good mill as something broke every few days. Most of the Mexicans spoke some English, but very few of their wives did or, at least, wouldn't. Nick had learned quite a bit of Spanish, but some of these Mexican women soon showed him that he had a lot to learn. They talked so fast and so much that he couldn't get it. One woman in particular got his goat and, for a long time, he hated to see her come into the store. She would start talking as soon as she opened the door and it certainly made her mad when he couldn't understand her. She would get him mad too and so confused — especially if there happened to be a little audience to laugh — that he was helpless. She sure called him some choice Mexican names.

Nick had never been around a sawmill so the first week he spent part of his afternoons down there. The mill was a couple of hundred yards below the camp by a large spring. It must have been a second-hand mill, because if it ever ran a full ten-hour day without having to shut down for something, it would be the main topic of conversation of the millhands as they sat on the store counter that night. Generally they were minor things — belt slipping off or the lacing breaking, or the steam nigger not getting enough steam pressure. The big circular saw used to break and fly to pieces too. Four or five Navajos worked in the mill — carrying lumber mostly — and they managed to get into the small saws occasionally.

Nick had only been there a short time when the foreman

brought a Navajo up to the store to be bandaged. He had rubbed up against a small saw and it had taken about a quarter of a pound of meat from his upper forearm.

The Boss had an agreement with the Army surgeon at Fort Wingate, twelve miles to the west, to serve as camp doctor and to come if needed. He was a big, loud-spoken man, very red of face. The Mexicans and Navajos were all afraid of him, so he was never sent for at their request. He had left some medicines and bandages at the store. The foreman, who brought the Navajo in, had tied a piece of the Navajo's shirt sleeve above the cut to slow up the bleeding. After Nick put medicine and salve on it and bandaged it good, he asked the Navajo if he should send for the soldiers' doctor. The Navajo assured him emphatically that he didn't need him, because he was going home and, as soon as he got there, his wife would go gather a plant which would be kept ready in the hogan to be chewed up and put on the cut if it got to bleeding too much. He explained all this to Nick with much talk and many gestures. He evidently wanted him to understand there was no need of disturbing the big white doctor. He probably thought the first thing the doctor would do would be to cut his arm off.

Nick's next patient was another Navajo. He had managed, in some manner, to step on one of the floor jump-saws and it took off about an inch of his heel. It was a bad looking cut and Nick was glad the Boss was there, but the Boss said he wasn't any good at that kind of thing and for Nick to go ahead and bandage it while he got a couple of good men to help him hitch the broncs, as he was going to take the Navajo to the doctor.

When he came back in the buckboard he hollered for Nick to help the Navajo out. When the Indian got to the store door he knew what the Boss had in mind and stopped. The Boss began talking to him, telling him he might die, that the doctor wouldn't cut his leg off, and that he would be all right in a few days. The poor fellow was too weak and sick to put up much of an argument so he got in.

About three weeks later the sawyer got into the big saw. No one seemed to know how it happened. The first thing anyone knew, the sawyer was in three pieces and quite dead. Nick was beginning to wish he was back with Roy. He hadn't known sawmills were such dangerous places. And when, not long after, a young logger was caught between two huge pine logs and killed, the rest of the lumberjacks and millmen went about their work more cautiously. They claimed bad luck ran in threes and there would be another death. There wasn't, however, but the way a Mexican worked over the stable boss with a pitchfork was enough to satisfy them.

Nick began to think it would be better if the Boss hired a doctor or, at least, a trained nurse to run the commissary.

Sundays, when Nick didn't ride down to the store to see Roy, Roy would ride up to the mill. "I like it up here all right; it's prettier country and more exciting, but I'd rather be down at the store with you," Nick confessed to Roy on one of his Sunday visits to the mill.

"Olson says they're trying to get someone for this job so maybe you will get back down there," Roy said.

"Hope they do. Well, what's new at the store?"

"Nothing much," Roy said, "except the weavers are sure turning out some swell Germantown stuff. They can certainly weave that readymade yarn. We're getting lots of pillow tops and throws. Bought a few of them twice though," he grinned.

"How was that?" Nick asked.

"Well, Thursday, I guess it was, I was delayed a little going to dinner. The others had gone ahead. I wanted to stop in the barn a minute, and as I passed the corner of the blanket room, I saw a pair of legs sticking out the window. I slipped over and saw they belonged to a Navvy, so I grabbed hold and yanked him out. It was Old Baboon's

33

boy, and he was what I call scared. I don't know how he got over the fence."

"What did you do with him?" Nick asked.

"I took him to the office and we waited for the Boss to come back from dinner. I told the boy likely they'd hang him. When the Boss came, he sent a rider for the Chief, Bicenti, who came in a couple of hours. He sure gave Baboon's boy a talking-to. Then the Boss and the Chief talked and decided that as long as the boy had no money, he was to come over whenever there was a car of hay, oats, or flour, and help unload. He has to put in thirty days' work. He'll come too," Roy laughed.

"Sure he will," said Nick.

Roy stayed for supper and then saddled up. "About time we went to see the girls again, isn't it?" he asked.

"If those lumber-hauling husbands ever stay up here overnight, I'll sure be down," Nick told him.

"Don't forget to let me know if they do," warned Roy.

"Don't worry about that and I hope it's soon."

"Well, so long," Roy said as he rode away.

Nick's hope was realized much sooner than he expected. Roy had been gone about an hour when Nick, who was sitting in front of the store, saw two freight wagons come down the hill and stop by the lumber piles. Then he recognized Smiley and Calico, the girls' husbands. Calico was Gracie's husband. He had been so named because one day, while buying some calico, he managed to slip a good-sized piece — which he had not bought — under his blanket. But the eagle eye of the Boss had seen this breach of store etiquette; walking quietly over behind the future *Na-h-get-ti* (calico), he yanked the blanket from Calico's shoulders and the stolen piece of cloth fell to the floor in full view of all. The Boss said not a word, just turned and walked into the office. The three or four Navajos in the store laughed uproariously at the much-abashed shoplifter, who had earned a new name.

Glacie's husband acquired his English name in a nobler way. His brown face was molded in such a manner that he always wore a perpetual grin, almost as if he were just about to burst into a hearty laugh.

Both husbands were men over forty and good steady freighters, honest and reliable. Calico's first attempt at stealing had evidently been his last. A Navajo hates to be laughed at and shown as a fool.

After unhitching and hobbling their ponies, the two Navajos came to the store. "What are you coming up here tonight for?" Nick asked in Navajo, as neither of the husbands spoke English.

"We came because we want to load and get back early tomorrow so we can go to Club Foot's hogan in the afternoon. Big sing for Club Foot's son. A Medicine Man from far out on the Reservation is in charge," Calico explained, as he got out tobacco and cornhusk paper and rolled a cigarette.

"That's fine," Nick said, "and there'll be lots of people."

"Everyone will want to go," agreed Smiley.

"We need some coffee and sugar," Calico said. "Will you open the store?"

"Sure," Nick told them, "come on in."

They got what they wanted and left. At dusk Nick was saddled and on his way down the mountain. He thought no one had noted his departure. It took him a little over an hour to reach the store. When he tapped on the window, Roy came at once and unbarred the great gate.

"Been expecting you," he said with a laugh. "I met Calico and Smiley on the way up as I rode down. I'll bar this again and we'll go out the front door. I'll also bring some candy."

"I'll lead the pony along so I won't have to come back here," Nick said when Roy came out.

It was a lovely fall night with a half-moon straight above, giving them all the light they needed.

"Navajos are practically always asleep by this time," Roy said as they approached the two hogans. "Now, we'll see if they kinda thought we might come tonight."

They slipped quietly up to Gracie's door; sure enough, they heard low voices and through a crack they could see the low flickering light from the fire.

"Open the door for two strangers who are lost," Roy said, trying to disguise his voice.

"Are the strangers white and tall and do they carry a sack that might be something sweet?" questioned Gracie, making no move to come to the door, although low giggling could be heard.

"We are not white, nor very tall," Roy answered. "We are your Apache cousins, so now let us in."

"We are alone and afraid," Glacie answered, "but Navajos do not turn their relatives away." She came and opened the door. "Welcome, cousins!"

Nick saw at a glance that the girls expected them. Roy walked over to where Gracie sat on a snow-white Angora skin. Nick lingered while Glacie closed and barred the door.

"How beautiful you are tonight," Nick murmured. His eyes took in her tall, straight, well-formed figure, encased in purple velvet shirt and heavily pleated sateen skirt. As he looked into her large dark eyes, she smiled. Then Nick knew why he had chosen her instead of Gracie. It was because of the crinkly little wrinkles that darted part way down her nose when she smiled. They originated in the inside corners of her eyes and always signaled the birth of her shy little smile.

They moved over and joined the other two. The sack of candy was opened and passed.

"I'm going to make some coffee," announced Glacie.

"That will be fine," agreed Gracie. "It will help keep our boys awake."

After coffee and more candy Glacie said, as she arose, "I must go see if my fire is still burning."

36

"Another joke," laughed Roy, "and, of course, Nick will have to go see too."

"Sure will," Nick said, and he and Glacie left for her hogan.

It seemed to Nick he had only been alone with her about ten minutes when some man just outside the hogan door was seized with a severe, but low, coughing spell.

"Smiley," exclaimed Glacie in a low voice. Then she went to the door and called, "What do you want?"

"I want to come in," answered Smiley. "I forgot something, so came back."

"You did not forget something and you are not coming in," Glacie told him. "You go right back to your work, you lazy man."

"There is someone in there and I know who it is," stated Smiley.

"What if there is, you no-good man who runs around in the night like a coyote."

"Chischilly is in there," Smiley said. "Is he too, a coyote?"

"You ride back to the mill, or do you want me to throw your saddle out?" she asked angrily.

Nick knew when a Navajo woman tossed her husband's saddle out of the hogan, that was all the same as divorce. But it was generally done when the husband was absent.

This announcement caused Smiley to pause a moment. Then he said, "He should give me something then, because I had a long ride."

Nick realized that Smiley knew he was there so he spoke up, "What should I give you?"

"Money," promptly answered Smiley.

"How much?"

"Five dollars."

"Too much," Glacie said sternly, "he will give you two dollars and no more."

"Three."

Glacie started to squelch this demand when Nick hurriedly said, "All right, three dollars."

"He will give it to you tomorrow. Now go back to your camp, you owl."

Nick supposed Smiley had ridden back but when, at two o'clock, he bid Glacie good-bye, he saw a figure arise from the ground a short distance away. He decided Smiley wanted company on the ride to the mill.

Roy came from Gracie's doorway then. Seeing the third figure, he asked who it was.

"That's Smiley," Nick answered. "Is it safe to ride home with him?"

"Sure," Roy laughed, "you owe him a little something, I guess."

"It was worth it and I would gladly have given him five dollars, except that Glacie felt that was too much for a bad man who sneaks around at night, like a coyote!"

# CHAPTER 3

NICK WAS BEGINNING TO FEEL like an old hand at the trading business. He had been in it almost four years now and had acquired a broad range of knowledge and many new friends. One night after supper, he was busy getting a Navajo freighter some oats when Jack Coddington came in for some chewing tobacco. Old Jack, as the boys called him, was a red-faced, white-haired, six-foot Irishman and a particular friend of Nick's. He had a monster barrel of a chest, great hairy arms, with one of which he could raise Nick above his head. The lower half of his left ear was missing, chewed off in a Michigan lumber camp fight, but, according to Jack, the ear chewer wouldn't chew any more ears with his own teeth because Jack knocked the front ones out.

"I heard you were going to town tomorrow, Nick, is that right?" he asked in his quiet voice.

"That's right, Jack, got to have a tooth either filled or pulled."

"How you going?" Jack asked.

"The Boss is letting me take the broncs and the buck-board."

"Got room for me?"

"Sure," Nick told him, "but what's the matter, you aren't quitting, are you?"

"Yeah," he answered, "I've been here three months and that's long enough for me to stay in one camp."

"The Boss will be sorry to see you go. Have you told him yet?"

"I'll tell him when he comes back," Jack answered. "I saw him going down to the store. What time you leaving?"

"About nine I guess. That ought to get us in town about two."

"I'll be around, Nick. Guess I'd better go shave and get cleaned up. See you in the morning."

"Don't forget to draw your pay," Nick laughed.

"Thanks for reminding me," and Jack laughed too as he went out the door.

The next morning when Nick went to the stable, Jack, with his duffle bag, was waiting. "Thought maybe you'd change your mind after talking with the Boss," Nick said.

"Nope," he answered, "and he didn't even urge me to stay."

The stable boss and Jack got the broncs hitched to the buckboard. Nick climbed into the seat and held the reins while the stable boss held their heads until Jack was firmly seated and with a good hold on his hat.

"Never will tame down, will they?" he said as the broncs raced along on a high lope. "Blessed if I know if I'd want a team like this or not."

"They'll be all right as soon as they've had their little run," Nick assured him.

After a mile they steadied down to a fast trot. The road was a pair of wagon tracks that stretched for miles down a valley, guarded on the higher side by tall pines, piñon, and juniper.

Talk was mostly of sawmills and logging camps, with Jack doing most of the talking. As they neared town, he abruptly changed the subject by asking Nick if he thought a man could lift a barrel of whiskey from a barroom floor and put it on the bar.

Figuring that a barrel of whiskey would weigh at least four hundred pounds, Nick said he didn't think so.

"Well, I can do it," Jack said in a matter-of-fact tone, "and if you'll believe me, there's the doggonest lot of people around saloons who think the same as you."

"What do you use, some kind of harness?" Nick asked.

"No harness, no nothing," answered Jack, "just my good strong arms and back."

"Then I don't believe it," Nick said, "and I'd even bet a little on it."

"Exactly," exclaimed Jack, "and you'd sure lose your money." Then he asked, "How much money have you got with you?"

"Sixty dollars," answered Nick.

"Well, I've got around a hundred so we can cover a few bets at least."

"We?" Nick said. "I don't feel too keen on this barrel lifting, but if you say you can do it, I expect you can."

"If I lose any money for you, I'll go right back to the mill and work until I have earned enough to pay you back. Fair enough?"

"Good enough for me," Nick told him.

"You know, Nick, I'm only forty-seven. It's this white hair that makes me look older. I'm a pretty good man yet."

They left the broncs and buckboard at the feed corral; then, after agreeing to meet at the Bon Ton restaurant for supper, Nick went to see the dentist. The dentist was busy so it was almost five before he got to Nick and filled the tooth. Nick met Jack at six. After supper, Jack said, "Now I'll do a little looking around, because it makes it a little easier for me if there's a good footrail and if the bar isn't too awful high. Also, I want to pick a good saloon where the customers look like they will have money. They'll bet freer if I seem a bit drunk, so don't be alarmed if you see me take a drink or two, because two or three drinks will make me lift all the better."

"Here's fifty dollars," Nick said as he passed it over. "Maybe I ought to kiss it first, though."

"Still think you may lose it, eh, Nick?"

"Seeing will have to be believing," he answered, "and, as I have nothing else to do and there's a train in, I'll go over to the depot and see how many poor Navvies are going to have to sleep without their robes tonight."

"What do you mean?" Jack asked.

"Most tourists think the Pendleton robe the Navajo wears is a genuine Navajo blanket, so they buy them right off the Indian's back to make sure they get the genuine article. See you later," and he started off.

"Oh say, Nick, when I get to bragging about lifting heavy weights, you suggest a barrel of whiskey. Come back about nine."

Nick fooled around the depot until ten minutes to nine and then strolled over to the Blue Light Saloon to see how Jack was doing. There were ten or a dozen others there and Jack already seemed to have their attention. He appeared to be a little drunk and was talking about wrestling. Then he got on the subject of lifting and how much he could lift when he was young and that he would bet that he could lift three hundred pounds right now. Some of the audience doubted this and would be willing to bet a little that he couldn't. Jack told them to trot out something that weighed three hundred pounds and make their bets because he would not only lift it, but would put it on the bar.

They all looked around to see if there was anything there for him to lift. This was Nick's cue, so he asked how about a barrel of whiskey; it probably weighed three hundred pounds. Someone asked the bartender if that was about what they weighed and he, although he knew they were much heavier, said that was about it. Then he sneakily passed the word around that a barrel of whiskey weighed nearer four than three hundred pounds. If the old fool wanted to throw his hard-earned money away they might as well have it as anybody and he, for one, would like to take fifty dollars worth.

Jack pulled out his roll, counted off fifty dollars and handed it to Nick, appointing him stakeholder. Jack's hundred was quickly bet and the barrel of whiskey was rolled over to the bar.

Nick couldn't see very well how he did it because the sports crowded around so close, elbowing him back, figuring he was just a kid and had nothing bet on it anyway. Jack got the barrel up on the footrail and then lifted it to his knees. He next kind of rolled and shoved it up, holding it against the bar until he put it almost level with the top. Then he gave a mighty lifting heave with his chest and the barrel of whiskey lay on the bar.

Those who had bet ten or fifteen dollars did not squawk any, probably thought Jack had earned it, but the bartender seemed to feel he had been cheated. Anyone could see he was quite peeved, although he had nothing personal to say to Jack except to tell him to take the barrel off the bar.

"Sorry, partner," Jack said, still puffing heavily, "but I only bet I could put it on the bar. Still, if you have any more restless money, I'll bet another fifty I can take it down." But the bartender wasn't betting on whiskey-barrel-lifting from then on.

The next morning after bidding Jack good-bye, Nick got the buckboard and broncs which, after the customary mile dash, settled down for the long jog home.

*     *     *

About a week later, the Boss, who had been down to the big store, drove into the stable. When he came to the store he seemed unusually serious. After a word of greeting he said, "Nick, I've bad news for you. I'm broke and this darned sawmill is the cause of it. I made a mistake going in this business, should have stayed with the Indian trading which is something I know about. Can't be helped now, but it's going to be hard for me to have to start all over again."

"I'm sure sorry to hear that," Nick said, "because I like working for you and I like my job. I have some money saved up and you are welcome to it, if it will help you any."

"Thank you, Nick," the Boss said with feeling, "but it wouldn't help. The creditors are taking over tomorrow. I am sorry I have nothing to offer you. I guess you know I have a little store at Zuñi and I'm going to send Roy up there if he wants to go, because he has been working for me much longer than you. But you're young and a good trader. You'll have no trouble finding a job."

"Don't worry about me, I'll be all right," Nick assured him.

"I'm sure I have enough money to pay off every man on the job," the Boss went on, "so you run tell Mr. Ramson to make the payroll and bring it over. Also, pass the word that we're paying off and closing down."

Nick did as he was told and after the last man was paid, the Boss said to him, "I'm going down to the Post now. Do you want to gather up your belongings and go with me?"

"Sure," Nick answered, "no use staying here, I guess. Suppose I'll be leaving tomorrow anyway." He thought of Glacie and wondered if he could get to see her before he left, at least tell her he was leaving. He did not want to leave but there was no job for him now. Perhaps it was best he was leaving; perhaps if he was with her a few more times he would want her so much that he would take her regardless. Perhaps he could get to see her tonight. 'Per-

44

haps, perhaps,' he thought, 'I've *got* to see her before I leave for good. She's too . . .'

"About ready?" the Boss asked.

"Just about," Nick answered. "I have a little bigger bundle than when I came. You can sure pile up a lot of stuff in four years."

"I hate to part with this team," the Boss remarked when they were seated in the buckboard and the broncs were freed and doing their customary mile dash, "but no way out of it, I guess."

"They're a powerful pair, all right," Nick said, "and I wonder what will become of them. I don't think many people would fool with such broncs."

"They're tough to handle, but they're fast and that's what I like. Maybe this is my last ride behind them so we'll let them go as they please."

There was no light visible in the store when they swung up to the big corral gate. "Guess there isn't anyone in there," the Boss said. "Here, you take my key and go through and open the gate."

Nick wondered where Roy was — maybe visiting Slick or Mike. After the broncs were put away and fed, Nick told the Boss he guessed he'd go see if he could find Roy. The cook shack was dark, so he walked across the track to Mike's little house. It, too, was dark. He would have liked a chat with Mike but didn't feel like waking him up. As he stood in the darkness wondering about Roy, it struck him. He turned abruptly and strode at a fast clip for the homes of Glacie and Gracie. In ten minutes he was cautiously approaching the door of Gracie's hogan. Girls' voices and the voice of Roy. Nick coughed and then heard someone at the door. Glacie asked, "Who knocks on my sister's door?"

"Another of your Apache cousins who is tired and hungry," Nick answered.

45

"My cousin is always welcome," laughed Glacie. "Come in and see your other cousin, Cousin."

Nick grabbed her in his arms and asked, "Where is the bad man who sneaks around like a coyote in the night?"

"He and the other bad man have gone to a sing. Didn't you know, or else why are you here?"

"I am here because I couldn't find Roy," he told her.

"Break away and come on in," called Roy. "There's coffee, mutton ribs, and blue bread here, and boy, it's all good. Guess you know we're out of jobs, so any free meals are just that much to the good."

"Told the girls yet?" Nick asked.

"Nope, because I had a hunch the Boss might bring you down tonight."

"It's going to be kinda hard for me," Nick said.

"We all have to part sometime, don't we?" Roy asked.

"Sure, but you never think ahead about that."

Nick ate large quantities of the delicious broiled mutton and blotter-thin blue bread, washed down by good old Arbuckle's coffee. Then he told Gracie and Roy he had bad medicine for Glacie and he would go to her hogan to talk with her.

It was after two when Roy whistled. Nick and Glacie arose and he said, "I must go now. Maybe I can come back and see you before long."

"It would be nice if I could go with you," she said, as he held her close.

"How about Smiley?"

"Oh, him! I could throw his saddle out in the morning and be rid of him. How foolish I talk. A white man shouldn't have an Indian woman."

"But you are half Navajo and half Spanish," Nick reminded her.

"And yet I'm all Navajo," she answered. "I have been very happy while you have been here. Now I must be sad."

46

"I will be unhappy too and will think and dream of you, and I promise to come back and see you."

Another whistle from Roy.

"Hold me tight once more, then quickly go," she said. Gently she pushed him through the hogan doorway into the starlit night.

At noon the following day Nick was in town, and by three o'clock he had a job in a trading store owned by a company that had several stores on the Reservation. He went to work the next morning.

*    *    *

The trading store in town was not as interesting as the one in the country; the Indians seemed different and were not as friendly. Nick worked there six months and then, late in the afternoon on the last day of February, 1911, the manager, Mr. Cross, came to him and asked him how he would like to go on the Reservation and run a store. Matthews, the Trader, who was running the Long Butte Post, had sent a Navajo in with team and buckboard, bearing a letter telling the company to get someone out there right away as he was sure leaving.

Nick wasn't certain he wanted to go forty-five miles out on the Reservation unless he had someone with him. Several Traders had been killed during the preceding years and their stores burned — Navajos most always set fire to the buildings after a killing — so he hardly knew what to say. Naturally, he was anxious to get a store to run.

Mr. Cross said sometimes the Indians were not altogether to blame for the killings, that there had never been any trouble at Long Butte, that he was sure Nick would get along fine, and that he would send a clerk as soon as he could find one.

The Navajo sent by the Trader at Long Butte was named *Hosteen Tso* (Mr. Big Man), and he and Nick started at seven the next morning. They hoped the ground would be frozen until they got over the mountains, but the night hadn't been quite cold enough. The horses' hooves and the wheels cut through the ice, snow, and mud. It took them from seven in the morning till nine at night to go twenty-five miles. In the middle of the day, when the adobe mud in the flats was real sticky, it would roll up on the wheels, dragging on the buckboard body and stopping the team. They could not pull — the wheels would not turn — so Nick and Hosteen Tso would have to get out and claw away the mud. Their feet would gather up such masses of it, they could hardly lift them. It was Nick's first experience with adobe, but not his last. He was worried for fear the buckboard or the harness would break, but old Hosteen Tso did not appear to be doing any worrying. He mostly laughed, saying the mud was no good, but soon they would be over where there was lots of sand and then they would go fast.

By nine o'clock when they finally got out of the adobe, the wind was terribly cold. They were both shivering. Hosteen Tso remarked that some whiskey would be fine to make them warm. Nick told him he had no whiskey, but Hosteen Tso said there was lots in the back of the buckboard. Nick asked him how he knew and he said he saw them put it in — a big jug in a box. The back of the buckboard had been loaded with the Trader's order of supplies while Nick was busy, so he didn't know what they were bringing out.

Nick knew there was a law against selling whiskey to the Indians. He couldn't remember ever hearing what the penalty was for giving one a drink, but if Hosteen Tso was as cold as he was, he considered Tso's idea a good one; so they got out, opened the box, and each took a good swig from the jug. The horses, after getting out on the wet, packed sand, covered the remaining twenty miles in about two and a half hours.

Matthews and his wife were in bed when they arrived,

but they got up and built a big fire in the fireplace. The adobe was frozen on Nick's overshoes so he couldn't get them off. He finally had to pour warm water over them and his shoes — to soften up the adobe.

After Hosteen Tso put the horses in the barn and fed them, he came in saying he was hungry. Nick was too, as he had only had a light lunch at noon. Mrs. Matthews wanted to start a fire and cook them something but Nick said he was too hungry to wait and a store lunch would do. When Matthews went out in the store to get the grub, Nick went too, as he wanted to see what it was like. Matthews lit a Rayo lamp which made a nice light. It wasn't a very large store, about twenty feet square. High counters were on three sides, set out pretty well from the wall which allowed plenty of space in back of them, but left a rather small "bullpen," as the customers' space was called. Good thing there was room behind the counters, as Nick found out later at Christmas. Seems that every Christmas Matthews had been there, he had, in the afternoon of Christmas Day, let ten or twelve of the lustiest *Yei-be-chai* singers go back of the counter, where there was a board floor, and whoop and stomp all afternoon. It was nice entertainment for the first half hour, but none too easy on the ears and nostrils in that small, hot, Navajo-filled room when they really warmed up and the perspiration began to flow. Indian dances are at their best when staged in the open.

"I know what Hosteen Tso wants to eat," Matthews said, "so what do you see that you'd like?"

"I might as well eat corned beef, pears, and crackers too," laughed Nick, who knew as well as Matthews did what a hungry Navajo likes. Corned beef — "cow-head meat," they call it.

They all went to the kitchen where Hosteen Tso and Nick quickly showed what two hungry men could do. Mrs. Matthews put out knives and forks. Hosteen Tso tried

49

these tools but after a fair trial, accompanied by muttered "go-to-hells," he shoved the knife and fork from him and proceeded to eat in a large and satisfying manner.

As Nick's fork couldn't hold as much as Hosteen Tso's fingers, the latter's pound of meat was gone before Nick's was half eaten. When Matthews asked if he wanted more meat, Hosteen Tso admitted that he did as he was very hungry. Before he was through with the second can, he ran out of crackers, so Matthews brought out two more boxes. He said Hosteen Tso was a good Navajo and he had had a hard trip, and if the stock of goods held out, he would try and fill him up. Hosteen Tso ate two cans of corned beef, two cans of Vienna sausage, three boxes of crackers, and two cans of pears. He assured them he was warm now; his stomach was full. Now, if Matthews would give him a sheepskin and quilt, he would go lie down somewhere and sleep.

Having arrived at night, Nick couldn't see what kind of place he had come to, but in the morning he was out the first thing to see what it looked like. The store building and living quarters were made of logs and were about twenty by sixty feet and maybe eight feet high — hard to tell, as the sand had drifted so heavily up against the walls. There was the store, rug room, wareroom, living room, two bedrooms, and a kitchen — all under a flat roof of sheet iron. The barn, henhouse, woodshed, and the other little house were made either wholly or partially of Arbuckle coffee boxes, roofed with sheet iron.

Next to the tin can, Arbuckle coffee boxes did more for the Southwest than anything. They were nice big boxes with wide, smooth boards. Most Traders opened them very carefully so they would not split the boards. As the Navajos hardly ever bought any coffee but Arbuckles, Traders generally had enough boards on hand; so if the Trader's wife suddenly wanted a henhouse, porch, or wash shed built, the lumber was right there to build it with.

50

It will never be known what the poor Navajos would have done without them. One might say they were ushered into the world on coffee box boards and, in the end, they certainly were carried away in them, as coffins. Two narrow boards made the back of the Navajo baby carrier. What could be shaped out more easily for this than a couple of coffee box boards? Traders always knew in advance when a young couple was expecting the first — of a probably large family. Newlyweds were quite fussy, and sometimes the Trader had to go to the warehouse and select a couple of boards from some unopened box. Often, after a new baby became a yearly event, they were not so fussy, and sometimes the lettering would be on the boards. One family brought in a new baby girl in a carrier. On one of the boards was the word "Ariosa" with a picture of the pretty lady with the wings (Arbuckle Bros. trademark). The Trader told them that was a nice name for the baby and they thought so too, although they pronounced it "Aliosa" because they couldn't make the *R* sound.

Long Butte Post was on the bank of a great arroyo and a more sandy spot would be hard to find. In the spring when the terrific windstorms were most frequent, there were times, Matthews claimed, when he could hardly see across the store. He said that fine sand seemed to come right through the walls and, as he had to keep the doors closed, he almost suffocated.

"You'll like it here all right," Matthews told Nick, "but you ought to have a helper or get married. Nick reflected that he would not even get to see Glacie out here. 'My wife helps me a lot," Matthews continued, "like when I have to go out to the barn for hay, or to the warehouse to weigh up wool; then all I have to do is call to her and she comes and watches the store. Until you do get a clerk, you'll just have to run the redskins out and bar the door."

Nick found later it was easy enough to say "chase them out," but not always so easy to do. The first time, after

Nick was alone, when a Navajo wanted some hay, he told the half dozen men in the store they would have to go out while he went to the barn. No one moved, so he told them again. Same result. Nick said, "All right, the horse will go hungry." The Navajo who asked for hay told him to hurry up as he wanted to go home. One of the loafers suggested that Nick give the barn key to the man and let him get his own hay. Another said Nick was probably afraid the man would steal the hay. Nick told them it was not that, but he was afraid the Navajo would not take enough and he did not want him to cheat himself. The idea of his not taking enough made them laugh heartily. They said they would all go out and see how much hay Nick gave for fifteen cents.

Matthews stayed two days to help Nick get acquainted with the Indians. When, on the third morning, they drove away, Nick watched them from the back door until they disappeared over a hill. He closed the door, and as he walked back through the living room, he sensed a change — it was too quiet. His footsteps on the floor between the rugs sounded as loud as those of a horse on a plank bridge. Human companionship had vanished over the hill. He was alone. Alone in the Indian country, surrounded by Indians — friendly or otherwise, he did not know. His nearest white neighbor was eighteen miles away. He had never been so completely alone before and he was afraid he was not going to like it. Now, if he had a wife, that would be different. "If" was not a very comforting word.

Going into the store, he opened the door, swept the floor, and started filling the shelves. Before long an old lady came in. She asked where the Trader was. Nick told her he had gone but she could buy from him. She handed out a string of rather poor Zuñi shell and turquoise beads, saying she wanted to pawn them for twenty dollars. He told her she could pawn them for three-fifty. She let out a yelp and, after telling him that he did not know anything, started in by calling him the very worst of her choice Navajo names. After running out of words — or wind — she smiled and said as he did not understand the value of good beads, she would pawn them for fifteen. Nick declined. Another cloudburst of abuse. Then he had a ten-dollar offer which he promptly turned down. Being pretty well winded by now, she only remarked that Nick was the stingiest American dog she had ever seen, so go ahead and give her the five dollars he had offered her in the first place, for she was all out of things to eat. Nick told her the offer was still three-fifty. Then the manhole lid really did fly off. If there had been a little audience to laugh at him, he would have weakened. "Coyote," "Bear," "Snake," and "Dog" were spit at him. She would not trade with him, nor would any of the other Navajos trade with him, for she would tell everyone that he was mean and stingy and could not tell good beads from bad. But she finally left with three and a half dollars worth of groceries.

Nick got along fairly well that first day. "Lazy Luke," as Matthews had named him, came in about ten and spent the rest of the day lying on the floor. "Crazy" came in too. She wasn't really crazy, just a harmless, half-witted woman who was almost deaf. She brought in a two-bit sheepskin and they had quite a time over it, as she seemed to think she could buy coffee, sugar, baking powder, and salt with it. Coffee was twenty-five cents a package, just what the skin was worth. Rather than have her spend the day repeating the other items over and over, Nick gave them to her.

The first night alone was the worst. After Nick went to bed he began to hear strange noises. He had probably heard the same kind of noises every night he had been there but paid no attention — the Matthews were there then. Then he thought he could hear footsteps and voices. By this time he was pretty nervous. He didn't have a gun but finally mustered up courage enough to get up and go into the store and hunt through the pawn case until he found a six-shooter. He felt easier then and, sometime after midnight, went to sleep.

The next day he became acquainted with a bright, intelligent Navajo boy who lived nearby and spoke good English. Nick made a deal with him to come work — and stay nights until he got a clerk. He would not have been much protection, however, because he was about the hardest fellow to wake that Nick had ever seen. He had thought Indians were supposed to be light sleepers.

It was over a month before a clerk arrived. Old Sam Goodluck, who ran the feed corral in town, brought him out. The young fellow had a letter of introduction from Nick's boss. It stated that the bearer's name was Bud Larson and that he seemed like a decent sort. He was being sent out on trial, so Nick could try him out and if he wouldn't do, ship him back to town. Bud was short, about five-foot-six, had an extra good set of shoulders, and looked to be just about of age. He was fair-haired and blue-eyed, and his pug nose gave him an Irish look. Nick thought, if first impressions went for anything, he and this young fellow would get along.

Sam said, as long as it was early afternoon, he guessed he'd feed and water his team and go back as far as Sweetwater to spend the night; then he could be back in town by noon the next day.

"I'll get a fire going and fix you up something to eat then," Nick told him.

"I'll go build a fire," offered Bud.

"Well, thanks," said Nick, pleased to see that Bud was ready to start right in helping.

After Sam had eaten and left, the boys went into the store. As no Indians happened to come in, they sat and talked. Nick learned that Bud was an orphan, that he had roamed around a bit, had been working in South Dakota

54

for the past two years, and hadn't landed in New Mexico broke. He still had over two hundred dollars in his pocket. As Nick had scarcely seen a white person since he had been there, it was good to have someone of his own race to visit with. By midnight when they went to bed, Nick knew he wasn't going to send Bud back to town. He hoped Bud would like the business and be contented.

One afternoon a couple of weeks after his arrival, Bud came into the store and asked Nick to go out and look at a horse an Indian had out there.

"What for?" Nick asked, "I don't know much about horses."

"Maybe I'll buy me a horse," said Bud. "He looks like a good one, got some size to him too. See if the fellow wants to sell him."

White Owl's Boy was in the saddle on a good-looking black horse.

"See what he wants for him," Bud said.

After some talk it was learned White Owl's Boy would sell the horse for thirty-five dollars. Nick thought this was too much and said so; then made an offer of twenty-five. White Owl's Boy laughed heartily at this; but finally, after much bragging about the fine qualities of the horse, he announced that he would take thirty dollars, silver, and that was final.

"Do you want him for thirty dollars?" Nick asked.

"Yeah, if that's the best he'll do, I'll take him," Bud answered.

"Well, he'll have to ride him home," Nick said. "He can bring him back tomorrow and get his money."

White Owl's Boy brought the horse about five the next afternoon, got his silver dollars, and left.

About six-thirty when the Indians had cleared out, Bud said he guessed he would try out his horse. He put on his boots, got a pawned saddle, blanket, and bridle, and carried them out.

Nick locked the store and went to the kitchen, built a fire, and started to get supper. About ten minutes later, Bud came in and went to his room. He came out with an Army blanket.

"I'll show that darned 'cayuse' whether he can pitch me off again," he growled.

"You mean that old Navajo plug threw you?" asked Nick.

"That's just what I mean," Bud said, looking rather sheepish, "but he can't do it again. I wasn't looking for any funny stuff from him."

"What's the blanket for?" Nick asked. "Will that hamper his bucking?"

"It'll hamper me from leaving the saddle so damn pronto," answered Bud. "I'm going to tie this blanket for a bucking roll on the front of the saddle."

"Oh, I see," said Nick, "but wouldn't it be better if I tied you in the saddle?"

"May have to, at that," grinned Bud.

"I'll have to see this exhibition of riding, supper or no supper," Nick told him.

"That don't look like an outlaw bronc to me," Nick remarked when they were outside.

"No sir, he don't," agreed Bud. He stood perfectly calm while Bud tied the rolled blanket to the saddle. "You might hold him until I get firmly seated," suggested Bud. "Okay, turn him loose and let's see how high I go this time."

The horse just stood there, so Bud gave him a couple of good kicks in the ribs. He came to life then and started right off in high gear, running about thirty yards; then he abruptly stopped, put his head down and went into his dance. No fooling about it, that horse could pitch. Bud stayed with him until about the fifth jump when, hampered or not by the bucking roll, he left the saddle and landed on his hands and left shoulder in the sand. He

56

looked terribly mad, but didn't say much except he thought the bucking roll had slipped. "I'll try him once more. If he throws me again, he can go to hell for all I care."

He readjusted the bucking roll and got on. But it was just the same thing over again, except Bud landed more on his back and it knocked the wind out of him. Also, this time, the horse probably decided he'd shown off enough for one day, because he lit out for home at a lively gallop.

"Well, cowboy, it looks like you're afoot in this here desert," said Nick. "Do you think you can make it back to the water hole?"

"I'm a little lame and stove up, but I guess I can make it," laughed Bud. "But how come that damn horse seemed so gentle with that Navajo?"

"He may be a better rider than you are," Nick answered. "Maybe he pitches the first time every day when anyone gets on him."

"Could be," agreed Bud. "Well, let's eat."

The Navajo brought the horse and outfit back the next morning and wanted to know how the horse got away. Bud was lame, and stiff, and plenty mad by now and wanted to fight the Navajo. The Navajo said he couldn't understand it — the horse was gentle; even his little boy rode him, but maybe he didn't like white men. Maybe they had a smell he didn't like. But he didn't want Bud to be mad. If he would allow him five dollars for his trouble, he would give back the rest of the money and take the horse home. Nick thought Bud was getting out of it cheap enough, as it was plain the horse didn't like him, so he told the Navajo to give Bud the money. About a month later when a horse buyer came, Bud had a chance to get himself a good pony for ten dollars — and he had fifteen hundred to pick from.

There were three wells in the arroyo just below the store, two of which were used by the Indians. Those who had wagons brought barrels which they filled and took home. The wagonless ones, who were in the majority, came with one or two ten-gallon wooden kegs, lashed on a burro. If there was a son-in-law in the family, it was his job to water the ponies. These were a squealing, fighting, kicking bunch, and it looked to Nick like it was about as much as one's life was worth to go among them. But the Navajo, with much yelling and cursing, would pull water until they had their fill.

It was different with the sheep and goats. What water they got was generally hauled up by a couple of little children who could hardly drag the pail from the well.

The Navajos had cattle too and, at least once a year, a cattle buyer would send out word to the Traders when he would be out to buy, so notice could be given the Indians to round up and bring in what cattle they wanted to sell.

Traders out on the Reservation had to carry big stocks of goods because they depended on the Navajos to haul their goods in with teams. Since the four-pony teams could only pull about a ton and roads were impassable at times, they usually kept a big reserve stock on hand. It had to be that way, too, because when the Navajos got money they could sure buy plenty of merchandise. They didn't plan ahead much, but enough so they would take their pawn out. In the fall they would buy quilts and robes, good ones. They were fussy about them too. If a quilt had a little tear or a spot on it, they would expect a reduction in price. But, as soon as it was theirs, they would throw it on the floor to wrap their purchases in — and the floor might be dirty with cigarette butts and tobacco juice, or even a wet spot where some Navajo child had let go all he had.

Not many white people came by that first summer, but the few who did generally stayed over night. Nick's room was off the big living room, Bud had a small room off the kitchen, and there was a nice little room off the screened porch. In the living room was a daybed, large enough for two people, which could be quickly made up.

58

A couple of mornings after Bud failed to win first prize as a rider, Nick was awakened at daybreak by a loud hammering on the store door. He got up and went to the living room door, which opened onto the screened porch, and saw Many Beads, a middle-aged Navajo, bawling and beating on the store door.

"What's the matter with you?" Nick asked.

"My wife is dead and I want her beads and bracelets and a new shawl to bury her in," he yelled.

"All right, all right, wait until I get some clothes on," Nick told him.

As soon as he was dressed, he went into the store. The beads and bracelets were in pawn, but Nick knew he would have to let him take them and hope Many Beads would pay some time. When it came to the shawl — Navajos always want a new shawl or robe for a burial — Many Beads chose the most expensive one in the store.

"Your pawned things come to over sixty dollars," Nick told him, "so I think this shawl is good enough," and he shoved out a ten-dollar one.

Then Many Beads flew all to pieces with rage. He lunged at Nick, but missed him. Then he grabbed at the high gate between the counters, but it was bolted and he couldn't open it. He was starting to climb over the counter when Nick said, as he tossed him the eighteen-dollar shawl, "All right, take it along. I won't fight you for it at a time like this." Many Beads grabbed it and the beads and bracelets, and dashed away.

Nick went out to the kitchen where Bud, who was up by now, was starting a fire. Nick told him about the death and Many Beads' willingness to fight for her shawl.

"Probably never pay for those things," Bud said. "If I'd been the one dealing with him I doubt if he'd have got anything."

"Then you'd have had a fight on your hands," Nick told him.

"Maybe so," agreed Bud, "but I haven't seen the Navajo yet who could make me run very far."

"Grief swings to violent rage doggone sudden with Navajos, remember that," Nick said, "and they have no love for white people anyway, so it will probably pay us to humor them a bit and not have any real trouble with them. You know there would be a good many against us two."

"Well, I'll try not to kill any of them," laughed Bud, "but still I don't want any of them to play too rough with me."

# CHAPTER 4

ONE EVENING AFTER CLOSING the store, Nick and Bud
went out on the little screened porch off the living room
to cool off before getting supper. As they sat talking and
smoking, Bud looked up and said, "Looks like we'll have
company for supper."

"Sure does," agreed Nick, as he watched a weary looking team pull a buckboard down the sandy hill. "Wonder
who he is?"

"Dressed in black as he is, he could be an undertaker,
preacher, or maybe a high-toned gambler," laughed Bud.

"Hope he's the last named," Nick said, "and maybe he'll
teach us some card tricks."

But Nick was wrong. When the stranger pulled up before the store and the boys went out, he introduced himself
as Reverend Cardican, Missionary to the Navajos, and he
would like to know if he could stop a few days and get
acquainted with the Indians in this section.

"Why yes, I guess you can, provided you can stand our
cooking," Nick told him.

"Maybe the Reverend is a better cook than we are," suggested Bud hopefully.

"I doubt that," the Reverend answered, "but I do know something about cookery, and will be glad to help."

"That's the Christian spirit all right," Bud said, "so you take your bag and go on with Nick. I'll unhook these broomtails and take care of them."

After showing the Reverend where he was to sleep, Nick went to the kitchen, started a fire, and prepared to get supper. When Bud came in, he washed and then set the table. Reverend Cardican offered to help but Bud told him there was nothing to do.

The Reverend was a large man, around forty or a little more, black eyes and hair. His mouth, nose, and ears were all too large, much too large. He seemed good-natured and laughed easily. The Navajos should like him, Nick thought. After supper was over and the dishes were done, the three went out on the porch to sit.

"You know," said Nick, "I've been wanting to go to town for some time. Hated to leave Bud alone, but since you're going to be here, Reverend, I think I'll go to-morrow. I'll stay a day in town and be back the third day."

"Then I *can* be of some help," the Reverend said, "and I will be glad to stay longer if you are delayed."

The reason Nick didn't like to leave Bud alone was that he was hotheaded and didn't understand Navajos or their language very well as yet. Being rather a small man and if he was there alone, some of the bucks might get smart, and then there would be trouble. Bud had already had two or three little run-ins with them.

One big husky fellow — Little Captain by name — a loud talker and a smarty, had already had his first lesson from Bud. Bud was doing some repair work on the back of the kitchen and didn't even know there was anyone around when, without warning, Little Captain landed on Bud's back with his arms around his neck. It certainly

62

staggered Bud but, being the powerful little man he was, he only had to take one staggering step forward to regain his balance; then, with a mighty heave, the Little Captain went over Bud's head to land on his back with a genuine thud on the hard ground, the wind completely knocked out of him. Bud whirled around to see if there were any more Captains — big or little — Majors, or even Generals, for all he cared, who might wish to climb his back and throttle him. There were none, so he yelled for Nick to come see what he could make of it and should he knock the hell out of this Little Captain.

When Nick got there Little Captain was trying to recover his breath and, at the same time, smile; but he was having a tough time of it. When he did have breath enough to talk, he said he was only joking with the "Little Man."

Bud said, "Tell him to get up and try out some of his other jokes, if he has any. Tell him I like to joke with him."

But Little Captain evidently couldn't think of any other good jokes at the moment, so he got up and, with his eye on Bud, backed away a bit; then turned and walked down to the well for a drink of water.

And one night a good-for-nothing silversmith hung around until dark trying to work Bud for some credit, until Bud got mad. The silversmith was twice as big as Bud, really a big fellow. Bud probably decided he needed more weight on his side this time, because he grabbed the two-by-four, used to bar the door, and swung it. The silversmith got through the door a split second before the bar landed right where he had been.

Then one afternoon when the store was full and the Indians all wanting to trade at once, one Navajo, after telling Bud to tear off two yards of velvet, decided he didn't want it after all. Nick was trading at the same counter near Bud and was surprised when he heard the Navajo say he wanted two yards of velvet, as it takes two and a half yards for a shirt, even for a small squaw. Bud knew

63

a short length of velvet would be hard to sell, so he told the Navajo he *did* want it, and shoved it over to him, telling him to hand over two dollars pronto. The Navajo said again he didn't want it, it was too short anyway, and he wouldn't pay for it. He started out. Bud started on a run around the counter to the gate and into the bullpen but, by the time he got through the gate, the Navajo was hollering, "Here's the money, here's the money!"

The Navajos had all gone home by the time Reverend Cardican arrived, so the next morning Nick sent word to Natonopah, the head man around there, for a good pony to ride to town. About noon Natonopah showed up, leading a little, wild-eyed roan pony, that looked like it might weigh six hundred pounds. But Natonopah assured Nick that it was a good pony and he would be in town by sundown. He saw to it that Nick had a good quirt, as he said Nick would need it going in because the pony, going so far from home, would pretend to be tired. The little pony was just as good as the old man said. Nick loped him practically all of the forty-five miles to town, and it was just dark when he reached the arroyo about a mile from town. Here he had trouble which delayed him quite a while.

This arroyo, which was deep and some fifteen feet across, was bridged. The pony had never had any experience with bridges, and the minute his front feet hit the hollow-sounding planks, he snorted and whirled away from that thing. Nick jockeyed him up again with the same result. He got off and tried leading him across, but the pony was stronger. Then he tried driving him across, using the lariat end as a persuader, and just missed having his belly kicked in. In the end the pony won and Nick had to ride a mile up the arroyo to a place where the pony could scramble down in and up the other side. Nick finally made the last mile, took the pony to a feed corral, where he told the stable man to just feed hay, as the pony had never seen any oats and probably wouldn't eat them.

After supper Nick strolled along Front Street, going into numerous saloons, now and then taking a drink, placing a small bet here and there on various games, until he suddenly realized he wasn't having much fun. He could go to the Red Light district at the west end of town, but he knew he wouldn't because tomorrow he was going to do what he had known he would do for a long time — he would go back to the old stone Trading Post and find Glacie.

Although he never spoke to Bud about her, he thought of her every day. The shy, quaint way she pronounced his name, the way her eyes snapped when she scolded poor Smiley, the last hug and kiss when they parted . . .

He went to bed early and, being tired, soon fell asleep. He was up early in the morning and, after a good breakfast, set out for the freight yards. He knew many of the freight conductors, as they used to come in the store while their trains were shoved in on the side track. When Nick got down into the yards, the first conductor he met was Frosty Sanders.

"You don't happen to be going east, do you?" Nick asked.

"If the damn boomers ever get my train made up and Old Eagle Eye can get her rolling, we certainly are heading east. Why?" asked Frosty.

"I want to go back to the old stomping grounds and would like to ride with you, if that's all right," Nick said.

"Sure can," said Frosty, "but I haven't got my orders yet. Don't know if we stop or not. But that won't matter because, with this drag, we won't be going over twelve miles an hour up that grade, so you can hop off where you please."

They didn't stop, but, as the train was crawling along, Nick easily stepped off the caboose step. As he walked toward the old store, he began to wonder, as there were no Navajos in sight.

Then he noticed the store door was shut. He stepped up and tried the door. It was locked. He looked in a window and saw the empty shelves. Funny that Frosty hadn't told him, probably supposed Nick knew. Then old Hosteen Kinne came around the corner of the building. After his loud and pleased greeting was over, Nick said, "Too bad the store is closed and all your friends gone. How long has it been closed?"

"Six months, maybe seven months," Hosteen Kinne answered. "Yes, too bad, Navajo all gone too."

"Smiley and Calico have left too, I suppose," Nick said.

"Yes, they're gone."

"Where did they go?" Nick asked.

"The men went to Red Rock to haul lumber after their wives threw their saddles out the door," Hosteen Kinne explained. "No one knows where the two women went. They just said they were going on a long, long journey."

"Which way did they go?" asked Nick.

"Someone told me they went west, but I don't know if they did," answered Hosteen Kinne. "Why do you ask about them? Maybe you liked those women."

"Maybe I did," Nick answered absentmindedly. Maybe he did like one of those women more than he cared to admit, even to himself.

"When did they leave?" he asked.

"Soon after you and the rest did," answered the Navajo.

So she pulled out right after I did, thought Nick. Probably thought I'd come back and talk her into living with me, maybe getting married, and maybe we would have. But she thought too much of me to have me called "Squaw Man." I suppose she's right, and I think more of her now than ever. But I wish I could have seen her just once more.

A westbound freight whistled. Then directly he saw they were slowing down to take siding. Nick had intended to have a visit with Mike Branagan, the pumper. But, somehow, now he did not feel like visiting with anyone, even

66

an old friend. When the freight pulled in, Nick got up and walked to the caboose and climbed on.

He was back in town at noon. He wasn't hungry. He was too blue and dejected to care for food. He went into a saloon for a drink. It tasted rotten. Then it dawned on him that he had had enough of town. He'd go home. He could make it by dark. He went to the hotel, got his packages, paid his bill, and went to the feed corral for his pony.

"Wish you travelers would buy yourselves horses instead of bringing these damn biting, kicking broomtails to my corral," grumbled old Sam Goodluck. "I passed back of this one of yours this morning and he let fly with both feet, didn't miss me over four inches either, the lousy, pie-eyed bastard. Makes me mad as hell to be kicked at."

"And how mad does it make you to be kicked?" asked Nick with a grin.

"They don't kick me," answered Sam. "I've been around horses too long. I take one good look at their heads and eyes, and right away I know the ones I can't trust. Well, do you want me to saddle this close-eyed bastard or will you? Naw, better let me. I'd like to cuff him around a bit for trying to kick my head off."

"All right with me," agreed Nick.

Sam went around to the head of the stall, climbed over the manger and untied him. Then he shooed him out and chased him over to where Nick's saddle, blanket, and bridle were. Trouble developed when Sam started to put the bridle on. He got the bit in the pony's mouth, but, when he went to put the bridle top over the ears, the pony jerked violently back and the bridle dropped to the ground.

"Looks like his ears are tender," Nick said. "The Navajos use them for handholds when they're breaking them to saddle."

"Yeah, I know how they do," Sam said. "I'll try him again." He tried, but with the same results.

"Maybe I can hold his head," suggested Nick.

"Nope, I'll get this headstall on this dang jack rabbit if I have to chop his head off and lay it on the ground to do it. But I've got another way to try first. Get behind him and shoo him over to this post and I'll snub his nose down to the ground and then we'll see."

The pony struggled and fought the bridle until he threw himself; then Sam sat on his neck and easily put the the bridle on.

"Now, you two-bit piece of crow meat, the bridle is on; and if I could, I'd put the saddle on you too while you're down, but I guess I'll have to let you up for that job."

The pony didn't mind being saddled. "Just his ears that he's proud of," said Nick.

"Does he pitch?" asked Sam, after Nick had paid him.

"Don't think so," Nick answered. "He didn't yesterday anyway. Maybe I can borrow one that's bridle broke next time. Well, so long." He swung up and set out on the long ride home. He decided to try crossing the bridge, thinking probably the pony wouldn't mind it in daylight. But the pony had a different idea. He wouldn't even put a foot on it, so Nick had to take his previous route a mile up the arroyo to cross.

Nick soon found that, instead of having to use his quirt, he was obliged to hold the pony back. Don't like town and wants to get home, thought Nick. When he rode up to the store soon after seven and gave a yell, Bud came to the door.

"Thought you weren't coming until tomorrow," he said. "Bright light hurt your eyes?"

"Nothing much to do, so I thought I might as well come home," Nick answered.

"Girls all run out of town?" Bud asked. "I better go next time. I can find something to do."

"Parson still here?" Nick asked, as he unsaddled and turned the pony loose.

"Oh yes," Bud replied, "he's quite a guy. He can cook

68

too, darn sight better than I can. He's getting supper now. We're late because I had quite a time buying a blanket. It was a good one, but small, and I knew you'd want it."

"Who brought it?" Nick asked.

"Come on in and I'll tell you about it," Bud answered.

Reverend Cardican came in and greeted Nick and said he'd go ahead with the supper.

"Well," began Bud, "you know this Rose?"

Nick knew her. He had named her "Rose," because the first time she had come to the store, she had smelled like a dog that had recently tangled with a badger. "Yeah, I know her all right."

"She came in about five with this nice little blanket," went on Bud, "and I offered her a darned good price for it — eight dollars. She was using her bum English on me. No, she wouldn't sell it for eight dollars, she wanted more. She wanted seven. That kind of surprised me, but I didn't want to give in too easy. I said how about eight and a can of peaches? Nothing doing. She wanted seven. I told her you'd probably be mad if I paid her so much, but finally said all right I'd give her seven."

"She's dumb in any language," Nick said.

"Sure is," agreed Bud. "She went ahead and traded out seven dollars and left. Well, a half hour or so later, here comes Rose and her mother, bringing all the things Rose had bought. The old lady charged across the bullpen and slammed the stuff down on the counter and then started to tell me off. I was a dog and a snake and a coyote; also a thief and a cheat and she knew, when she let her daughter come alone, that the cheating *Belacona* (American) would cheat her out of her blanket. I had only given seven dollars worth of goods when I had promised nine dollars worth. Then she cussed me plenty and demanded the blanket back."

"Like to have heard her, bet it was good," said Nick with a grin.

"It must have been good," laughed Bud. "What I could understand of it was good. When I got a chance to bust in I told her Rose asked for seven dollars. Rose said I was a liar, she had said nine dollars. I told her she better go back to school another year and find out where seven showed up, just in case she ever wanted to count up to ten."

"You gave her the other two dollars, I suppose," said Nick.

"Sure," answered Bud, "and I told Rose it was all a joke, and she better forget the English and stick to Navajo when she was dealing in terms of dollars. But the old woman didn't think it was any joke. She couldn't see it, and, as far as she's concerned, I'm still a cheat and a liar; so let's go eat."

After the meal was over and the dishes done, they all moved to the porch.

"Reverend, here," said Bud, "is new to the country and has been pumping me about the Navajos. I told him I didn't know an awful lot about them myself, but to wait until you came back."

"As I suppose I will be working among them for some time, I would like to learn all I can about them. What about their religion?"

"I don't know much about that," Nick replied, "except they seem to think what they have is as good — and maybe as old — as what we have, and my guess would be you're up against a tough proposition."

"Bad as that, eh?" the Reverend said. "But there must be some way to reach them."

"Maybe," Nick answered. "Anyway I can tell you how to get a crowd to your meetings: serve plenty of doughnuts and coffee. They'll come long distances for a free feed."

"Otherwise?"

"You'll have very, very slim attendance," Nick told him.

"Don't know if our meager budget would stand that for long," mused the Reverend. "What do they live on mostly

70

— I mean during hard times when they might not be able to trade much at the stores?"

"Bread, mutton or goat meat, and coffee," Nick answered. "Of course they have to buy the flour and coffee, but they'll get those somehow. Then there'd be rabbits, prairie dogs, and piñon nuts, with an occasional mountain lion or wildcat. No ducks, geese, or fish, as Navajos won't eat anything that lives in or on the water."

"Do they eat snakes?" the Reverend asked.

"I should say not," Bud said. "They won't even kill them, will they, Nick?"

"That's queer," the Reverend said. "Do they get bitten often?"

"Not as often as one would think, considering women or children are out all day with the sheep and there are plenty of rattlers around here."

"Looks like I have a job cut out for me," said the Reverend, "but I'm not going to start out by being discouraged."

"That's the system, Reverend," said Bud. "They're slow to get acquainted with, but I'm predicting they're going to like you."

"I hope so," he said; then changing the subject, "That was funny about the girl, and the blanket Bud bought."

"Yeah, and that old mother of hers would have packed that blanket out, too, if I hadn't ponied up another two dollars," Bud told him.

"They're sure queer, excitable, single-track people with funny ideas," Nick said. "We always try to give the weavers just about what we think we can get for the blanket. We can afford to do this because we make a nice profit on the goods we sell. So, when they really begin to squawk about our prices and begin carrying the blankets away, we can generally figure the reason — some Trader has sold a big bunch of blankets, more than he has on hand, so is paying a bit extra until he has his order filled. This Trader may be thirty miles away. No matter. The Navajo hitches up his ponies, buys a couple of dollars worth of hay and grain, and sets out on a two- or three-day trip to get ten dollars for a blanket we would have given him nine for right here."

"Looks foolish, doesn't it?" the Reverend remarked.

"Sure does," agreed Nick, "and you can talk to them until you are blue in the face, explaining that they are out a dollar on the deal before they started — buying hay and grain — but they can't see it. The only angle they can see is that they got a dollar more for the blanket."

"Queer people is what they are," the Reverend said. "Well, I hope I can do something with them. By the way, Bud says you made the bread and cake I've been enjoying. I'm glad you know how to bake. Homemade things are so much better."

"I'm sure glad too," Bud chimed in.

"Bread, biscuits, cake, and pie are easy to make," Nick said. "Of course that white cake is the only one I make. Got the recipe from a Crisco can. Bread recipe I got from a yeast cake package."

"How do you get your meat?" asked the Reverend.

"We can get a quarter of mutton from the Indians most any time. Then during June and July we get kid — you know, young goats—and they are good, aren't they, Bud?"

"Best darned meat I ever tasted," answered Bud. "They aren't very big and we roast the whole thing at once. One doesn't last long with us."

"Do many travelers stop here?" the Reverend asked.

"Yeah, quite a few white people and, of course, a lot of Tight Pants."

" 'Tight Pants,' who are they?" asked the Reverend.

"Oh, government people; they wear riding breeches and high tops or boots. We don't care much for them. They want service and expect it free of charge, which is all right, I guess, as we seldom charge anyone — unless we don't like them. But these Tight Pants, before departing,

72

always have one of us sign a voucher — just to show they have been here. So they say! We feel pretty darned sure they fill it in afterward with a suitable amount and put it in their expense account."

"And we've had a good many guests promise us presents — cigars, candy, cases of oranges, et cetera — to be sent us when they reached home. But the poor souls never made it; all were lost or perished before they reached home. But we don't care, do we, Bud?"

"We're doing all right," agreed Bud.

"Well, I was on a long saddle path today. Guess I'll go to bed," said Nick. "Good night to you, gents."

The days, weeks, and months slipped by. Nick could hardly realize the time had gone so fast when Bud approached him one spring morning and said, "Well, Nick, two years ago today I landed here."

"My gosh, it doesn't seem possible," exclaimed Nick. "Well, how do you like being an Indian Trader?"

"I like it fine and I've learned a lot. Speak pretty good Navajo too, don't I?"

"You sure do, Bud, and I guess I do too, for that matter. And I guess we've each got a nice little wad saved. Don't know where else we could have done so well. Another year or two and we can buy a place of our own. Maybe they'd sell this one, but I guess not."

"We'll keep our eyes peeled and sooner or later we'll get what we want," Bud said. "We're young yet. Let's see, you're twenty-two and I'm twenty-three this fall. Plenty of time yet, I'd say."

"Even if we don't find what we want before we're thirty, we'll still have time to make a wad before we're too old," said Nick.

"Another thing we ought to plan on," said Bud, "is that one or both of us should get married, nice to have a dishwasher around. I mean, of course, when we get a place of our own."

73

"Well, I don't know," answered Nick, "we hardly ever see a girl and I don't seem to think much about getting married. You got any prospects?"

"None," he answered. "I don't know just how we would go about getting girls. Probably have to take a month off and go somewhere where they raise them and pick us up a couple.

"Well, when the time comes, I'll let you go first and see how you make out. Hello, why's old Hungry Man in such a hurry?"

Bud stepped to the window and looked out. He saw Hungry Man riding lickety-split down the hill. Then, when he came to the fence, he tied his pony and sauntered into the store.

The Navajos always did it that way when they had news to tell. He strolled up to the counter where the free tobacco and papers were and rolled a cigarette. There was always a cigar box on the counter with free tobacco for the customers. When it was first put out, Nick and Bud were amazed at how fast the box became empty, so Bud hit on the bright idea of driving plenty of nails up through the bottom of the box. This allowed a Navajo to get a thumb and finger in the box to pinch up enough tobacco for a cigarette, but prevented his getting a handful to put in his pocket.

Hungry Man smoked a bit and then informed Nick and Bud — and three or four Navajos — that there was a very funny wagon without horses over in the next arroyo, and it couldn't get out. It made much noise and smoke and shook with rage, but it couldn't move from the sand in the bottom of the arroyo.

He went on to say that the two *Belaconas* had shoveled heaps of sand, and Hungry Man had tied a rope from his saddle horn to the strange wagon while it was quiet. But, when the noise started, his pony became frightened and jumped and lunged sideways, so the saddle turned and

Hungry Man was thrown off and the pony broke the rope and he had to chase the pony a long way before he could catch him, because the saddle, under the pony's belly, frightened him and hurt his legs, so that he ran and pitched until he was tired out. This recital caused much laughter.

Hungry Man paused for breath while he pinched out tobacco for another smoke. Then he resumed. His opinion was that it would take at least four ponies, with harness, to pull the thing out of the arroyo; so if any of the Navajos in the store had wagons, they better go over, as the white men would probably be so glad to get of the arroyo, that they would pay a good price for help.

It happened that there was one team and wagon down at the well and one of the other Navajos said he would go and get his. About two hours later the automobile arrived at the store. It had high wheels, no fenders, two high seats, no top, and was chain driven. The drivers had been three days coming the seventy miles from the River but thought, as the remaining road to town wasn't quite so sandy, they could make it in one day. Nick and Bud thought so too, if there happened to be teams handy to pull them out of the several arroyos — none was bridged.

Bud told them they'd better get hauled across this arroyo while the teams were there to do it, as it was the toughest one on the road. It was a hundred yards across and pure sand. After the auto had been dragged across, the two men came back to the store. They were leading the half-grown Russian wolfhound the boys had noticed in the back of the auto. Wanted to water him, they said.

As it was about noon, Nick invited the men to dinner. Bud took a great fancy to the dog, got him a pan of water and gave him all the food left from dinner. As the dog still seemed hungry, Nick said to get him a can of corned beef and see if that would fill him up.

One of the men, Rollins by name, said, "You boys seem to like my dog pretty well, don't you?"

"I know I do," Bud said, "and I wish he'd get away from you and come back here."

"He is a nice dog," agreed Nick. "He has a terrific appetite. Must keep you broke buying meat for him."

"He hasn't been fed yet today," Rollins told them, "and he won't be hungry all the time after he's full-grown."

"Would you think of selling him?" Bud asked.

Rollins said, "Well, he is quite a problem for us. Why, would you boys like to own him?"

"I think it would be nice to have a good dog around here," Nick said. "Don't you, Bud?"

"Sure do," agreed Bud, "except I've heard these dogs are worth plenty."

'They are," said Rollins, "and this fellow is a thoroughbred. Petrovich is his name. Now, I'll tell you something. We had decided Pete — that's what we call him — was a little more trouble than we had figured on; so, we had decided to sell him when we got to town. But now, I have a better idea. You boys were so nice, surprising us by sending over those two teams and inviting us in for a good hot dinner, and seeing how you both have taken to Pete, I'm going to make you a present of him."

"Well, mister, that's right fine of you," exclaimed Bud, "but we could pay you something for him."

"No, he's yours. I can see he's going to be treated right and have a good home, and that's all I want to know. Say, any rabbits around here?"

"Lots of them. Why?" asked Nick.

"Fine," Rollins said, "because in a couple of months this fellow will be able to catch a rabbit before the rabbit finds out what's after him. Make him a nice dinner, too."

"Well, it looks like we own a dog," Bud remarked after the men had gone.

"We ought to have some fun running coyotes," Nick said.

But later on when Pete was full grown, they found that this was not to be. Pete would have nothing to do with

76

coyotes. Bud thought maybe Pete had chased a couple and they had turned on him and nipped him a bit.

Cottontails and jack rabbits were his dish and he could sure catch them. Generally he would grab them by the back and throw them high in the air. Sometimes he would run right past them, maybe to show them what the rear end of a good runner looked like.

One afternoon a Navajo woman came into the store carrying two dead kids. She threw them up on the counter, exclaiming that the big white dog had killed them, and they were going to have to pay for them or she would tell the Agent at the Fort.

"Do you suppose Pete did kill them?" Bud asked.

"He could if he wanted to," Nick answered, "but I don't know why he'd want to." Then to the woman he said, "Maybe it wasn't our dog."

Oh yes, it was. She saw him. He ran into the herd and grabbed one kid, throwing it high in the air (and she grabbed a dead kid and threw it to the ceiling, knocking down two coffee pots and a lot of dust). Then, she said, the dog grabbed another kid and did the same with it before she could chase him away. Both kids were dead when she picked them up.

"It sure sounds like Pete's hunting technique, doesn't it?" Nick said. "I guess we may as well pay."

He got a dollar and tossed it on the counter, considering this fair pay for two kids. But it wasn't. Oh no, a dollar apiece was the price. Everybody knew a goat was worth a dollar, so hurry up so she could go back to her herd.

Nick tried to explain that these were not goats. They were not even half as big as goats and fifty cents was a good price for the little things. She snorted and laughed derisively at this silly idea. A goat was a goat, big or little, because a little goat would grow into a big goat.

Nick told her a big goat had a hide that was worth twenty-five or thirty cents, while the skins of the little ones were worthless. Fifty cents was a big price for the kids.

Yes, yes, but the hides on these would have been worth thirty cents by fall, and a dollar each was what she wanted. And a dollar each was what Nick had to give her. Before the afternoon was over — and before Pete came back — Nick had settled with two other Navajos for five more kids. Seven dollars seemed quite a lot for one afternoon's sport; so Pete was kept tied daytimes until the kids grew large enough not to be mistaken for rabbits.

A couple of days later, a squaw came into the store and said she had a hindquarter of calf in her wagon down by the well, and wanted to know if Nick wanted to buy it.

"I guess we could use a small quarter of meat," Nick remarked. "Bud, you might go down and look it over. If it looks bright and fresh and like it might have been butchered instead of dying of some disease, have her bring it up."

Bud came back saying it was fresh-killed, at any rate, so he weighed it, paid for it, and hung it up to cool. The next morning Bud decided on steak for breakfast. He went to the wareroom, cut a slice from the quarter and fried it. It was a little tough and seemed to have a sweetish taste.

"I'm not too dang sure about this meat," Nick finally said. "The more I eat, the more I have the feeling that Hunchy's wife has put something over on us."

"I have that same notion," agreed Bud. "Let's go take a right careful look-see again."

"This fat, what little there is, don't look just the right color," Nick said, "and the general shape isn't right. I don't think the critter ever sucked a cow — horse, maybe, or mule or burro — *quien sabe?*"

"Guess I don't eat any more of that," Bud stated firmly.

Later on when a Navajo came in, they took him to the warehouse to get his opinion. After a good look and smell he said, *Tlee* (horse). Very nice meat, he claimed, and could he buy some. He could, and all he wanted. He took about half of it.

That evening a white man came along with a bunch of cattle. He had four Navajo herders and they wanted meat. Bud took him out and showed him what he had and, by making a special price, sold it all. The white man didn't know it was horsemeat and Bud didn't mention it. The man evidently cooked some for himself, because ever after when he came along, he would stop in to inquire if Bud had any old sore-back pony meat. Then he'd laugh and say it was all right, because his herders ate every bit of it.

A few mornings later a young buck came into the store and said he wanted a box. His baby had died during the night. The boys had made a good many coffins. The little ones were not so hard to make, but once in a while they'd have a call for a full-sized one. Generally, bodies were stuffed into some crevice in the rocks. For an adult-size coffin, something stronger than Arbuckles coffee box lumber was needed for the bottom, and this was seldom to be had. One large box that Bud made had to be carted to the final resting place and then the body put in, because when it was put in at first and unwilling hands laid hold to put it in the wagon, the bottom of the box AND the departed one remained right on the ground. Bud had exclaimed in Navajo, "He don't want to go," and he burst out laughing. But he quickly changed it to coughing, and moved fast down to the corral, where he laughed for fifteen minutes. He had never liked the departed before he was a corpse.

Bud, who was quite a carpenter and always made the coffins, asked the young father how long the baby was. The man held out his hands to show the length and Bud took a rule and measured it. He allowed a couple of inches more and started to saw a board, when the Navajo stopped him saying it had to be longer. Bud told him he didn't have much lumber and he had allowed a little extra, so that length would have to do. The Navajo grabbed the hammer and would have beaned Bud if Nick hadn't grabbed his arm.

"Now, what in hell is the matter with him?" growled Bud.

"I don't know what set him off," admitted Nick. "Maybe he has something else he wants to put in, bowl of food or something. Darned if I know."

"Well, all I know is that he has his heart set on a certain length," Bud said, "so, if you will please put that hammer back of the counter out of his reach, I'll saw this board anywhere he puts his dirty finger. I'm sure not going to fight him. He's feeling bad enough as it is."

"You see what I mean, though, don't you, Bud? Grief and sudden rage go arm in arm with these fellows."

# CHAPTER 5

"WHO'S THIS COMING?" asked Bud one October afternoon. He watched a buckboard, pulled by a slick looking pair of mules, come down the hill. "My gosh," he exclaimed, "it's a one-armed man!"

"Sure enough," said Nick, as the driver swung the mules up in front of the store.

The boys went out the door and the stranger asked if he could spend the night with them. He said he was a government stockman and an officer of the law and was looking for a Navajo who had escaped from jail at the Agency.

Government man — not so good. Nick and Bud were not too pleased to see a government man on that particular day for this reason: a couple of weeks before, they had unloaded and put in the warehouse, four barrels of pop. Pop was packed ten dozen to the barrel. They had already used three of them, and this afternoon when Bud went out to open the fourth barrel, he came quickly back to inform Nick that they were all out of pop, but did have a barrel of nice cool beer. Someone at the storage plant in town had made a mistake. "Tough on our customers to be out of pop but rather nice for us," Bud said.

Traders weren't supposed to have liquor or beer on the Reservation, but the beer tasted fine and the boys had already had three or four bottles each when the government man drove up.

Of course, there was nothing to do but take him in, so Bud unharnessed the mules and put them away in the corral, although the man said not to think he was helpless as he usually harnessed and unharnessed them. He also said that his name was Bill Lott and he preferred to be called Bill. Then he asked the boys their names.

He was a big powerful looking man, probably around sixty-five years of age. He was sandy complexioned with a heavy head of white hair. His huge eyebrows and moustache were also white. He had a rather stern, fierce look until he smiled.

Bud came in from the corral, went to the warehouse, and piled empty pop bottles on the beer so it would look like a barrel of empties. The boys tried to keep a respectable distance from the government man so he wouldn't smell the beer on them. They found out later, he had smelled it at once. They also learned that he hated all Indians. As a young man, he had had several fights with the Apaches and, in the last one, had his left arm shot off. Bud wanted to know how he would handle a bad Indian when he had to take one in. He said that was easy. He would make some other Indian or the prisoner's wife tie the bastard's hands behind his back, and then they'd shove him, head first, up under the seat of the buckboard where Bill could keep his foot on the prisoner's neck if necessary.

"I'm an inspector too," Bill announced, after they had visited for a time, "so while I'm at it, I'll look around and see how clean you boys keep this store."

"Go right ahead," urged Nick, because he felt the store was always fairly neat and clean.

Bill first complained about the mixed candy. This was kept in a bin large enough to hold a thirty-pound box, as that was the size box the candy came in. This mixed candy, heavy with gumdrops, was the only class of candy the Indians ever asked for, and it certainly sold fast.

"This here candy should be kept covered," said Bill. "Keep the flies and dust from it — not but what it would be good enough for the Long Hairs even if a skunk played around on it, but suppose some white people come along and want some?"

"Yeah, bad all right," agreed Bud.

Then Bill noticed the bread piled on a shelf. A box of a hundred loaves was ordered every time a freight wagon went to town. Bread wasn't wrapped so it was generally quite hard by the time it reached the store. The Navajos didn't care how hard it was. It tasted different from their baking powder bread and, anyway, it could be soaked in coffee until it was soft enough to eat.

"You really should have a good tight box to keep bread in," Bill said, as he picked up a loaf. "Good Lord on high! That's harder than the hardtack we used to try and eat. You couldn't cut this bread with an axe. You mean these Indian friends of yours buy this stuff?"

"Sure and glad to get it," answered Nick.

"Well, I'll be doggoned," was all Bill said.

Of course when he spotted the caked sugar on the floor, he did have a reason to squawk. That should have been kept cleaned up.

"Now, right here," announced Bill, "is something I wouldn't have believed and just goes to show how shiftless you boys have become."

That sugar had been piling up there on the floor for years. The sugar bin was built under the counter and swung out from the top. During each day a little sugar would get spilled on the floor and then each morning before they had a chance to sweep, it had hardened and caked. By now it was a couple of inches thick. Bill told Bud to get a hatchet and chop that mess up and then scrub the floor. It took Bud a good hour to get it clean enough to suit Bill.

Along about closing time, Bill said he was sure he smelled beer — or something — and he felt it his duty to look the place over, at the same time remarking what a serious thing it was to have any intoxicants in one's possession on the Reservation. Generally this meant having one's license revoked. He seemed to think the wareroom would be the logical place for illicit goods, and the boys were quite nervous as they followed him there. When he came to the barrel and took the few empty bottles off the top uncovering the beer, they knew they were sunk.

"Ha, ha," he said, "a whole barrel of it. Now it does look like you are in for it, because I firmly believe this is beer, but there is only one sure way to tell. Where is the opener?"

Bud produced an opener and handed it to Bill, saying, "All right then, so it's beer."

Bill opened one and drank it without ever taking the bottle from his mouth. "Yep," he said, "it's beer all right, and just as I suspected." He opened another and drank it. Then he roared with laughter. He had never had so much fun in his life . . . government inspector . . . ha, ha . . . and now to find a barrel of nice cool beer . . . he'd camp right there with them until it was all gone.

"I'm no officer," he said, "I'm just a plain government stockman. I like you boys and I haven't much to do right now so, if you'll forgive me and can put up with me, I would like to spend a few days here. You really shouldn't hold it against me for having Bud clean up that sugar mess because if it had gotten much thicker, someone might have fallen over it and broke a leg or something."

"Oh, that's all right," laughed Bud, "and I'm not going to let that sugar get a start on me again."

84

After supper Bud said he guessed he'd better make a little blaze in the fireplace as the nights were beginning to get chilly.

"Yeah, a fire will feel good," agreed Bill. "I suppose you boys have quite a few people stop here. Seems like there are more people crossing the Reservation than ever before."

"Yeah," Bud said, "we've entertained everyone from governors and generals to fallen women, bandits, and murderers."

"Who was the governor?" asked Bill.

"The first governor of New Mexico, after statehood," answered Nick. "He and party were on their way to the river and Bud and I got them a pretty good meal coming and going. The governor was certainly a swell fellow, wasn't he, Bud?"

"He sure was," agreed Bud, "and he certainly was interested and surprised to see how well we lived out here. General Scott was a grand old fellow too. That was a nice letter he wrote us after he returned to Washington. We ought to keep that."

"I've got it," Nick answered. "He stopped here twice. First, when on his way over to Beautiful Mountain to settle that so-called Indian uprising. The old general was a damn sight better natured than I'd have been after being jerked and bounced over forty-five miles of muddy roads in a four mule carryall. He was behind the cavalry; they got here the night before."

"Boy, and were those troopers scared of the Indians," laughed Bud. "You know, they camped so close to the store, we were afraid their campfires would set the place on fire."

"Yeah, and the stuff you told them about the poor Navajos didn't ease their minds much," Nick said.

"I only told them that the Indians were always on the lookout for a few scalps, that they hated soldiers and were pretty well worked up over their coming, and if they did

85

attack, it would be just before dawn so it might pay to be on the alert about that time. They swallowed it all too."

"Do you know Sandy Tilton?" Nick asked Bill.

"No, I guess not," Bill answered. "Why?"

"Oh, I just thought of him because he was here the night the soldiers were here. He chipped in his two bits worth, too, on how bad and treacherous the Indians were. Sandy was an ex-bandit who got caught after a holdup of a Santa Fe train that didn't go quite as planned. He served a stretch in the Pen, only three or four years though."

"Wish he'd come through while you're here, Bill," Bud said. "He can sure tell some interesting and funny things about the time he was with those train robbers. Oh yeah, Nick, we must tell Bill about Silverton Liz."

"Who was she?" Bill asked.

"She was quite a character," Nick answered. "She stepped into the store late one afternoon, and I don't mind saying she was a startling looking creature. She was a full six foot tall, broad-shouldered and big, but not fat. She looked to be thirty or more. She was wearing a big floppy hat and carried a dinky little bag. But the outstanding thing about her was she had no nose. This caused the few Navajos in the store to murmur and giggle, and one woman said she hadn't known before that white men cut off the noses of their women."

"Do the Navajos do that?" asked Bill.

"Maybe they used to," said Bud.

"Yep," agreed Nick. "Well, this dame began inquiring how she was going to get to Gallup. I asked her how she got here and she said she walked. She had stayed at Farley's the night before, eighteen miles from us. I told her I didn't know how she'd get to Gallup unless she walked. Well, she said her feet were pretty bad and before she did any more walking, she'd have to have a good rest. We sure didn't want her here but, as we couldn't see any way out of it, we figured we'd have to put her up for the night."

86

"I asked her if she could ride a horse. She said she didn't know, but she guessed it would be easier than walking, so I asked the Indians if any of them would come and bring an extra horse and take the woman to town. None volunteered. Then Lazy Luke said if we needed a load of goods, he would go to town and the noseless giant could ride in with him; but he would insist on his wife going too, because he didn't think he should go alone with this woman who had her nose cut off."

"And you bet we took Luke up on his offer," said Bud. "We got Liz some supper — we assured her we only ate twice a day and had already eaten. There would have been no use trying to eat with that face before us. We fixed her a bunk on the porch, but she talked a great deal before she went to bed. Among other things, she claimed she wasn't so bad looking when she wore her nose. She generally had a putty nose but she had lost it. We told her we would love to see her with it on and knew she must feel half-dressed without it. We both assured her we could tell at a glance she would be a knockout with a nose, although we could only guess what a putty nose would do to that mug."

"And you can bet we got her off on the freight wagon the next morning," put in Nick. "Then about noon a Navajo came with a note from old Moab Farley — where Liz had stayed the night before — wanting to know if that thieving, noseless old pickpocket was with us and, if so, to hold her and send word right back. Seems Liz had gone through the pockets of Moab's coat, which hung in his bedroom, and swiped a ten dollar bill. We sent word right back that Liz — thank God — was gone, so it looked like he was out the ten."

"We found out later that she was a pretty tough number and had been run out of Silverton," added Bud.

"A nice dame to be hanging around a couple of innocent boys like you," Bill said with a grin.

"Only unescorted woman that ever stopped here," said

Bud. "Too bad, though, that a couple of pretty ones didn't drop in on us."

"They won't," said Nick. "We had a murderer spend the night with us too," he went on. "But I don't know if he was a real murderer. He had killed a man over in Colorado and maybe the guy had it coming to him anyway. This fellow, who said his name was Smith, was a nice quiet little fellow. We liked him and we sat and talked until after midnight. After breakfast next morning before saddling, he insisted on paying us for keeping him. We told him he didn't owe us anything, but we finally did take a dollar for horse feed."

"The next night the sheriff and a deputy arrived and they stayed with us overnight. They told us who our previous guest was and according to them, it was just plain murder, but we still think the guy probably had some good reason that the sheriff didn't know about."

"We had another shooter stay with us," Bud said. "He'd killed a man in a gun fight and the sheriff came after him, got him too, we heard."

"Suppose they think the Reservation is the best place to head for," remarked Bill.

"Yeah," Nick said, "but it should be the last place. Probably due to the fact that they may ride hours without seeing a Navajo, they get the idea that the Navajos don't see them. That's where they are wrong, because plenty of Navajos will see any rider who passes through this country; and, believe me, they can describe him to anyone who makes inquiries."

"I guess those buggers don't miss much," said Bill, "and even if the bad men only rode at night, they'd notice the larger tracks of an American horse."

"That's right," agreed Bud, "but all travelers don't ride horses. Remember, Nick, that gang of I.W.W.'s who came along?"

"Yeah," Nick said, "that time our dog, Pete, woke us

up about midnight. Bud slipped on his boots and said he'd go see what was going on. He took his six shooter as he's always hoping he'll get a chance to use it on somebody. Pete was barking out back, so we went to the kitchen door and when Bud opened it, it sounded like there was a small army down there in the arroyo. We supposed they'd come to the store when they filled up on water, so we went and put our clothes on. Sure enough, they soon were yelling and pounding on the store door. We went out on the screened porch to see what they wanted. They seemed to be a mixed bunch of foreigners and one of them said they were miners on their way from Arizona to Silverton and wanted something to eat and a place to sleep. There were twelve of them and they seemed to have had plenty of whiskey. We opened the store and let them get what they wanted to eat. Then we told them they could sleep in the barn."

"They were pretty good fellows at that," Bud said. "Left us a quart of darned nice whiskey, didn't they, Nick?"

"Yeah," he said, "and that whiskey apparently brought us an unwelcome visitor, the way the beer brought Bill."

"Well, I like that," said Bill.

"You heard me say *apparently*," Nick told him, "but wait until you hear this. About closing time we mixed a good drink; then a little later while getting supper, we had another and then we heard someone at the door knock and holler."

"I went to the door," Bud said, "and there was a portly priest, who said he'd like to spend the night with us. He introduced himself and I told him to go on in and I'd put his team away. Nick and I had heard of him. He was a great friend of the Navajos and they all liked him."

"Well, he came in and I told him who I was," Nick said, "and you can bet I was worried because he was sure to get a sniff of whiskey on one of us. Bud came in and visited with the Father while setting the table. A little later I was quite surprised when I heard Bud ask him if he'd like a little snifter before supper."

"Sure," said Bud. "I knew he could smell whiskey and he'd had a long drive, so why not be open and above-board about it."

"Damn sight more above-board with him than you were with me," remarked Bill.

"Well," went on Bud, with a grin, "this priest was Irish and had an honest face and a twinkling eye, and I had a hunch he'd take a drink."

"He did too," Nick said. "Had a couple before supper and then, in the evening, we sat and listened to him while we killed the rest of the quart. Bud and I were feeling quite good by bedtime, but it never fazed the Father."

"I've known some priests like that," Bill said, "and I could never see that a few drinks hurt them any." Then, changing the subject, he said, "I see only a few chickens around here. Why don't you raise lots of them, be nice to have plenty of fryers and eggs."

At this, Bud burst out laughing. "What's the joke?" asked Bill.

"Want to buy a good incubator and brooder, Bill?"

"No, I guess not. Why?"

"You tell him, Nick," replied Bud.

"Well," began Nick, "we had the chicken idea — but in a big way, so a year ago last spring, we ordered an in-cubator and brooder, a hundred egg outfit. After the outfit was here, we ordered the eggs — a hundred and twenty-five, because we had to allow for some breakage coming out on a freight wagon. As soon as they arrived we put them in the incubator and filled and lighted the lamp. Of course, we had to watch that lamp a good deal, because the days were warm and the nights were cold."

"Yeah, we used to set the alarm clock for two and take turns getting up in the night to see that the temperature was right," laughed Bud.

"Then we had to sprinkle them and turn them every day. We must have done everything just about right, because darn near every one of those eggs hatched out a nice Rhode Island Red chick. The second day we put them in the brooder. We turned the lamp up high so they'd be warm during the night, but I don't know if they were, because there were eleven dead ones the next morning — trampled and smothered."

"I thought maybe they were weaklings and would have died anyway, but I was wrong," said Bud.

"You sure were," agreed Nick, "because the next morning there were fourteen dead ones. Then Bud had a bright idea and spent the afternoon dividing the brooder into enough little pens so he could put five in each. That worked fine too, although, of course, we lost some more. But if we raised sixty percent it would be plenty, and we were sure we would. Then Bud said how about sending for a bunch of turkey eggs; it would be swell to have turkey when we wanted it. We sent for a hundred and twenty turkey eggs and started them cooking."

"I've heard they are hard to raise," remarked Bill.

"We know a whale of a lot more about that than you," laughed Bud, "but they're awful easy to hatch. We got ninety-two out of a hundred eggs, didn't we, Nick?"

"Sure did," he answered, "and we didn't lose as many in the brooder as we did chicks. We only kept them in the brooder three or four days because a Mormon came along and, after looking at our old log hay barn, he said if he was doing it, he'd move them right out there in that nice dry place and they'd do a lot better. But the big bull snakes found out about it and they got a lot of them. Also there were little holes around the bottom of the barn where the turkeys could get out."

"We never knew how many Pete ate because we didn't know he was eating them until one day when I was walking out to the barn, I met him coming from that direction and, just as he reached me, he burped up a turkey. He evidently swallowed them whole. How many at a time, I don't know."

"Yeah, and he might just as well have eaten them all," Bud said, "because one afternoon when they were all out, a sudden hard rain came up, and they just stood with open mouths pointed to the sky and drowned themselves."

"No!" exclaimed Bill, "they didn't really do that!"

"Well, they might as well have," Bud said, "because the next morning they were all dead, except four. In a couple of days more there was only one left. We brought him in on the back porch and made a pet of him. He liked flies, so we'd swat them for him."

"Yeah," Nick said, "if we wanted him to follow us, we'd just pick up a fly swatter. But after he got big and we put him out of doors, a Navajo dog got him, so we never got one meal out of our ninety-two turkeys."

"Well, now, that's what I call tough luck," Bill said. "Chickens did better, I guess."

"In a way, they did," said Nick, "but nothing to brag about. We got chicken wire and made a nice pen for them. There were about fifty left and they were just getting big enough. We figured in another week we'd begin eating some young roosters, when a skunk got in the pen — at night, of course — and cut the throats of thirty-two. Why he didn't finish the job, I don't know."

"Well, I'll be damned," exclaimed Bill.

"Oh, we ate two roosters," Bud told him, "but we'll probably set a few hens next spring. Since we put the wire fence around the yard, we may have better luck. But no more mass production for us."

"That's right," agreed Nick. "Say, Bud, I was going to tell you what Lazy Luke told me this morning. I asked him why the Navajos were all pigeon-toed. He said he would tell me. A long, long time ago, his people lived far to the north where it was very cold and there was much snow. That was a hard country to live in, so finally their chief decided they should all move south where, perhaps, they would come to a warmer country. As they had no horses, they packed the few things they owned on their backs and started out, with the chief leading them. For many moons they traveled through the snow, each setting his feet in the tracks of the one ahead. But it happened that the chief's toes pointed in; so by the time they reached the warm country, all turned their toes in when they walked."

"The darned old liar," Bud said, "he's always stringing me too. Well, it's ten thirty. Guess I'll hit the hay."

"Guess we all will," said Bill, "so good night."

Bill stayed four days. Before he left, he said, "I have sure enjoyed myself here, and if I'm not too much trouble to you boys, I'll be seeing you every once in a while. This is a swell place to hide out."

"Come as often as you like," urged Nick.

"And here's another thing," went on Bill, "you sign this voucher and I'll pay my board."

"You don't owe us any board," Nick said.

"Nevertheless, here it is, and you'll take it," he said. "I'm allowed so much for that purpose. Don't come out of my pocket, you know."

Nick didn't want to take it, but rather than argue, did.

One afternoon a couple of weeks later, Jesse, the boy who had worked for Nick before Bud arrived, came into the store.

"White Eye wants you two to come and see his daughter married," he stated.

"What time is this here *Banderogio* set for?" asked Bud.

"If you come at four or four-thirty it will be all right," he answered.

"Well, I don't know," said Nick. He was not too keen about accepting, because they had previously been to a couple of these little night healing ceremonies and found that after they once got in the hogan and the Medicine Man started chanting, it was not so easy to get out and it had been awfully late when they got home.

"First I'd like to know how long it's going to take to join this happy pair. In other words, what time do we leave?"

"Oh, you don't need to stay more than a couple of hours," Jesse answered.

"All right then, we'll take a chance," agreed Nick. "You'll have to bring me a pony. Bud has his."

"Yes, I'll bring you a pony," Jesse assured him.

Jesse's last name was James. The government school teachers named a good many of the wild little Navajo children when they came to school — Grover Cleveland, Abe Lincoln, George Washington, Thomas Jefferson, and Jack Johnson were examples of the teachers' originality. Of course, a Navajo has the real name his mother has given him when he is a baby, but he very rarely tells anyone what that name is.

In due time Jesse came with the pony, so Bud saddled his and the three set out.

There was quite a gathering at White Eye's hogan. About the time the boys were through with greetings and handshakings, the groom, his father and mother, and a few friends were seen coming with the price of the bride.

The boy, Notai, was dressed in a new pair of overalls, fancy new shirt, boots, and a big hat. The girl, Kahon-abah, stayed in the hogan. Of course Nick and Bud knew her, a fat, dumpy girl and certainly no beauty.

Her mother and father came from the hogan to see the ponies, which were the bride's price, to make sure the number was right — six — and that there were no cripples in the bunch.

"Well," said Bud, "if they'd left it to me, I'd take the ponies, and they're nothing to get excited about either. I wouldn't give one of them for that girl."

"Well, the boy has to have a wife, don't he?" said Nick. "What the hell, they don't marry them for looks anyway."

"Sure looks like a swap, don't it?" Bud said, as they watched the ponies being herded into White Eye's corral. "I thought there might be an argument on that old white horse."

Everyone now started going into the hogan. Inside, they sat on the dirt floor around a big kettle of boiled mutton — or goat. Nick and Bud dipped into this with their fingers, as did the others. Kahonabah's mother passed around Navajo bread and cups of black coffee.

"The grub isn't too bad," Bud remarked, "although I won't be surprised if the stew gets to tasting a little horsey before long with so many fingers dipping in the pot. I didn't notice anyone washing after handling horses, sweaty saddle blankets, and bridles."

"Don't give it a thought. I won't," said Nick, "even if I have had enough stew, because I wasn't too hungry."

"I get you," said Bud.

There was much laughter and many coarse jokes and one woman sang a little song, which probably was entitled, "Go Easy With My Daughter."

Jesse told them how the ceremonial bread or mush for the wedding was made two days before the nuptials. The girl digs a pit and builds a fire in it. Then she grinds what corn she needs and mixes up a thick batter. When this is done she cleans the fire and ashes from the pit, lines it with cedar bark over which she puts cornhusks, and then puts in the cornmeal batter. Over this she places cornhusks, more cedar bark, and then covers the whole mess with dirt. This generally is left for a day and a night. The day after she makes the bread, she kills a sheep or a goat and gets it ready for cooking.

"I've always felt sorry for the sheep or goat that is to be killed," Bud said. "I've watched some old woman with a dull knife saw away on a throat for what seemed five minutes at least. Used to wonder why they didn't use the point to get a start, until I found out they don't use the point of a knife. You never see them stick a knife in a melon either — the point of a knife is for enemies."

"Well," said Jesse, "it's pretty hard to knock a sheep out by hitting him in the head, would spoil the head and brains and, probably, the eyes."

After visiting and smoking awhile, they all went to another hogan where the wedding was to take place. The groom's family took their places on the north side and the girl's folks on the south, where Nick, Bud, and Jesse also seated themselves.

After a bit the boy came in and sat down in the place of honor, just north of a line drawn from the door in the east wall to the west wall, where some sheepskins had been placed for him. Then an Uncle brought in the girl, who seated herself to the right and just a little back of the boy.

White Eye, who had remained outside, now came in with a Navajo *Toh-je* (water jar) and a gourd dipper. The water jar was a vase-shaped woven jar, covered with piñon gum to make it waterproof. Each family had one or more.

The girl got up and took the jar, knelt before the boy, and poured water on his hands while he washed them. Then he took the jar and poured water while she washed her hands. A Wedding Basket was then brought in, filled with the mushy corn meal bread that the girl had baked, and was placed beside the couple with the opening in the basket design facing the east. Next White Eye took out some pollen from a little sack. This was supposed to have been gathered by a Bluebird — but wasn't — representing the symbol of happiness. From between his fingers and thumb, White Eye dribbled the pollen across the bread, first from east to west, next from south to north. Then,

96

starting at the basket design opening, he made a circle around the inside of the basket. This program was repeated by the boy's father.

Kahonabah dug her hand in and took some of the mush from the east side of the basket and handed it to the boy, who gulped it down like Pete had the young turkeys. He took some from the same side and gave it to the girl, who also gulped it down. This was repeated from the south, west, and north sides, and, finally, from the center of the basket.

Now Kahonabah poured some water into the gourd and handed it to Notai, who drank; then he poured her some and she drank. This concluded the ceremony — they were hitched. Nick and Bud, after sampling the wedding mush and visiting a bit, left. The Navajos would stay, eating, joking, talking, and singing until dawn, when the boy's folks would leave.

"Well, you see how it's done now, Bud," Nick said, as they rode along. "Anytime you feel like getting married, we can fix it up in no time. The girl furnishes everything."

"Yeah, how about the ponies?" Bud asked.

"Well, yes, that's right," Nick answered. "I guess you'll have to find yourself an orphan."

"And I guess I won't. You know something, Nick, I still think my wife is going to be white."

"I know that well enough," Nick told him. "Me, I don't know. Time will tell." But inside, he didn't feel quite that calm and indifferent. He was still thinking of Glacie, and maybe time was running out. What was he waiting for — or afraid of?

Back at the store they unsaddled. Jesse would get his pony in the morning, as he had no intentions of leaving before the party was over.

"Guess we better have some supper," Bud remarked. "I don't just feel what we had was a real meal."

"We aren't very sociable, are we, Bud? Suppose we should go out among them more. Oh, well."

* * *

Snow came early that winter, accompanied by howling winds, which made it difficult to heat the store and living rooms. The cold weather lasted for almost three months and the Navajos said it was the worst winter for many years. There was plenty of coal in the coal house. Even if there hadn't been, there was plenty in an arroyo, three miles from the store. This arroyo had cut down about fifteen feet, exposing a vein of very good coal, which the Navajos would hack out and deliver for three dollars a load.

The big potbellied stove was kept roaring and the bullpen was plenty warm, but back of the counter it was really cold. The Navajos would come in, wrapped in their robes and, if it was snowing and the robes were wet, so much the worse — they would make for the hot stove and hover so close that they steamed and scorched their robes. That scorched wool smell, mingled with the odor of sweaty, unwashed bodies, along with the cheap tobacco they smoked, was just about all a white man could take.

"May I be excused from complaining," growled Bud, "but this business is getting too much for me. Let's divide the days into shifts. Say you stay in here an hour — if you can stand it that long — and then I'll come in and relieve you. We'll get sick, just as sure as hell, if we breathe this smell all day."

It wasn't quite that bad, but they were mighty glad when spring came and the doors could be kept opened.

About ten one nice May morning, White Horse came bursting into the store. He had a cut in his upper arm and the blood was slowly running down and dripping from his hand. He was terribly excited and wild-eyed and he wanted a gun. "What do you want a gun for, and what's the matter with your arm?" Nick asked.

"What he wants most is to get that arm bandaged, I'd say," remarked Bud. "I'll go find something to tie it up with."

But no, the arm didn't matter, he wanted a gun.

"Just forget the gun," Nick said. "First, we'll take care of this arm. How'd you get this cut?"

"Little Man struck me with an axe, and I'm going to kill him," answered White Horse.

"The killing can wait," said Nick. "Unless you want to bleed to death, and besides you'll get no gun here."

Bud came in with some cloth and a handful of salt. He didn't care much for White Horse.

"What's the salt for?" asked Nick.

"To stop the bleeding," he answered. Then, as he rolled up White Horse's bloody shirt sleeve, he said, "This will hurt a little but will stop the bleeding," and he slapped the salt on the cut.

White Horse jumped and yelled and tried to jerk away from Bud, but Bud hung onto the arm and kept the salt in place. "That made him forget about the gun," grinned Bud. "Now help me get a bandage on."

Between them they tied up the wound, with White Horse still yelling and squirming.

"That really must have stung. Will it help any?" asked Nick.

"Sure it stung and sure it'll stop the bleeding, or so I've heard," Bud answered. "And another thing, don't these kindly creatures throw a handful of salt in the wound after they have castrated a colt? Now he knows how the colt feels."

Nick got the patient a bottle of pop and some cookies. After he calmed down a bit, they asked him what happened.

Well, he had, for some time, been watering his sheep over at the pond by Little Man's place, and this morning his son, a boy of about ten who herded the sheep, had taken them to the pond as usual. But evidently Little Man had noticed how the water was shrinking in the pond and decided he would save what was left for his own sheep. When he saw the flock of White Horse's coming, he ran to head them off and tell the boy he could not water them there anymore. But, as everybody should know, it takes more than a man and a boy to stop sheep when they are thirsty and near water. Little Man ran back and forth, trying to head them off and getting very hot and mad. Then he picked up a big stick and began beating any he could reach and crippled two or three. The little boy began to cry and ran all the way back to his father's hogan to tell him that Little Man was trying to kill their sheep. White Horse left his son at the hogan and set out for the pond.

The sheep were by the pond and had drunk. Little Man wasn't there, so White Horse went to the hogan. Little Man was terribly mad and he and White Horse got into a very bad quarrel, so bad that Little Man grabbed the axe and cut White Horse on the arm and chased him away. Now, if they would please give him a gun, he'd go back and kill this bad man.

"No, you don't get any gun from us," Nick told him. "You go home and have your boy round up the sheep. Then, when your arm is better, you go to the Agent and let him settle this row."

"And you'd better water your sheep somewhere else, because it looks to me like Little Man doesn't want you watering at his pond," added Bud.

# ChAPTER 6

AS A COUPLE MORE YEARS PASSED, Nick and Bud felt the impact of changing times. In 1912 automobiles began coming by, sometimes as often as two in a week, but they all had trouble. None made it through the big sandy wash by the store. They simply did not have power enough. The Model T's had the best chance because they were not as heavy as the other makes. The Ford drivers were optimists. They would come in the store to let Nick and Bud know they had conquered half of the distance across the Reservation, and to brag about the "bearcat" they were driving. They would all pooh-pooh the idea of needing help to cross the wash. Some would make it a quarter of the distance across; occasionally one would drive his "bearcat" halfway before it was buried in the sand. They generally tried some shovel work first, but that was no use. The sand was too deep, and it either slipped or blew back in the tracks faster than it could be shoveled.

Soon they would come sheepishly back in the store asking for help. Most always there were Navajos in the store, or more likely outside laughing at the ease with which the white man got stuck. If it happened to be a Model T in the arroyo, a couple of riders with ropes tied to the saddle horns and assisted by the Model T's feeble power, would do the trick. The grateful driver would then slip the Navajos two bits or a half dollar apiece and be on his way.

If it was one of the heavier makes of cars in trouble, that took a good team and some pushers. This was a different proposition and a deal that called for some negotiating, especially if a Navajo had to go home for a team. But in time the deal was consummated. Time is what the Navajo had the most of and he loved to dicker and argue.

Some drivers could not believe they were really stuck. They would get mad and rock the car back and forth, getting nowhere, except deeper in the sand. Sometimes this wound up in a broken axle or drive shaft; then Nick and Bud would have company for a few days.

One afternoon a man and woman drove in from the North in a shiny new 1914 Buick to see if they could get some gas. They could, because a month before Nick had ordered five barrels sent out. While Bud was getting the gas, the man asked about the road ahead.

"Except for the arroyo here, I guess you can make it all right," Bud answered. "This arroyo is the toughest on the road."

"It will have to be tough to stick us," the woman said.

"Except when the sand is a little wet, it sticks them all," said Bud, "although I haven't seen any car like yours try it yet."

"Well, you're going to see this one try it, and also make it across."

Bud shrugged. "Okay, put it in second gear, hit it hard, and hope for the best."

He joined Nick around back of the kitchen to watch

them. They sailed right along until they reached about the middle; then the car slowed down and stopped. The lady got out and walked around the car. Bud and Nick could hear her order the man to back up a little.

" 'Little' is a good word," said Nick, because a foot back was as much as the car could make.

Then she told the man to go ahead; and, while he was switching gears, she moved over back of the car, just in time to get showered with the sand the rear wheels kicked up.

"What the hell are you trying to do, put my eyes out?" she screeched as she clawed at her eyes.

"Goodness, gracious," said Bud, "the lady swears."

"Just stay out at the side and you'll be all right," calmly answered the man. Then he got out to take a look. The car was down to the running board by now.

"Get your shovel," she ordered. All the cars carried shovels. He shoveled for fifteen minutes or more.

"Now get in and try it. Give it everything it's got," ordered the lady.

The car crawled forward about three feet. The man started to change gears to back up again.

"Don't do that!" the lady yelled. "Keep going ahead, you fool!"

He tried ahead again.

"Keep at it; it moved a little," she said.

"Yeah," said Bud, "a little *down*."

At the third try, something happened, because the motor raced. But the wheels didn't turn.

"Well, by the Eternal, Sparks, if you haven't set right there and busted up this new car. What in hell do you suppose you've done to it?"

"Calm down, Pigeon," he answered, "your guess is as good as mine as to what's happened."

Although Bud knew very little about automobiles, Nick felt he ought to go take a look anyway.

"Well, Sparks has managed to break something," the woman said, when Bud got to them. "Oh, I'd better tell you who we are. Our name is Sparks, what's yours?"

"Bud Larson is my name," he answered. "Guess you shouldn't have tried to buck this sand. I suppose you've busted an axle. Start her up again and put her in gear and I'll see if the drive shaft turns. If it does, it must be an axle. Yeah, it turns."

"Well, Sparks, what are you going to do now?" she asked.

"I hardly know," he answered.

"Well, you'd better know. What can the old fool do, Bud — you said Bud, didn't you?"

"That's right," he told her. "Well, first, we'll have to get the car hauled up in our yard. It'll take two teams to do it, and will probably cost five dollars. Okay?"

"Sure, Sparks is plenty able to pay," she answered. "He's got plenty of money, if he hasn't anything else."

"We'll have to find out which axle is broken and send a rider to town for another. I'll go see about getting some teams."

"We can stay with you then?" she asked.

"Yeah, we can take care of you, have to," Bud told her, and left for the store.

"Ha, ha, comrade," he said to Nick, "we have guests, so prepare the bridal chamber. May and September have broken an axle on their chariot; and, the way I size up May, we are in for two and possibly three hectic days."

"Give me a drink too, so I can 'ha, ha,' " Nick said.

"I've had no drink," Bud assured him, "but I wouldn't doubt September has a bottle; he just naturally has to have one to take the abuse he seems to take."

"What are they like close up?" Nick asked.

"Well, let's see," Bud answered. "Pigeon — that's right — is red-headed, freckled a bit, has blue eyes, a good form, and is maybe thirty-five. Not a bad-looking dame at all.

Probably was a hash slinger before she hooked Sparks. He's tall, as you could see, at least a six-footer, lean, dark hair, good-looking man of fifty-five or so. Probably a Texan, calm sort of gent and fond of Pigeon — or why would he call her that? Well, we'll have to get another team — I see one wagon outside — and get the car up; then get someone to ride to town."

"Here they come," said Nick. "You can show them around."

At five-thirty when Bud went to the kitchen to start the fire, Pigeon trailed along. She wanted to help get supper, she claimed. Bud emptied the last of the coal on the kindling, saying he'd get some more.

"Where do you keep the coal?" asked Pigeon.

"Out there in the coal house," he answered.

"Well, Sparks can get the coal. Sparks, come here and get some coal. Snap out of it! And from now on see that you keep these scuttles full." She hustled him out. "My God," she went on, "don't you ever wash the windows?"

"Sure," answered Bud, "last year — no, I guess it was the year before — I washed them myself. Why?"

"Well, the first thing in the morning, I'll get after them. This stove could stand a little cleaning too," she said. "Maybe scrub it up while I'm washing the windows."

"You're not a government inspector, are you?" Bud asked.

"No, I'm not," she answered, "but I can't stand dirt."

"I can't stand dirty food or dishes," Bud said, "but I don't expect to spend much time washing windows or stoves. They just get dirty right away again."

When Sparks came in with the coal, Pigeon said, "We need fresh water. Pour that out and go fill these pails. Well's down there, isn't it?"

"Yeah, but I can sure get it," Bud answered.

"Nothing of the kind, Sparks will tend to the coal and water, kindling too, and probably a lot of other things. Who does he think he is, busting up new Buicks!"

After supper Pigeon started right in scraping the plates, getting them ready to wash. Bud and Nick watched her put the bones — there had been lamb chops for supper — in a clean dish.

"Here, I'll take those," Bud said. "Pete is waiting for them."

"Who's Pete?" she asked.

"Our dog."

"No dog gets these," she stated. "I'm going to make some nice soup with them."

"Soup!" exclaimed Bud. "Who likes soup? And anyway Pete has to eat."

But Pete didn't get them.

Next morning Pigeon announced she was going to start in and give the whole house a cleaning.

"All right with me," Nick told her, "although I thought we kept it fairly clean."

"Clean," snorted Pigeon, "look at those window curtains, and I hate to think what I'll find under the beds."

"I'll admit it's hard to sweep under beds," said Nick.

"Ever think of moving them?" she answered.

"Yeah, I suppose we could have at that," agreed Bud. "Well, anyway, I'm sorry I can't help, but I've got an awful lot to do today."

"Oh, that's all right," she said, "Sparks will be glad to help. Get those curtains down, Sparks, and be lively about it."

"Looks like a bad day for Sparks," laughed Nick, when they were in the store.

"Sure does," agreed Bud. "She'll have him so he'll sleep tonight, unless he's too tired. Wonder if our house *is* that dirty."

"Well, let her go to it, if that's what she likes," said Nick.

During the morning, Sparks came in many times, always with the same quiet question: "Pigeon wants to know if this is any good, or should she throw it out?"

She found time to set the table and serve the soup, which the boys had agreed to praise heartily. She made Bud hunt the place over to see if he could find some paint. She wanted to paint the kitchen.

"It wouldn't do you any good if I did find some paint," Bud told her. "We haven't any brush."

On the third day, Pigeon ran out of cleaning. She had been quite good-natured when busy, but, with nothing to do, she was restless and fussy — and poor Sparks suffered.

"I'll bet you get the axle tonight," Nick said, on the fourth morning. "Also bet they had to send to Albuquerque for it."

"I'm sure getting damn sick and tired of sitting around here with nothing to do," Pigeon said.

"Well, then," suggested Bud, "why don't you bake us up a mess of bread, pies, and cakes. We can always use them, also have something to remember you by."

"Well, I might at that," agreed Pigeon, "but I'm not so all-fired good on that stuff, am I, Sparks?"

"Why now, Pigeon, I think you're a marvelous cook," beamed Sparks.

"Now, don't be a damned liar," she answered. "A man who was brought up in a cow camp is no judge of anything. Okay then, I'll do some baking today. Your dog can eat it if you can't."

Sparks must have been right for once, or else Pigeon had extraordinarily good luck, because the things she baked were all very good. That afternoon, about four, the Navajo came with the axle. Just as Nick predicted, they had to wire Albuquerque for it. Bud put it right in. Nick sent word to Cledge to bring his mules over in the morning to help get the Buick across the wash.

When it came to settling up the next morning, an argument developed. Pigeon insisted that Sparks give Nick twenty dollars for the accommodations. This Nick refused to take.

107

"After you putting all your time in working," Nick said. "I guess not."

"That was fun for me," Pigeon answered. "Now, don't be a fool, Nick. Sparks has — I don't know how many — oil wells on his land. And if you don't take this, we're going to be plenty mad at you both."

'Pigeon is right," agreed Sparks. "Buy yourselves something extra with it, cigars or liquor maybe."

"All right, all right," said Nick, "we'll take it, but you know you were welcome here without paying. We sure appreciate all the cleaning and cooking Pigeon did for us and we hope you'll come through again."

After they were gone, Bud said, "You know, they were darned nice, weren't they? And I could see that darned Pigeon thinks the world of Sparks, even if she does abuse him scandalously. Say, not that we're talking of dogs, but did you see Pete yesterday?"

"By gosh, no," answered Nick, "wonder where he is."

"Maybe a lady friend," Bud suggested.

"Anyway, we'll ask the Navajos," said Nick.

But no one had seen him, and, when a week had passed and Pete had not come back, the boys felt sure he had been stolen. That must have been it, for they never saw him again.

A month later, a freighter camped there one night, and, after learning that Pete had been stolen, said he had a good dog they could have. He was a white bulldog and, as they missed having a dog around, they decided to take him. He was a nice friendly dog with the name of Mike. He couldn't eat as much as Pete and he didn't seem interested in chickens. He stayed in the store a good deal, generally asleep back of the counter in front of the pawn case, from which spot he did not care to be disturbed, so Nick and Bud obligingly stepped over him many times a day.

Mike had been in his new home some three weeks when an old woman — the one Nick had the argument with about pawning beads when he first came — raged into the store. Since Nick was in the kitchen, Bud had to stand the first onslaught. Nick heard the screeching and came in to see what it was all about. He soon found out, because, now that her audience had doubled, so did her rage.

Nick gathered, when she wasn't cussing them and their dog, that Mike had killed one of her rams, a ram that she had bought from the government for twenty-five dollars. She made it very plain that she was going to have twenty-five dollars or know the reason why.

The boys had become attached to Mike. He seemed so well-behaved and gentle and was, at the moment, sleeping innocently and peacefully by the pawn case.

"Must be some mistake," said Bud, as he walked over to Mike. "See, there's no blood on him."

"Of course there's no blood on him," she screeched. Hadn't she run as fast as she could with a stick in her hand, and chased him away before he could eat on the ram, and didn't they suppose she could tell one dog from another.

"Well, it still looks fishy to me," Bud said. "Mike gets plenty to eat. I don't like this old canner and will still bet she's lying."

"Anyway you go over and take a look at this high-priced ram, and see what you make of it," Nick told him.

The old woman went along to show him where the dead ram was lying. When they returned, Bud said, "Well, the old lady is right in every particular. It was Mike all right. We followed his tracks right back to the store."

"Guess we're in for it then," said Nick. "Maybe that's the reason that freighter gave him to us so promptly — he's a sheep-killing dog."

"It was bad enough buying those dollar kids that Pete killed," Bud remarked, "but Mike has really reached up in the upper bracket."

"Now give me the twenty-five dollars," demanded the old lady.

"Well," said Nick, ignoring the old woman, "we can't have a sheep-killing dog running around. Either we have to keep him in, or give him away. Why did he have to grab the head of the flock instead of a two-dollar sheep?"

Bud then told the old woman that Mike wasn't really their dog; a man had left him with them, but, if the white man came back, she could talk to him about paying.

Oh, no, she knew better than that. Mike was their dog all right, but if they weren't lying, then just give her the twenty-five dollars and Nick could collect from the white man.

"All right, then," said Nick, "there is only one thing for us to do. Our dog killed your ram, so after we close the store, we will take the dog out and kill him. That will make it even."

Yes, yes, that was the way to do it, so now give her the twenty-five dollars and she would go back to her sheep.

"Oh hell," said Bud, "we're hooked! Make the best deal you can and we'll pay it."

Nick finally settled for fifteen dollars cash. Navajos didn't see much cash on the Reservation and fifteen silver dollars looked like a lot of money to the old woman.

"Well, there goes most of the cigar and whiskey money that the Sparks gave us," laughed Bud.

"That's right," agreed Nick, "so we aren't really out anything at that. We'll try keeping Mike at home from now on."

\* \* \*

The day after the ram killing — in the middle of the afternoon — a man, woman, and two girls arrived in a new Studebaker car. Of course they stopped in, and, of course, they were warned about the arroyo. The man was not too braggy about his car. Still, he felt, after what they had come through, that he would try crossing the wash without help.

"Don't believe there has been a Studebaker along here before," said Nick, "so maybe she will make it. But, anyway, when she stalls, let her set, because if you try to buck that sand, you'll probably break something."

"Boy," said Bud, after the party had started off, "one of those girls is an easy looker, isn't she? Wouldn't mind having her stop here a few days."

"Oh, yeah. Well, let's see how they get along."

The few Navajos left the store too, so Nick and Bud followed them out.

"By gosh, I believe he's going to make it," exclaimed Nick, as the Studebaker plowed along. "He's more than halfway across now."

"Yeah, but she's beginning to slow down," said Bud. "Oh, oh, she's stopped. Looks like she only lacked about ten or fifteen feet of making it. Boy, that's a good car."

"Now, if the damn fool takes my advice and don't try to buck his way out, he'll be all right."

But the man evidently thought, as it was such a short distance to go, that surely he could make it out. He tried to go ahead. No go. He put her in reverse. He tried this a couple of times and then suddenly the motor raced and no wheels turned.

"Axle," said Bud. "Well, Compadre, we have guests again, and am I mad!"

"I can see you are," said Nick. "She sure is pretty though, but probably married."

"Well, I'd better go down and help the poor old man carry some bags up."

"Yeah, he looks pretty weak and helpless," Nick said sarcastically.

Bud was introduced all around and answered all the questions about what and how to do, and then they all waded through the sand to the store, where Nick was introduced to Mr. and Mrs. Berger and their daughters, Marge and Jessie.

Mr. Berger was a good-natured, ordinary looking man of about fifty. His wife was a bit younger, very nice looking, and very well-dressed. The daughter Bud thought so good-looking was named Marge. She had brown hair, brown eyes, a clear complexion, and her nose was slightly on the pug order. Her five-foot-six-inch body was perfectly formed. Bud found out later that she was twenty and her sister was eighteen. Jessie had the same brown hair and eyes and nice complexion that Marge had. She also was nicely formed and about the same height, but that was as far as it went. She just wasn't as pretty and attractive as her sister.

"Now, you are sure you can put us up without inconveniencing yourselves, are you?" Mrs. Berger asked.

"Oh, sure," answered Nick. "May not be as nice as some places, but you'll be fairly comfortable."

"The girls and I will be glad to do the cooking," she went on. "We can, at least, do that much to help."

"Fine," agreed Nick. "Bud, you show them where they sleep. The bed linen is clean. Then you make a fire. After that we'll see which axle is broken so we can get a Navajo started to town first thing in the morning. No one will bother the car, except we'll get it pulled out of the wash."

Cledge, who lived about half a mile east of the store, soon showed up with his mules. Nick had told him it would be a safe bet for him to drive over every time he heard an automobile, because he was always needed and he was sure of making three dollars — his charge for pulling a car out of the arroyo. Cledge promised to have his son-in-law, Curley, over the first thing in the morning to take the broken axle in. The broken axles were always sent in so there would be no mistake made.

When supper was over, Marge said she'd wash the dishes and Jessie could dry them.

"I'd better dry them," Bud spoke up, "I know right where they belong in the cupboard."

112

"Well, thanks," laughed Jessie, "and I might put a plate or something in the wrong place." Bud wasn't fooling her any; she could already see that he thought pretty well of her sister.

The others seated themselves in the living room. "You should have dried those dishes, Jessie," said Mrs. Berger. "I don't think it is any treat for Bud to do them."

"It seems to be," she answered, "or sounds like it is by the way he's laughing and talking."

"He's a nice boy, isn't he?" Mrs. Berger said to Nick.

"Yes, he is," Nick answered, "and it was lucky for me that he was sent out here. He and I are partners and, as soon as we find a Post that suits us and is for sale, we're going to try and buy it."

"You like this business, I judge," said Mr. Berger.

"Well, we understand it and get along well with the Navajos. I suppose they like us as well as they do any white people, so I guess we'll stay right in this business."

"What's the soft, murmuring sound I hear?" asked Jessie.

"Owl," answered Nick. "I like to hear them. The Navajos don't, though. They say it's a sign of bad luck, although not for the white people."

"Coyotes are bad luck too, aren't they?" asked Mrs. Berger.

"Oh no, except for stealing lambs," Nick answered. "They think coyotes are the smartest of animals and don't kill them, although they seem pleased when we kill them. They'll shoot at them when they come around their sheep, but they're mighty careful not to hit any. They are superstitious about coyotes. I was riding to town one time when, about thirty miles from here, a Navajo rode out from a hogan and joined me. He had a rug tied to his saddle and was going to town to sell it.

"We had ridden along some six or seven miles, when a coyote came running toward us from the left and crossed the trail about a hundred yards ahead of us. The Navajo swore softly; then pulled up his pony and said he had changed his mind and would wait until the next day to go to town. Of course I knew he thought it was bad luck for him to go on after a coyote had crossed the trail before him, and I tried to talk him out of it, but nothing doing. He explained that coyotes were very smart, and this one had run very fast to warn him. He said I could see for myself that the coyote wasn't running from anything, nor was he going anywhere because there he sat, a short distance away, watching us.

"The Navajo also thought, as this seemed to be a special warning, that I'd better turn back too — although he didn't really think a coyote would warn a white man, because white men killed coyotes. I told him I'd go ahead anyway, but he sure didn't. I did have a little hard luck though; my pony went lame about five miles from town, so I had to leave him and borrow another."

Marge and Bud came from the kitchen, and Bud announced that they were going up on the hill and watch the moon come up. "Some wait!" thought Nick, although he said nothing. The new moon had gone down an hour or so earlier.

"Are the Navajos honest and trustworthy?" asked Mr. Berger.

"Well, some are and a lot aren't," answered Nick, "although practically any one of them, if given charge of something, will see that it is taken care of. Suppose Bud and I have to lock up and leave here for a week. All we'd have to do would be to get a Navajo to camp here and you can bet everything would be all right when we came back. Our money for wool buying — we always pay cash for wool — is usually sent out on a freight wagon, two or three thousand dollars. It is generally packed in a box of dry goods or notions and they show the Navajo freighter which box the money is in, and tell him to see that it reaches us. It always does. But, if you'd happen to leave a pair of gloves on the counter, that same freighter would have them in his pocket before you could turn around. They'll take anything that isn't nailed down."

"Well, I suppose you folks are tired and would like to go to bed."

"Yes, I think we will," Mrs. Berger said. "Good night."

When Bud came in the kitchen the next morning, Nick commented, "You doubtless enjoyed watching the moon rise last night."

"We sure did," Bud said, with a silly grin.

"What time did this phenomenon take place?" inquired Nick.

"Must have been along about midnight, because we came in right after that."

"Oh, yeah," laughed Nick. "Got quite a crush on her, haven't you?"

"She's sure some kid," Bud answered, "and, if they have to send to Chicago for that axle, it won't make me mad."

"Yeah, and she's probably engaged to some nice fellow anyway."

"Oh, no, she isn't," Bud answered, "although she goes with one fellow pretty steady."

"Good luck to you, Amigo," Nick said. "We could use a housekeeper at that."

The Navajo arrived with the axle on the fourth day, but too late in the afternoon for the Berger family to resume their journey.

"Why don't you go kill two or three of those young roosters," Nick said to Bud. "Maybe the folks are tired of lamb and kid. They're swell people and we ought to spread ourselves tonight, although it's probably the last night we'll ever see any of them."

"Want to make a little bet on that?" Bud asked.

"What inside dope have you got?" asked Nick.

"Might as well tell you," Bud said. "Marge and I are engaged. I've got her ring size and I'm going to get her a right nice ring and I'm going to find out what Mr. Berger thinks of me before he leaves."

"My gosh, you're a fast worker, aren't you?" exclaimed Nick, as he put out his hand. "Put 'er there, Amigo! But why a swell girl like she is, should fall for you is one of those things, isn't it? But, on the other hand, she could do a darn sight worse. And you be sure to mention to Mr. Berger that you have money, that I have too, and that we'll have a good place of our own before too long."

"Thanks, Nick. I'll sure tell him. Guess I might as well go see him now. It's a job I don't like, but here goes."

Bud soon came back, feeling quite well pleased with himself. "Wasn't as bad as I expected," he announced.

"Maybe it wasn't as great a shock to Mr. Berger as you thought, "Nick said. "Marge has likely mentioned her passing fancy for you to her Mama, and the same was probably relayed to Mr. Berger."

"Passing fancy, my eye," exclaimed Bud. "But don't be alarmed. We won't be married for a year. Marge is going to college another term. That may give us a chance to get our own place."

"I sure hope so," agreed Nick. "Well, you're a lucky guy. I guess she must like you if she's willing to live out here, away from everyone. She should have some interesting experiences to tell her grandchildren."

"Yeah, and you'd better get busy and find a nice girl this year; then we'll have a double wedding."

Small chance, Nick thought, the only girl I know is Glacie and I don't even know where she is.

"Maybe I'm not cut out for a married man," he said, with a smile. "Well, you'd better run along and slay those roosters if we're going to have that fine farewell supper."

The next morning, Mr. Berger's offer to pay for their stay was flatly turned down by Nick. As Cledge had been notified to be ready for a towing job and was already awaiting on the further bank, they were ready to leave.

116

Mr. Berger was to give her the gas and go as far across the wash as he could, then Cledge would do his stuff.

"Naturally I hope you don't break another axle," grinned Bud, when they were ready to start.

"You keep your fingers crossed, young fellow," warned Mr. Berger. "Well, good-by, boys," and he threw in the clutch and was off.

The boys followed around to the corner of the building and watched as Mr. Berger put her in second and raced down the slope into the arroyo. The car swayed from side to side, but Mr. Berger held it in the tracks.

"He's got her rolling faster this time," said Nick.

"She sure is pulling good," agreed Bud. "Old Cledge won't have to haul him far."

"Well, I'll be doggoned," exclaimed Nick. "Cledge isn't going to pull him any. He's made it across."

Mr. Berger stopped on the other side and got out and waved. "Write that down, if it's any record or anything," he yelled.

"Just the first car to cross under its own power," answered Nick.

But Cledge appeared disgusted until Mr. Berger went over and handed him some money. After all, he was there with his team ready, so Mr. Berger probably thought he should have something for his trouble.

"Suppose it will seem a little dull to you now," said Nick, as they went back into the store.

"Oh, I don't know," Bud answered. "I've got something to look forward to, and what's a year anyway, the way time flies around here?"

"We've just got to find some Trader who wants to sell before the year is up," said Nick. "Be a lot better if you and I own a place before you bring Marge out. I know what I'll do: next time I go to town, I'll talk to Leyton of the Merc. He always knows when a Trader wants a change."

A few mornings later a white man opened the screen door and stepped into the store, causing Bud to exclaim in Navajo, "What do you call this?"

"I don't know," answered Nick.

He was certainly a strange looking character. His sole attire was a faded shirt and a pair of pants that reached midway between his knees and his ankles. A piece of rope was tied around his waist for a belt. His eyes were a pale blue and his nose was straight and narrow. His blond hair reached his shoulders and his beard was six or seven inches long. He was a small man and was probably between thirty-five and forty years of age. All he carried was a quart canteen. He came forward to the counter and asked if he could get his canteen filled.

"You sure can," Nick told him, "but you could probably get colder water from the well. But I'll fill it in the kitchen."

"I wish you would because I'm very thirsty," he said. "I ran out of water last night."

"Where are you heading for?" asked Bud.

"Wherever the Lord directs," he answered. "Where He leads, I follow."

"Well, He hasn't been along here," Bud said. "Looks like He has directed you into a tough country. Haven't you any shoes?"

"I do not need shoes," he answered.

"Probably not," admitted Bud, "but if you happened to step on a cactus or a rattlesnake you might change your mind."

Nick came back and handed the canteen to the stranger, who drank deeply.

"I gather this fellow is an apostle of some kind," Bud told Nick. "Wonder if apostles eat."

"The Lord will provide," announced the man solemnly.

"Might as well let Him do it then," said Nick, although he knew all the time that he wouldn't let the fellow leave without feeding him. "We had thought maybe a can of corned beef, bread, and some peaches might taste good to you."

"It will be kind of you and the Lord will bless you," the man said.

While Nick was opening the cans, Gambling Woman came in. She dropped a couple of sheepskins on the floor. Then she moved a little closer to get a better look at the barefooted stranger. "Is he an American?" she asked Bud.

"I don't know. I guess so," he answered.

"You're going to give him something to eat. Why don't you give him some clothes and shoes?" she asked.

"Why should we?" Bud asked. "It's enough to feed him. Let him go to work and earn his shoes and clothes."

"Maybe he's crazy," suggested Gambling Woman.

"Something like that," agreed Bud, as he weighed her sheepskins. He gave her fifty-five cents. She picked the money up, and then, on a sudden impulse, stepped over and handed it to the stranger.

The man looked surprised and said, "Sister, I thank you, but I don't need money," and handed it back to her.

"What does he say, and why does he give the money back," asked Gambling Woman.

Nick interpreted, "*Ah-ka-hay, she-dazh-ae, peso do-niz-en-da.*"

"Yes, he's crazy, the poor man," Gambling Woman stated firmly. "Well, give me some coffee and the rest in sugar."

"These Indians are kind people; they invite me into their homes and feed me," the stranger said.

Sure, thought Nick, they think he's crazy so naturally they look after him. Aloud he said, "Yeah, they'll always feed a traveler."

The fellow picked up his food and went out to eat.

"Now, right there is probably the king of the nuts," stated Bud, "and if he ain't nutty, then I'm a watchmaker."

Soon the man came back in and laid the spoon, Nick had loaned him, on the counter.

"What's your name?" Bud asked. "Just in case the Sheriff comes along."

"My name is Joseph," he answered.

"Joseph, just Joseph, and where is your spotted coat?" But Joseph didn't get it. He thanked them and went out.

That was the last they saw of Joseph, but not the last they heard of him.

A couple of mornings later Snoopy came into the store, and, after noisily inhaling a couple of cigarettes, asked if the boys were going to the top of the mountain with all the *Din-ney* (the People) as the Navajos call themselves.

"What for?" asked Nick. "Going to be a little *Yei-bi-chai* (dance) up there?"

"No, no *Yei-bi-chai*," he answered.

"Then what are you talking about?" Nick asked.

"Don't you know about the big flood that is coming with the new moon?" he asked.

"Big flood?" exclaimed Bud, looking at Snoopy incredulously. "Who says there's a big flood coming?"

"White man's Jesus Clis says so," stated Snoopy.

"Oh, oh, Joseph," said Nick.

"You don't suppose . . . but let's see if we can find out about this," suggested Bud. "Maybe Snoopy is kidding us."

But Snoopy wasn't. Two nights before this, Jesus Clis had wandered into Natoni's (chief-headman) hogan. Natoni's daughter, a school girl, was there and asked him what he wanted. He was hungry, so they brought him some bread and meat. Old Natoni had a headache and was doing some heavy groaning. Jesus Clis asked the girl what was the matter with her father. She told him he had a headache. Jesus Clis said, "Tell him I will cure his headache." So he went and knelt behind where Natoni sat and rubbed his head this way and that way, and pretty soon Natoni said the headache was all gone. Then the stranger

120

sat down and began to talk, with Natoni's daughter interpreting what was said, to her father.

This man who could stop headaches was the Son of God, and he had come to warn the Navajo of a great flood that was soon coming. It was going to rain for forty days and forty nights. If the Navajos wanted to save themselves, their horses, cattle, and sheep, they must all go to the top of the mountain.

"Well, now, I have heard everything," exclaimed Nick.

"What do you suppose this is? A big joke? Or is that Joseph crazier than he looked?" asked Bud.

"You got me," Nick answered. Then he said to Snoopy, "But the Navajos aren't such fools as to go to all that work and trouble of moving, just on the word of a crazy white man?"

"Maybe not," answered Snoopy, "but the night Jesus Clis was there, Natoni had a dream. He stood on the mountain top and looked down across this great valley and all he could see was water. The hogans and hills were covered, nothing in sight but water. Then he knew that the white man spoke the truth. Yes, everyone is hurrying and getting ready to leave."

"That does it, I guess," Nick said. "They sure do put a lot of faith in dreams."

"Remember old Crooked Nose and how he dreamed his dead father came to the hogan and told him he positively had to meet him in eight days. Crooked Nose went up in the mountains four days before the date set and sat down. And in four days more, he was sure with his Papa, remember?"

"Sure, I remember," Nick assured him. "Well, we'll certainly have a loafing time until the poor fools find out they've been cheated."

"You going to stay here and be drowned?" asked Snoopy.

"We'll stay here and we'll laugh at you when you come back," Nick told him.

A great many Navajos came in, during the next few days, buying large quantities of provisions and always urging the boys to come with them.

"They all really believe that bunk, don't they?" remarked Bud, as he watched four wagons go up the hill.

"Sure they believe it," answered Nick. "Even the skeptical ones don't dare take a chance and stay."

The new moon came in a clear sky. The wind blew some, as it generally did, but that was all. When the moon was a quarter full, the Navajos began trekking back. They avoided the store as long as they could, as Navajos hate to be laughed at.

"Let's not say a word about it," suggested Nick. "That will make them feel even more foolish."

And that was the way it was. Nick and Bud greeted and traded with them as if they knew nothing about Jesus Clis or about Natoni's dream. The Navajos seemed grateful, and were very careful in their topics of conversation.

# CHAPTER 7

A FREIGHT WAGON with a load of goods had arrived and Nick and Bud had just finished unloading and checking it. After settling up with the freighter, Nick untied the package of letters. Any mail for them was brought over by the Navajo teamsters. Most of the mail was for Bud, as usual, and his letters were all from Marge.

"Well, well, I get one," exclaimed Nick. "Wonder what this is. Well, what do you know? We're going to be on a Star Route and have mail service twice a week."

"Say, this country is really getting civilized, isn't it?" Bud remarked. "Automobiles and now mail delivered at our door. What more could you want?"

"Yep, going to run from Sweetwater to Lone Point, about a forty-mile trip each way. Say, you know what we're going to do now? We're going to subscribe to a daily paper. How about the *Denver Post?*"

"Swell," agreed Bud, "we'll sure keep up on world events, sports too, and say, I can hear from Marge a little more regular too."

"Oh, yeah, and we got to get a leather pouch and pad-lock with two keys, one to be kept at Sweetwater so they can open at that end, and one for us," Nick told him.

"When does this here Pony Express start?" asked Bud.

"My gosh," exclaimed Nick, "it starts day after tomor-row. They sure don't give us much notice. How can we get a leather pouch that quick?"

"When was that letter written?" asked Bud.

"My gosh, no wonder," Nick answered. "Let's see, why this was written fourteen days ago."

"We better send a rider in tomorrow and see if we can get a pouch," suggested Bud.

"We'll have to get a bunch of stamps too," said Nick.

About noon, two days later, there came Hosteen Yazzi, riding the Lone Point Trader's big bay horse. Back of his saddle was tied a regular leather mail pouch. One glance was all it took to see that Hosteen Yazzi was a proud and important man. Upon being questioned by the four or five Navajos in the store as to how come he was riding the Trader's American horse, where he was going, and what was in the leather bag, Hosteen Yazzi, after helping him-self to tobacco from the free box, broke out in a big rash of talk.

Yes, sir, he was now working for "Washingtone," a very easy job too, and he was getting two dollars and forty cents for this day's ride, and two dollars and forty cents for to-morrow when he rode back; and then, in five days, he would be right back here, making that much more money. Four times a week he would make two dollars and forty cents. If that wasn't very good pay just for riding forty miles, he would like to know what was.

He then told Bud to give him fifteen cents worth of cookies and a bottle of pop for his lunch. Lazy Luke sug-gested, inasmuch as Hosteen Yazzi was doing so well, he should buy the other Navajos a bottle of pop. Sure, sure, he would, so Bud opened pop for the rest of them.

"I'll write a note for Hosteen Yazzi, and if there should be any mail for us, he can put it in his pocket. We should have our pouch by next trip."

"You'd better order the *Denver Post* too, while Hosteen Yazzi is eating," said Bud.

"That's right," agreed Nick, "I'll do that right now. That way we're sure to get mail every trip."

"Yeah, and I'd better write Marge a note, telling her my new address," Bud said.

The new mail service was fine. Hosteen Yazzi was a very efficient carrier, arriving each trip at just about the same time of the day. He always had first-hand news of any little events that had happened at either end of the route. Lazy Luke made it a point to be at the store mail days, as he generally could work Hosteen Yazzi for a bottle of pop. But what was a dime for a bottle of pop to a man who was getting two dollars and forty cents just for riding forty miles? And, anyway, Luke was his *ce-za-de* (cousin).

That night about eight o'clock, someone came pounding on the door to the screened porch. Bud was shaving, so Nick went to see who it was. There was a big Navajo at the door who said he was going to town for the Lone Point Trader and wanted to get in and get some groceries. It was about dark and Nick couldn't make out who the freighter was, but he said he'd let him in.

Nick lit the big hanging lamp and then unbarred the door. Now he saw who the fellow was; he was one of old Sugar Nose's boys, a big tough fellow who had had some schooling. Nick had only seen him a couple of times before, as he lived beyond Lone Point. His name was Sammy and most of the Navajos seemed to be afraid of him. He threw a little old buckskin on the counter and said he wanted to pawn it for five dollars. If it had been a good thick buckskin, Nick wouldn't have taken it, because they were not taking any pawn and hadn't for over a month. When Nick informed him he wasn't taking pawn of any kind for any amount, Sammy immediately got mad and began shooting off his mouth, telling Nick he had to take pawn or he'd go tell the Agent and have Nick put off the Reservation. He could see Nick was no good anyway and didn't know anything about running a store.

Nick told him to go right ahead and tell anyone he pleased, but the fact remained that he wasn't taking any pawn. Sammy was blowing off real nasty and loud, and Nick was about ready to rush for the pick handle when the living room door opened and Bud stepped in. "What's the matter with this loud-mouthed so-and-so?" he asked.

"He's got a little old buckskin he's going to pawn, or he's going to put us off the Reservation," Nick explained.

"He and who else?" said Bud. "Maybe he'd like to start with me. Shall I toss him out? Who is this important party anyway?"

"He's the son of your lady friend who wears her blanket over her face," answered Nick. "Now, Sammy, you better walk right out under your own power, because this little fellow here doesn't like bad Navajos and hasn't the patience I have so, if you don't get right out, he's liable to mess you up bad." Nick spoke in English, knowing Sammy could understand most of what he said.

But Sammy wasn't through talking yet and, as he was almost as big as Nick and Bud together, he saw no reason to be alarmed — which showed he hadn't heard much about Bud.

"He's fairly big," remarked Nick.

"Which means he'll make just that much more noise when he falls," Bud answered. Then he said to Sammy, "All right, big fellow, clear out. We want to lock up," and he opened the little gate and stepped out into the bullpen.

"I kill you," snarled Sammy, speaking in English for the first time.

"No, no, you won't kill anyone," laughed Bud, as Sammy charged at him. Quick as a cat, Bud leaped, lowered his head, and rammed Sammy in the stomach; and, as he did so, he reached down and yanked on Sammy's legs. Poor big Sammy, with no wind in his body, crashed on the back of his head on the hard adobe floor and lay still.

"Nice work, Bud," gloated Nick. "Use your head and save your hands, eh. Seeing he's a heavyweight, I'll help you carry him out." They each took an arm and dragged him out and then covered his face and chest with the buckskin he didn't pawn.

There was a wagon with four ponies out in the road. The boys barred the door and went into the living room. After a while they heard a wagon moving away, so they knew Sammy was all right and must now understand why the Navajos called Bud, "Little Strong Man."

One evening late in the fall Sandy Tilton, the ex-train robber, rode up in front of the store, dismounted and came in. He was carrying a grain sack which contained three quarts of Scotch whiskey and a thousand dollars in gold and silver with which to buy cattle. The Scotch was to balance the weight of the money tied on the back of the saddle. Sandy was a lean, fast-moving red-headed man of around forty. He had served one year in the Pen for being a member of the Johnson gang that held up the fast Santa Fe mail train. The would-be robbers were quite surprised when the train stopped, to be met with a blaze of rifle fire. Some were wounded but not Sandy. He reached his horse safely, climbed aboard, and rode south as far as St. Johns, where he was picked up by the sheriff. As he was only twenty at the time, they let him off easy. He was appointed deputy sheriff and always wore a six-gun, a forty-four Colt. The Indians named him *"Hosteen Hosh-kay"* (Angry Man), probably because he talked rather loud while out in the corral. He would look a cow and calf, or steer, over very carefully; then tell the Navajo what he would pay, and that was it. No arguing. Take it or leave it.

In three days Sandy had the thousand dollars spent so

he hired a couple of Navajos to help drive his herd to town, and the following early morning they headed the cattle south. Sandy left the two unopened Scotch bottles for Nick and Bud.

That evening at supper time, old Moab Farley rode up. When the boys heard the booming voice and the heavy knock on the door, they knew who it was.

"He don't need to holler, I'd recognize that cane of his anywhere," laughed Bud. "I'll go put his horse away for him."

"Open up here! You've got company," Moab announced. "Got to go to town. First time in fourteen months. Got a good Navajo watching the place, so everything is all right. If not, I'll cane that Navajo within an inch of his worthless life."

"Go on in, you old horse thief," said Bud. "I'll take care of your horse."

Moab, with his limping, lopsided walk, moved on in. "How are you, Nick? Long time since see. Hear you're getting civilized, mail every day or so. Me, I don't need any, never write a letter and never get one. How about a medium-sized drink, although I don't suppose you got one."

"Well, now," answered Nick, "this is just as good a time to fool you as any." He went to his bedroom and came back with a bottle.

"Goodness, gracious, land's sake!" Moab exclaimed. "How did you happen to save that for me and with this here Bud around too?" He winked at Bud who had just come in.

"Hold everything, my good Jack-Mormon friend," said Bud. "That Scotch is being saved for Christmas. Nick is just showing it to you."

"Oh dear me, good Lord, no," exclaimed Moab. "Can't be, and me an old man of sixty-eight, who has just ridden eighteen miles — and may not live until Christmas."

"I suppose since he asked for a drink, and I gave him the impression that I could give him one, maybe we'd better open it," Nick said.

"And I only asked for a medium-sized drink," Moab added.

They had a drink, and then another.

"We're having scrambled eggs and red-hot chili for supper. Like that?" asked Nick.

"Good Lord, yes, and the hotter the better," Moab answered.

He was a Mormon but not a very good one, because he smoked and drank. He didn't swear, except on very rare occasions. He had been thrown from a horse when a boy and his left leg was some three inches shorter than the other. He carried a very heavy cane, the bottom end fitted with a tin ferrule to protect the wood, because Moab often used his cane as a poker for the fireplace. It had other uses too, and saved Moab many steps. He usually sat on a stool behind the counter and had his best selling items nearest him. His cane didn't have the regulation curved handle but was more the shape of a hockey stick. Anything asked for from the shelves, was promptly hooked by the cane, and as it fell, he neatly caught it and passed it over to the customer. When sheepskins were laid on the counter, out of reach of Moab's big hands, out went the cane to drag them over. Coffee pots, frying pans, lariats, and lanterns, which hung from the ceiling, were juggled down with the cane. If a Navajo became sassy, the cane would dart out to the back of his neck and the surprised gent would find himself face to face with Moab.

At one time he rigged a pin in the end of his cane. The front of the counter, from the floor to the top, was faced with chicken wire, so the Navajos could see the goods displayed below. Some of his customers would stand, with their backs to the counter, and gossip for long stretches instead of doing their shopping. Moab found that a good lively pin jab in the butt would turn them around to make them remember what they came in for — and start getting it. While they never caught him harpooning them, they knew the pain originated from his direction; so in a short time no native of that locality cared to trust his or her butt near the counter.

Moab was, as he said, sixty-eight but looked ten years younger. He was hale, hearty and healthy. He was a good six feet when he stood on his good leg, big, not fat, and still a powerful man. When he was a young fellow he had freighted in Arizona and California, had soldiered in Arizona, and had lived for a while in Mexico. He told the boys of a tribe of Indians in California who, when such things were in season, seemed to thrive on bugs, worms, and grasshoppers and of others he had seen butcher and eat cows that had died of blackleg.

Several times before, he had stopped with the boys, so they were well acquainted and great friends.

"Supper's ready," announced Bud. "Suppose we'll have to give old Seldom-Fed an appetizer now."

"Gracious, yes," grinned Moab. "A small one this time."

After the drink they sat down to the table. "Spare the chili and spoil the eggs, I always say," said Moab, after he had taken a big mouthful of scrambled eggs and chili, "and I will say you didn't spoil these eggs and you have a right potent brand of chili."

"You claimed you liked it hot," Nick reminded him.

"Sure do and hope you made plenty. That ride made me hungry. Bud, you eat like you're constipated. Mustn't get fat or you'll be a burden to the pallbearers."

"A little lit, isn't he?" grinned Bud.

"Did you know Bud's going to get married next June?" Nick asked.

"Of course not," answered Moab. "Good for you, Bud. I'm glad to hear that. Suppose you'll be next, eh, Nick?"

"Oh sure, if I find a girl."

"Hear about my robber?" Moab asked.

"No, who robbed you?" asked Bud.

"An ornery Navajo, but he didn't make a very good job of it. This was a couple of weeks ago. It was about eight o'clock at night, I guess, when I heard a faint sound like breaking glass. I couldn't figure what that could be but thought maybe I'd better take a look around anyway. I didn't strike any matches, because I know my way around. Store seemed all right so I slipped on out into the ware-room. There was just a sliver of moon, enough so I could see the glass was busted in the little eighteen-by-twenty-inch window. I sidled over to it and flattened myself against the wall. In a minute a head came through, for a look around and to listen. I just naturally reached up with my cane and hooked his neck and bore down. I guess there were some pieces of glass still in the frame and I doubt if his Adam's apple was resting comfortable, because he sure hollered and squirmed. I lit a match to see what I had trapped. It was Big Thumb and he was yelling that I was cutting his throat."

"He had it coming to him," Bud said.

"Sure," agreed Moab, "but anyway, I loosened up a little and told him a few things. He sure made some good prom-ises, so I finally told him to bring me five dollars in the morning and I wouldn't say anything about it. But, if he didn't bring the money, so I could get a new window, I'd sure ride him down and give him a mighty good licking with my cane."

"That was fair enough, too," Nick said.

"Fair enough, but I've never seen him since," laughed Moab. "He's moved away, which is probably just as well, as he was no good anyhow. Gracious Peter, but I'm sorry that bottle is empty."

Nick got up and went to his bedroom, returning with the other bottle Sandy had left.

"Well, bless my soul," Moab exclaimed, "you're a lad

after my own heart; and when I come back from town, Bud, I'll be able to replace your Christmas cheer."

They sat and drank, smoked, and talked. Always the talk was about the Indians and things pertaining to the trading business. "We sure need rain over our way," Moab remarked.

"We had a short, hard rain a few days ago, and boy, what lightning," said Nick.

"We'll get some then, I guess," Moab decided. "And lightning, say, I was in some real lightning one time, eight or ten years ago, I think it was. I was coming across the mountain and one of those quick, hard, black ones came up. I never saw such lightning nor heard such crashing thunder. I was dodging and ducking and my horse was trying to jump out from under me and every so often it would pop a pine tree. Then I spotted a hogan, off to the right of the road, so I made for that. They're a pretty safe place and I could get out of the rain, although, of course, I had my old yellow slicker on.

"When I got to the hogan, I found it was a *chinde* (spirit or devil) hogan — you know where someone had died and they had left the body inside. But any port in that storm, so I kicked the half rotten door down and went on in. A skeleton lay on one side, so I sat down on the other and waited for the storm to blow over. And, after it let up, I went out to take a look at the sky to see if the storm was over. Just then two Navajos rode along the trail, which was some two hundred yards from the hogan. Say, they took one look through the misty, purplish light at my flopping figure coming from that hogan, and they were a half mile down the road before I figured out what was the matter with them. They thought I was the ghost of that dead Indian."

By two o'clock the second bottle was empty so the party broke up. Nick and Bud were not accustomed to such heavy drinking and though quite wobbly, got to bed safely.

The next morning at six Moab was up, loudly demanding breakfast, as he had a long ride ahead of him.

"If you want breakfast, you just hop to it," Nick heard Bud say. "I'm not well and I'm going to sleep until morning."

"Good land of Goshen," exclaimed Moab. "Nick," he roared, "get right up. Bud is sick."

As Nick failed to answer, Moab went to see why. "What's the matter with you fellows, ain't you going to get breakfast and Godspeed me on my journey?"

"I'd rather God-you something else," growled Nick. "Let Bud feed and speed you. I'm sick."

"Gracious sakes alive, now I have two sick young men and no breakfast. I can't believe they could both be stricken the same morning. They're lazy, that's what's the matter," and he threw the covers back and lifted Nick out of bed and stood him on his feet.

"You old devil," said Nick, with a sickly grin. "Why can't you be human?"

"Scotch didn't agree with you, eh? Come on, snap out of it. You'll live. Now, I'll go get Bud."

He did too. After some coffee, eggs, and toast, everyone felt better, and Bud was able to saddle Moab's horse for him.

Four days later around five o'clock, Moab came riding up. "Well, children, here I am again, fresh as a dewdrop after that grueling ride."

Nick and Bud went out to welcome him. "Bud, are you able to take care of my horse for me, or are you sick and, if you ain't, I'll try and have you sick again in the morning. Step lively, kid, because I've got four Scotch in this here grain sack, and I'm just about ready for a medium."

"Thanks, Amigo, but I just had my shoes shined, and, anyway, I don't use the stuff."

"Land of Goshen, oh me, oh my, did you hear that, Nick?"

133

"Yeah, I heard him. Come on in. Here, I'll bring the sack."

"Where are all the Navajos?" asked Moab.

"Plenty here this morning, but darned few this afternoon," said Nick, as he carried the sack into the living room. Moab had, as he said, four bottles of Scotch; also two five-pound boxes of good candy, two boxes of cigars, and quite an assortment of things for himself.

"Candy and cigars are for you fellows," he said. "Scotch is for anyone who wants it, so let's try it. Whiskey is good for you, once in a while."

Bud came in and Nick got the glasses. "Guess two glasses are all we need," Moab remarked, "seeing as Bud don't use the stuff."

"The morning after you left, I said I never wanted to even see a bottle of Scotch again. But I have felt so good ever since, that I guess I didn't mean it, although I'm going to be a little more cautious this time."

They sat and talked for about an hour. Nick was thinking he'd better get started on supper when Bud said, "Someone just drove up out there." He got up and went to the door. "Squint Bozeman and another fellow." Nick and Moab followed him to the door.

They all knew Squint. He worked for Sam Goodluck at the feed corral in town. He was a small sandy-complexioned man, a native New Mexican of about fifty-five and he liked his liquor. He was decidedly squint-eyed which gave him a shrewd look.

"*Yat-ta-hey*," said Squint, "got room for us tonight?"

"Sure, we can fix you up," Bud answered. "Come on in, you're just too late for a drink."

"Now don't you start fooling me," warned Squint. "I want you to know Mr. Shaw here," and he went on to introduce them. "Mr. Shaw is an Englishman on his way to Ouray, where he owns a silver mine or something, so I'm going to drive him over to the River where he can

134

catch the narrow gauge. He wanted to drive across the Reservation so he could see some wild Indians and maybe a few buffalo. Buffalo been bothering you lately?" he asked with a wink.

"Not right lately," answered Moab, "but you never can tell. Say, if I'd known you were coming, I'd have waited and ridden along with you."

Nick got Mr. Shaw's two bags out of the buckboard and Bud took Squint to show him where to put the horses. Nick put Mr. Shaw's bags in the bedroom off the porch. They'd make Squint a bed on the floor or out in the store on the counter. "The can's right out there and you can wash in the kitchen," Nick told Mr. Shaw.

"Perfectly all right. I'll go wash now," he said.

In the living room, Moab greeted him by saying, "You're just in time for a little drink; that is, of course, if you do drink."

"Oh, yes, I drink," he answered, "but let me furnish the liquor, I have some in my bag."

"Great Scott, no," roared Moab, "we positively never let anyone furnish any liquor, do we, Nick?"

Mr. Shaw accepted a medium, a tumbler half full. A large drink, according to Moab's standard of measures, was a full tumbler, and, while Mr. Shaw seemed a bit surprised at the quantity, he drank it down.

Mr. Shaw was a six footer, fair-haired, blue-eyed, and freckled. He spoke with a pronounced English accent and smiled easily. Nick knew they were all going to like him right off the bat.

Mr. Shaw went to the kitchen and washed. Bud came in and said, "You know, Squint just told me Mr. Shaw is a Duke. What do you know?"

"Gracious Pete," Moab said, "then we better call him Duke. Make him feel at home."

"Wonder what Dukes eat," mused Bud, "but then we wouldn't have any of it, if we did know."

"I say, feed him like you did me the other night — chili and eggs," suggested Moab.

When the Duke came back, his face glowing from a vigorous scrubbing, Nick asked him if he liked chili. He said he was very fond of it. What was it?

"We haven't any fresh meat, so we'll have a cowboy supper — a mixture of scrambled eggs, corned beef, and chili, with a can of peaches for dessert. Do you think you'll like that?"

"I am sure I will," Mr. Shaw answered. "That sounds like a noble dish."

"Come on, Bud, let's get at it," said Nick.

"Goodness me, how time flies. Let's have a drink before you start," suggested Moab. "The Duke has had a tiring ride." Moab poured out five mediums. "And remember what I always say about sparing the chili, Nick."

"I'll use plenty," laughed Nick.

"We're getting the worst of this," Bud remarked, after being in the kitchen awhile. "This hot kitchen isn't hindering the working of those drinks any."

"Sure isn't," agreed Nick. "Wonder if I put enough chili in this to suit old Moab? Maybe I'd better put in a little more. We can eat is as hot as he can, although I don't know anything about the Duke."

"He can probably handle it hot," Bud said.

Just before they sat down, Moab came with the glasses and filled them half full and set them on the table.

"A little drink to go with the chili," he said.

It might be the chili got stronger with age, or else Nick must have been far too liberal with it, because, after tasting the mixture, Nick had to admit it was what even a Mexican sheepherder would call hot. Nick put a glass of water at the Duke's place, just in case.

After the Duke put a large forkful in his mouth and Nick was just about to ask him how he liked it, Nick saw he was in trouble. The tears streamed down his cheeks

136

and his neck and face seemed to swell and turn red. Moab said afterwards that if it had of been him, he would have spit it out regardless. But the Duke was too polite for that. He gasped and gulped, endeavoring to swallow, shooting his head forward like a chicken trying to swallow something that is too big.

He finally seemed to get it down, but the fire was still raging, so he grabbed for the glass of water, but got the glass of whiskey instead, and gulped in a great mouthful before he discovered his error. That mouthful of raw whiskey must have added considerable heat to his already blazing mouth, because he didn't even try to swallow that. He gave a great sputtering cough, turned his head to the right and the whole dose shot out, hitting old Squint, who sat next to him, full in the left ear and eye.

Squint started cussing something terrible and rubbing his smarting eye as he leaned over to let the whiskey run out of his ear. Mr. Shaw was strangling and gasping for breath, his eyes blinded with tears. He rose from his chair, his hand groping for something to steady himself with, found Squint's bowed head and his fingers clutched into the bushy hair.

"Unsnag him from my hair before I get mad and chaw his leg off," roared Squint.

During one terrific spasm of coughing, Nick thought he saw something shoot from Mr. Shaw's mouth, but wasn't sure. He went around the table to see what he could do and Moab yelled, "Get the Duke some water; lead him to the water pail," then he added in an awed voice, "Good Lord on high, look at him! His face has settled in!"

It was true too. He looked awfully queer. His face had certainly changed, but anyway, Nick got Mr. Shaw's clinched hand free of Squint's hair, led the still coughing man over to the pail, and put a dipper of water to his mouth.

Then Squint, who had lurched back in his chair, yelled,

"What the hell now? Something is punching a hole in my back."

The Duke, much helped by the big drink of water, mumbled, "Teef, teef." They all looked at him in surprise and then turned again to Squint, who was peeling off his shirt.

"The Lord bless my soul," exclaimed Moab, "what do you make of all this business? I suppose Squint thinks he's got a snake down his back, but it's the Duke I'm worried about; he sure looks bad to me. Wish we had some cold beer. That's the best chili extinguisher I know of."

Squint got his shirt off just then and something dropped to the floor. Mr. Shaw heard it, dashed over, and grabbed up a set of upper teeth, which he popped into his mouth.

"Is my back bleeding?" Squint asked, as he turned around.

"Nope," Moab answered, "but you've sure got a pretty set of teeth marks low down on your back."

Mr. Shaw, whose face was still very red, had stopped coughing enough so he could talk. He apologized for his disgusting behavior, hoped they wouldn't think him a sissy, but he was sure some of the chili got in his windpipe.

"Anyway," said Nick, "I'm going to fix you up a nice plate of cowboy hash — without any chili."

"Take a good drink," ordered Moab. "That's what you need now."

Mr. Shaw took a stiff drink and, when Nick brought him the special dish, without chili, he ate — as Moab said — "con mucho gusto."

"Well," remarked Bud, after supper was finally over and the dishes washed, "I guess I'd better light up the fireplace. These nights are getting chilly."

"A bully idea," said Mr. Shaw. "I do think a fireplace most cheerful. Excuse me a moment," and he left the room, immediately returning with a bottle of Scotch.

"Good gracious, you didn't need to do that. We have plenty here," Moab told him.

"I think we should use some of mine," Mr. Shaw answered.

They pulled their chairs up near the fireplace, Moab taking his rocker very close. Nick brought out and opened one of the boxes of cigars Moab had brought with him. Mr. Shaw asked question after question about the Indians. Moab did most of the answering, because he had been among them for so long. They talked and smoked and, frequently, had a drink. About nine-thirty, old Squint, who seemed pretty well oiled, said, if someone would show him where to sleep, and if he could make it that far, and if his chawed back wasn't going to be too tender to lie on, he believed he'd call it a day and go to bed.

After he staggered off, Mr. Shaw resumed his questioning. He seemed to doubt some of the things Moab told him and, at times, started to say so, but Moab paid no attention to him.

"Now you occasionally hear of a white man being killed by an Indian," he remarked. "Whenever that happens, I generally figure there's a woman mixed up in it. And, while there are some right desirable Navajo women, I'll be side-stitched if I've ever seen any who are worth getting killed over. I remember one time I saw what was awful close to a killing, but it wasn't a Navajo who had the gun."

"Tell us about it," urged Mr. Shaw.

"This has to do with a preacher and a Navajo woman who took to the depths of an arroyo," began Moab. "This person was called *Bo-who-giz-hi* (he who lost a tooth), and he wasn't exactly my idea of a God-fearing man or shepherd enough to lead stray lambs into the fold. To me, it looked like some Missionary Board back East had had something put over on them. I was helping a Trader out by staying with him until he could get another clerk. I didn't see the start of the fracas, but God love me, I saw the finish. This *Bo-who-giz-hi*, who seemed to be a lazy, worthless, harmless, tobacco-chewing dude, was married to

139

an outsize woman of around two hundred pounds. For some reason they had no children, which seemed queer, as you'd expect a poor outfit like that to have at least a dozen young ones around.

"This Navajo woman, Josephine, was a fairly good looker of thirty or so, married to a worthless, lazy old gambler. She had been to school and spoke more or less English. She told me about the start of the mix-up. Seems on this particular day she had been helping the Trader's wife with the washing, and, when finished, had started for home. She had walked about a quarter of a mile when the Reverend Bo-who-giz-hi caught up with her. She knew him, of course, and they laughed and talked as they walked along, he, no doubt, shooting tobacco juice through his missing front tooth gap. When they went down in the arroyo, a little time was spent before they came out on the other bank and parted company.

"The Trader, Freeport, hadn't had any luck getting a clerk, so I stayed for darned near a year. Freeport asked me one day if I'd ride over to the parson's and see about his making a little payment on his grocery bill. It was after eleven when I got there and the Reverend wasn't home — out rabbit hunting — but his wife said I could expect him back by dinner time, unless he shot a leg off. He showed up about noon and asked me to eat. We were just about to sit down, when in walked this Josephine with a baby on her back. Indians don't knock; they just walk right in."

"One of your converts, I suppose," remarked the Reverend's wife. "Well, what does she want?"

"Why don't you ask her? She speaks English," he answered.

"I come now to show him little son," says Josephine.

"You what? Who's little son?" asked the big woman.

"This his baby," continued Josephine in her calm voice. "Maybe so Josephine live here now in nice house. Maybe so you get out. You no good wife. You no get him baby. Josephine get him fine boy."

The parson's wife looked from Josephine to her husband. And, by cracky, old Bo-who-giz-hi sure did look guilty and was already edging for the door. That big lady's face and neck turned red and she seemed to swell like she was going to bust. She couldn't speak so she hissed. Then she saw the shotgun Bo-who-giz-hi had stood in the corner when he came in. In one mighty leap she had it. But, when she leaped, old Bo-who-giz-hi also leaped and, while she was cocking the gun, he bounded through the open door and slammed it shut. There was a deafening report as the two barrels of that shotgun blew the upper half of the door to hell and gone.

"The recoil knocked her back and she lost her balance and flopped with a jolt that rattled the dishes. Likely this all looked very funny to Josephine, because she began to laugh, but not for long. The big dame on the floor began to hiss even harder and louder than before, and started to rise, still clutching the gun. For all Josephine knew, it might go boom next in her direction. She decided maybe the big woman wasn't going to join her in a laugh, and there could be another shot in that gun so probably, as it was noon anyway, she'd better be getting on home. And it sure looked like when she made up her mind to leave, she *left*. She jerked what was left of the door open, and right now she was running her very best.

"When she went out the front door, I went out the back because I don't understand white women any too well and I wouldn't know just what to say in a case of that kind anyway."

"Did the preacher ever return?" asked Mr. Shaw.

"Oh, yes," answered Moab, "they patched up their quarrel — and the door. Bo-who-giz-hi got Josephine to say she was only joking about the baby. But I'll bet he was a little more cautious after that."

"But, Duke," went on Moab, "I don't want you to form a wrong opinion of the Navajos, because they have their good points too and, if the white people will leave them alone, they'll get along somehow. I don't know of any other race that get along with less trouble or fewer quarrels than they do. They'd be a darned healthy race if it wasn't for T.B. and trachoma. I wonder what it is they eat — or don't eat — that keeps them free of cancer. Appendicitis, among them, is as rare as a dead mule. Maybe it's the colored corn they eat so much of, or maybe it's that powerful Billy Goat meat."

Moab poured himself a drink; then he continued, "Navajos are not supposed to eat raw meat, but, by cracky, I've seen them eat prairie dogs that I wouldn't say were cooked to a crisp. They have a saying that red meat must not be eaten without salt, and, from the large amount of salt they buy, I guess it never is. That doesn't apply to fat or tallow, however, because I have never seen any people who are so fond of raw, unsalted beef fat or sheep fat as they are."

"Yeah," said Nick, "whenever we order a quarter of beef or lamb, we have to tell the Navajo to leave all the kidney fat on or we won't buy it. I remember one day, after a nice fat quarter of beef had been brought in and put on the counter, Bud and I went to the wareroom to weigh up some wool. There were two squaws in the bullpen — a mother and daughter — who we knew were all right and wouldn't steal anything. When I came back in I noticed them picking at the meat and told them to get away from it. But it was too late, because they had just about cleaned that quarter of fat, probably three or four pounds of it. I was sure mad, which seemed to surprise them, as they said they didn't think I would care if they ate a little fat."

"Goodness me, you mustn't be so stingy, Nick," laughed Moab. "Well, Duke, you look tired. Guess we'd better be getting to bed. I'll be riding eighteen miles with you in the morning, so we can visit some more then."

142

The next morning, Mr. Shaw tried to pay for his lodging. When he found he couldn't, he brought in a quart of Bourbon, which was very beneficial in case of cold — a better remedy than Scotch, he said.

# CHAPTER 8

IN THE FALL OF 1918, there was an unusually large piñon crop. A good piñon crop didn't happen every year, maybe every four or five years. The Indians said the big crop came every seven years. Nature arranged that part of it nicely too, because if there was a large crop every year, the price would be too low to make them worth picking. The piñon nuts were rich and oily with a very fine flavor, but they were so small that few white people would fool with them, unless they could get them already shelled.

A Navajo put a handful into his mouth at a time, spitting out the shells as he ate the kernels. This trusting way of putting a handful into the mouth was rather risky, because too many sheep grazed under the trees and little round things were apt to get picked up that were not piñons.

With most Traders, a big piñon crop was worth more than the lamb or wool business. It gave the poorer Indians a chance to stock up on robes, shawls, blankets, quilts, shoes, and clothing — and they certainly did it.

Nick had received a letter saying he could pay fifteen cents a pound, which was a big price, because generally they were worth eight or ten cents.

"Boy, we'd better begin getting some wagons to town," he said. "We're going to need an awful lot of goods. We'll sure make the company a wad this fall."

"I'll say," agreed Bud. "Order plenty of bags and seamless sacks. Yeah, and hardware cloth too." This last was large-holed wire screen that the Indians used to screen the nuts through.

By the first of October the nuts were coming in at a lively rate, and from then on the boys were kept busy. One evening they were sitting before the fireplace, Bud rereading a letter from Marge, while Nick read the *Denver Post*. It was dated October 3, 1918. It had taken only three days to reach them. Not bad, thought Nick.

"See there's an epidemic of influenza in the East," he remarked. "Seems to be bad, too."

"Yeah," said Bud. "Well, I hope it stays there."

But it didn't. Each paper they received had more alarming news. The flu was spreading rapidly over the country and there were many deaths. "Between this and the war," Nick said, "there won't be many Americans left."

A few days later it began to rain, a cold, drizzling rain, and, as Nick said, when it began to rain in the fall, it generally kept it up for a week or two. And then they began to hear of sick Navajos. One day Hosteen Yazzi came in with the mail, saying there were lots of sick people in town and many had died. The people were running around like scared rabbits, and lots of Indians were dying too, and what was this sickness that killed so many.

"Must be getting pretty bad," Nick said and then he told Hosteen Yazzi, "The white doctors don't know much about this sickness or what to do for it, except to go to bed and keep warm."

"Which won't help the Navajos any, because they won't

go to bed, and, if they did, it wouldn't be warm, that's a cinch," said Bud.

The next day Yellow Man came down from the foothills where he was camped. He said he had gone to where Snag Tooth was camped, and had found him, his wife, and baby all dead, and that another woman had died in another camp the night before.

"You'd better tell all the Navajos who are up there to let the piñon nuts go and move back to their hogans and stay in by the fire where they can keep dry," Nick told him. "And tell them not to come to the store, except when they really need to, because it is better to keep away from other people."

The next day when Hosteen Yazzi came in again, he said the Trader at Lone Point was very sick, but his wife was all right, so she fixed the mail.

"You know what I'm going to do?" Nick said, after Hosteen Yazzi had left. "I'm going to write a note to Moab and send over to find out if he is all right. He's all alone and if he got sick, it would be pretty tough." Yellow Man was still there and, when asked, said that for two dollars he'd go.

Four hours later he came back with a note from Moab. Yes, he was all right so far and probably he was too tough to get sick, but a great many Navajos were sick and quite a few had died. If Moab did get the flu, he would send a rider and Nick or Bud could come over and attend to his needs.

But by the next day, Nick was not able to go see anyone. Just before supper he began to feel bad, and by eight o'clock he was in bed.

"Well, I've got it and I'm sure feeling bad," he told Bud.

"Don't you worry, pal," said Bud. "You just keep covered good. I'll get a slop pail and bring it in; then I'm going to give you a good physic and a dose of quinine. You'll be better by morning."

146

By midnight Nick had a burning fever and at times was delirious. Bud had a job to keep the covers on him, and it took all his strength to keep Nick in bed.

About six in the morning, Nick fell into a fitful slumber and Bud dozed for an hour or so. When he awoke he looked in, and, as Nick appeared to be sleeping, he went to the kitchen and built a fire. Then he made coffee and boiled some eggs. After washing the dishes, he took Nick a cup of the strong, hot coffee.

"How are you feeling, Nick, better, aren't you?" he asked.

"I'm awful sick, and I've got to use that pail."

"Fine, fine, just what I've been waiting to hear you say," Bud told him, as he helped him up. "And now," he went on, when Nick was back in bed, "drink this coffee while I rush the growler out."

When he came back, Nick said, "I read in the paper that a doctor in Kansas City claimed whiskey was the best remedy for the flu."

"My gosh, and we've got that quart the Duke gave us," exclaimed Bud. "I'll mix you up a good stiff hot drink right now. But you drink that coffee."

Then Bud came back with the drink. "This will make you sweat, but you keep covered good just the same," he ordered, "and then you try to sleep. I hear some Navajo, so I'll go see what he wants, but I'll look in every little while."

When Bud went back to see Nick, he found him wide awake and coughing huskily. "I'm going to give you another drink; maybe it will put you to sleep," announced Bud. "Also I'll go get you a bottle of Grandma's Cough Syrup to stop that coughing. We'll have you on your feet by tomorrow. Feel like eating?"

"No, I couldn't eat," he answered.

At noon, Bud started some mutton broth, and in the middle of the afternoon, he made Nick drink a cupful.

Nick had another bad night, but did finally get to sleep

about two. Bud, who kept a fire in the fireplace night and day, sat down there and immediately fell asleep. At seven he awoke and went to Nick.

"How long have you been awake and why didn't you call me?" Bud asked. "Want anything?"

"Not long awake," answered Nick, "and I'm thirsty."

"Okay then, I'll get a fire going and make coffee, after which you get another slug of Duke's whiskey."

"Feel any better?" Bud asked, after Nick had had the coffee and hot toddy.

"No better, but maybe no worse," he answered.

"When that broth warms up, you are going to have some of it," Bud told him.

The day wore along. Not many Indians came. At noon Hosteen Yazzi arrived, reporting many more dead Navajos. The Trader was very sick but not dead yet.

Nick slept some during the day. His face was very flushed and hot, and sometimes when he coughed, blood came, although he tried to conceal that from Bud. The next morning he said he felt a little cooler and really believed he was some better.

"That's the stuff, pal, I knew you'd be better today," said Bud. "How about a couple of poached eggs?"

"Maybe by noon," Nick answered.

At noon Hosteen Yazzi arrived and told Bud that the white men were dying so fast in town that they couldn't get enough boxes to bury them in. Hosteen Yazzi hoped he would not get sick because he did not think anyone else could carry the mail as well as he could.

Bud got a letter from Marge. She said the flu was very bad in Colorado too, and she was so worried, thinking of Bud and Nick all alone. There was a letter in a government envelope for Nick, which Bud opened. The Agent ordered them to close the store. Let no Indians in, although groceries could be passed out to them through a window or warehouse door.

"The poor fish," muttered Bud, "as though a locked door would keep the flu out."

"Okay," he told Nick, "I'll do it, if that's what the Agent wants." But he never did, because, by the middle of the afternoon, he began to feel queer, and in another hour he was very ill. He locked the pawn case and the store door, then went out and filled the two pails with fresh water and carried coal and wood which he piled beside the fireplace. There was enough bourbon left for one good toddy. He fixed it and took it to Nick, who said he would drink it later. There was half a bottle of Scotch in Nick's room, so he got it and drank about half. He also took quinine and a laxative. By eight o'clock, he was burning with fever and could scarcely hold his head up. He drank the rest of the Scotch, got his pajamas, piled the fireplace high with coal, and went to Nick's room.

"I've caught me a cold," he told Nick, "and I'm going to get in with you, so if you want anything, I'll be right here. Also, you know, misery loves company."

"I'm sure sorry you feel bad, Bud, and hope it isn't the flu. I believe I feel better, but I'm so weak it's pitiful."

Nick got little sleep that night. Bud seemed to be in a stupor, although he tossed and turned and was burning with fever. Nick knew he would have to have help. Where to get it was the problem. He felt that he was out of danger now, but he was too weak to take care of Bud. Then he thought of Moab, but maybe he was in as bad shape as they were. Anyway, it was a chance, and, if a Navajo showed up, he would send word by him.

The long night passed and it began to get light. Then sunlight struck the window. Nick looked at Bud. He sure looked bad. He spoke to him, but got no answer. He reached for the toddy Bud had fixed the night before. No, he better keep that in case a Navajo did come. It might give him strength enough to get to the door. The long hours dragged slowly by, and then, in mid-morning, he heard a Navajo pound on the store door, demanding to be let in.

Nick gulped the toddy as fast as he could. He waited a bit until the big drink began to warm his blood. He knew the Navajo wouldn't give up and leave until he had tried all the doors. He sat up, then, with his hand on the table, stood up. He was too dizzy so he sat down again. Maybe he couldn't make it to the door, but still he knew he had to, because there might not be another Navajo show up all day.

He tried it again with the same result. Then he had an idea. He got on his hands and knees and started slowly creeping toward the door. He didn't hear the Navajo now; maybe he *had* gone. Reaching up, he turned the knob, opened the door, and there, with his face pressed against the screen was Wart-on-Face.

"Are you sick?" he asked.

"Very sick," Nick answered, "and Little Strong Man is very sick. You must ride fast and tell *Gomale* (Moab) to come here quick. Can you do this?"

"Yes, I can go, but I am hungry."

"Tell Gomale to feed you and your horse. I can't get you anything to eat." Nick started coughing.

"Go to bed," said Wart-on-Face. "I can wait to eat," and away he went.

Nick crawled back to bed shivering. At about four o'clock that afternoon, a large face appeared at the bedroom window and a booming voice asked, "How's a critter to get in to where you boys are?"

"Back door, but it will take me a little time to crawl that far," Nick answered.

Moab went around the house and waited while Nick slowly crept to the door. When it was opened, Moab said, "Good gracious Peter, why didn't you send for me before?" He picked Nick up as if he were an infant, tucked him under his arm, and side-winded into the bedroom.

"Bud was all right until last night," Nick answered.

"Seems to be in a sort of trance, doesn't he?" Moab remarked. "I'll have to go put my horse away and then we'll have to work him over. I'll be back in a few minutes."

He came back carrying two bottles of Scotch. "These are the two I brought from town last trip. Glad I didn't drink them. But I don't like to drink alone. Now, I'm going to get this Bud roused enough to get a big drink in him. Got any eggs? Good. Then I'll boil some and make some toast and coffee. You fellows need food."

Moab forced Bud to take the whiskey and then gave Nick a drink. Next he came with two glasses. "Baking soda," he announced, "my remedy for everything, except broken bones," and he forced some into each of them. "You got quite a fire going in you, Bud, haven't you?"

"Terribly hot and sick," murmured Bud.

"Cover up good now. I'm going to open this window for a little while. This room fairly stinks."

"It's that pail," Nick told him.

"God bless me, so it is," he exclaimed. "I'll empty it now, because when that soda begins to bear down, you boys will be fighting for this pail."

By mid-afternoon Nick was feeling very much better and Bud certainly was no worse. Moab moved Nick into the living room onto the day bed so Bud would be more comfortable.

"Four or five Navajos out there," Moab told Nick, "want me to let them in?"

"Sure, let them get what they need," Nick answered, "and, if they haven't any money, give them the stuff."

"By cracky, that's the way I feel about it," Moab said. "I'll fix them up. They're going through a bad time."

Moab slept in a rocking chair by the fireplace that night. Occasionally he put more fuel on the fire and at four he stayed up. At six he brought a wash-basin so Bud could wash; then he did the same for Nick. Next came the

151

whiskey and baking soda, then breakfast. Nick felt good, but weak. Bud was better too, as the fever was gone.

"By Gumbo, another day or two and I'll have you young squirts on your feet again," said Moab.

"I'm sure I'll be fine by tomorrow, Moab," said Nick. "I know you should be over at your store."

"Why?" asked Moab, "I've neither a cat nor a dog, nor a chick nor a child; and, unless that Navajo I left to look after the place has died, everything's all right. No, I'll stay until I know you kids are in good shape."

Hosteen Yazzi came and Moab let him get something to eat and gave him the mail sack. He thought the worst was over now and those who had not died, were getting well. The Trader at Lone Point was getting better.

Two days later Moab prepared to leave. Nick felt good again, except he was still pretty weak and still coughed. Bud was able to sit by the fire, so Nick knew he was doing all right.

"Well, I expect I should go home," Moab said, "but by Juniper, if you boys have a relapse, just send for me."

"Sure will," agreed Nick, "and we'll try and get even with you for all you've done."

"Good Gracious Peter, what's a neighbor for if he can't help when needed? I know you'd do the same for me, and, anyhow, you know I like you rascals. Well, so long. I'd better get going." With one last grin, Moab left.

"He's a right guy, ain't he?" asked Nick. "Guess that soda was good medicine."

"Yeah, and I don't see how we could have got along without him, although maybe we would have," said Bud.

"Well, we'll take it easy for a few days," Nick told him. "You know, I doubt if I could have crawled to the door to send for Moab, if I hadn't had that big drink first."

"Yeah, I'll bet the whiskey had a lot to do with us get-ing over that damned flu," agreed Bud.

The days passed on, and, as they did, the boys began

to get an idea of the number of Navajos who had perished with the flu.

"I don't suppose we will ever know how many did die," said Nick one day. "We gradually hear of this one and that one but, since they do not report the deaths and don't like to speak of the dead, all one can say is that a whale of a lot of them died." He had a sudden vision of pretty, vivacious Glacie — and a fear that she might be one of them.

A week before Christmas, Nick had a letter from Mr. Leyton saying he believed, if Nick was still interested in buying a post, that he might make a deal for the Blue Rock place. The Trader there had died of the flu and his wife was anxious to sell. This store was some thirty-five miles across the mountain and in higher country.

"Well, what do you think, Bud?" Nick asked. "I've always thought that was a good place. It's rather high up, around seven thousand feet, and they must get real winters there."

"Yeah, but if there's a good business there — and Mr. Leyton should know — who cares?" said Bud. "You better make a trip over. Start in the morning. Trails are still open and it don't look like snow."

"That's right," agreed Nick, "we don't want anyone to beat us to it, provided we do want it and she doesn't want too much for it."

"Well, we've got to get a place of our own," Bud said, "so don't let a few hundred dollars spoil the deal, if you like the setup. But, whatever you do will be all right with me."

"Thanks, Bud, I knew it would be."

Nick was ready to leave the next morning at sunrise. Bud had been out early to feed and water his pony and now had him saddled and raring to go. Nick's heavy Mackinaw, with a lunch rolled up in it, was tied back of the saddle.

"It's cloudy this morning and we may very well get

some snow later," Bud said, "but anyway I'm sure it won't snow today."

"It's a slow, rough trail, but I'll make it by two or three this afternoon," Nick said. "So long, Pardner."

"Good luck," called Bud, as Nick rode away.

The pony was in good shape and willing, so Nick traveled fast until he reached the foothills where the trail started up. By ten-thirty he was on top and starting across the long, flat meadows. At noon he halted, took off the saddle, and ate his lunch. Two o'clock found him on the rim where the trail started down. He paused to gaze over the great valley that spread below. "Boy, that's beautiful country," he exclaimed to the pony. "If Bud and Marge won't like this, they're hard to please. I believe I know where that store is; sure looks like buildings and a corral way down there in the foothills. But, boy howdy, it looks like a regular old he-trail down from here."

The mountain on that side was no gentle slope. It seemed to drop right off and then slope down for miles. After the pines petered out, almost as far as he could see, were smaller trees — piñon, juniper, and cedar. The whole country was green and, in the far distance, he could see a large lake. It proved to be a tough, rocky trail. In places he got off and led the pony. After he was down he was pleased to see the trail headed south in the direction of the buildings he had seen.

The trail led through heavy oak trees and brush now. Suddenly the pony gave a loud snort and stood trembling. To the left Nick heard, and then got a glimpse of a large black body — a bear. He had thought they would be denned up before this.

In another half hour he reached the store. It was a larger place than he expected to see. Gosh, he thought, it'll take a lot to buy all of these buildings.

Nick rode around a corral and barn, back of which was the store and warerooms. On the south side of the barn was

154

what looked like a two-roomed cottage with a porch across the front. Across from the store, separated by a driveway, was a six- or seven-room one-story house. Back of this was a long narrow building which Nick later found was the wood house and laundry. He got off his pony and went into the store. There were three Navajos there and a white boy behind the counter. Nick introduced himself. The boy's name was Ned Smith.

"Are you Mrs. Smith's son?" Nick asked.

"No, I'm her nephew," he answered.

"Is Mrs. Smith here?"

"She's over in the house," Ned answered. "You can go over there if you want to see her. Go around to the kitchen door."

"Thanks, I will," said Nick.

Mrs. Smith was busy baking, but she invited Nick in. She was a tall thin woman who looked to be around fifty. She was pleasant and friendly and Nick liked her at once. There were some freshly baked cup cakes, nicely frosted, on a bread board. Mrs. Smith got a plate and put three on it, saying to Nick, "Bet you're hungry. Try these and let me know how they are."

"Thanks," said Nick, and then, after a big bite, "They're certainly good, so good I'm afraid I'll eat all of them."

"If you do — and I hope you do — I'll think they must be good." She smiled at him.

Nick thought he might as well let her know what he had come for, so he asked her if it was true that she wanted to sell.

"Yes, I do," she answered. "It's just too lonesome for me since George died, and I don't think Ned and I can carry on the business like George did. Ned is a good boy, but he's just too young to handle these Indians, and, though he speaks quite a bit of Navajo, he hasn't had the experience it takes to be a Trader."

"Well, then," said Nick, "the first thing to find out is

how much you want for the place and how you want it. Maybe it's beyond our reach."

"I can tell you that easy enough," she said. "I want ten thousand for the buildings. The stock of goods goes at cost. As you can easily see, I'm putting these buildings in at much less than their real value, but that's because I really want to leave here."

"Yes, I'm sure it would take a great deal more than ten thousand to replace these buildings," agreed Nick. "I suppose you will sell the house furnishings too."

"Everything except my personal things," she answered.

"Have you any idea what the stock will inventory?" he asked.

"I suppose the merchandise and pawn will run around three thousand. We haven't much pawn right now."

"Probably around fourteen thousand in all, including the furniture," Nick guessed.

"About the way I figure it," she answered.

"Then the next, and most important question is: How much do you want down on it?"

"Half," she answered, "and the balance at six per cent interest."

"Well, I don't know," Nick said, "we have saved up six thousand, but maybe we could borrow a thousand. I've never tried to borrow money, so don't know."

"But you do have the six thousand cash," she said. "All right then, I'll take six thousand. And do you know why? Because Mr. Leyton told me all about you and your friend. He said he would be pleased if I would give you first chance on it, as you two boys were honest, industrious, and steady, and he was sure you would pay it out. He also thinks you will give him some business when you are on your own."

"That's mighty nice of Mr. Leyton and awful nice of you, Mrs. Smith," Nick said, "and my pardner, Bud, will be very grateful to you. He's going to be married next summer, and I know how pleased and happy his girl will be when she sees this place. When do you want to leave?"

"Will the first of March suit you?"

"Why, yes, that will be fine. But that would give us the spring wool business, or hadn't you thought of that?"

"Yes, I thought of that." She smiled. "I want to see you off to a good start."

Well, now, here was a swell woman, thought Nick. Any other Trader would never leave until after the wool season. "It's a deal, then," he said, "and you have certainly been more than fair. You don't know how happy I am to think I'm going to live at this lovely spot."

"It is nice and, if George were here, I would want to stay. Do you want anything to show you've been promised the place?"

"Your word is good enough for me," Nick told her.

"And I'm sure your saying you will take the place is good enough for me, too," she said. "Now, you go look around. You've just bought a pig in a poke, although I don't think you are going to be disappointed in anything. We'll have supper about six-thirty. My, it sure does look like snow."

"I would like to see how the house is arranged, so I can tell Bud," Nick told her.

"Go right ahead, that's what I want you to do. Ned can show you the store and everything else, too."

Nick went from the large kitchen to the dining room. It was a room fourteen by sixteen with double windows on the west side. The next room was a living room. It was larger than the dining room and it had double windows on the north side as well as the west, with a large fireplace on the south wall.

Between these rooms and the three rooms on the east side, ran an eight-foot hall, the full length of the house. There was only one door from the hall on the east side. Nick stepped through it and found there were two bedrooms and a sitting room between. The front, or north, bedroom was much larger than the other two rooms. That would be Bud's and Marge's room. He'd take the back one.

He stepped out onto the screened porch which ran the full length of the north and east sides of the house. Then he crossed the driveway and went into the store. It faced east and was large compared to the one Nick was used to. The northeast corner was built into an office, wainscoted up four feet and then screened. Back of the counter on the west side, was a large blanket room, and opening through a wide door were the two large warerooms — one for merchandise, the other for wool, pelts, and piñons. A pretty swell setup, Nick thought.

The cottage had two good-sized bedrooms and would be used for guests.

Nick stayed in the store visiting with Ned and the Navajos until supper time. After supper, Ned went out to get kindling for the morning fires and came in saying it was snowing hard. "May be tough going over the mountain tomorrow," he said.

"Probably won't get so very deep by morning," Nick answered, "and it would take me three full days to go around."

"Longest way 'round is sometimes the shortest way home," laughed Mrs. Smith.

In the morning there was about five inches of snow, not as much as they had expected, but it was still snowing.

Ned had fed the pony earlier so after breakfast Nick went to saddle up. Then he went to the store to get some lunch. Inside he found White Rock, an Indian from home.

"What are you doing here?" Nick asked him.

"I came over two days ago to visit my uncle," he answered. "What are you doing here?"

"This is going to be my home in three months," Nick told him.

"Shall we ride together?" asked White Rock. "There will be deep snow on the mountains."

"Do you think we can get across?" Nick asked, as he valued his opinion.

"Oh, yes, I think so."

After bidding Mrs. Smith and Ned goodbye, they set out, White Rock in the lead. Nick was glad to have company and White Rock would surely be able to keep the trail. They trotted along until they came to where the trail started up. It certainly was a bad trail when it was covered with snow. About half way up, White Rock's pony slipped and fell. It was a dangerous place, but the pony had sense enough not to struggle or was too winded, so they cleared the snow and got him up. They led the ponies the rest of the way to the top.

There they found traveling much better. On their side of the mountain the trail down was much easier and by midafternoon the snow had ceased. They reached home before sundown.

After supper Nick began telling Bud what a nice home they would have in the spring and what a fine deal Mrs. Smith had made them. He assured Bud he would be able to bring Marge to one of the nicest Trading Posts anyone could possibly wish for. He thought a little wistfully that it was just the place he would like to bring a wife of his own.

# chapter 9

THE NEXT TWO MONTHS passed slowly, but, finally, the big day came — February 25, 1919 — when Nick and Bud were to leave the place that had been home to them for eight years.

"A fellow kinda hates to leave a place he has been at so long, doesn't he?" remarked Bud.

"You're right," Nick answered, "but when you see the place we're going to, you'll soon forget this little spot on the desert."

The Navajos had protested when they heard that the boys were leaving and all said that when they moved to the mountains in the summer, they would go down the other side and trade with Nick and Bud.

A Trader — Dawson by name — and his wife had been at the store two days, getting acquainted with the Navajos.

The boys found that a lot of stuff had accumulated in eight years, and it took quite a number of boxes to hold their possessions. These had already been sent in on a freight wagon to town as the road over the mountain would be deep in snow for some time yet. Bud had arranged with Cledge to look after his pony, and, as soon as the trail over the mountain was open, he was to bring him over.

The company manager, Mr. Cross, arrived about noon in his new Hupmobile, so, finally, the boys had a chance to see a real "bearcat"; the Hup came wallowing through the wash without a pause. Naturally Mr. Cross was sorry to have the boys leave, but couldn't blame them for wanting to get into business for themselves.

Now they were leaving. From across the wash, the boys turned and looked back on the old familiar buildings.

"Damn it all, I'm really sorry to leave that place and all my Navajo friends," exclaimed Nick.

"Me, too," chimed in Bud, "I really am."

"Guess the Navajos are sorry too," Mr. Cross said, "and say, while I think of it, I want to tell you that I'm going to take you out to Blue Rock tomorrow. I've never been there."

"That's swell of you, Mr. Cross," said Nick. "We sure will appreciate it."

They left town early the next morning as they did not know what kind of road they'd have. They found the road to the Agency fairly good, but from there up the valley it was different. In July and August, during the heavy rains, the water ran down the slopes until it hit the road. It ran down this, cutting deeper and deeper until sometimes the former road became a deep, wide arroyo.

Mr. Cross had to take to the sagebrush many times, and once he misjudged a high center and ran up on it so the two front wheels were off the ground. This delayed them a good half hour and caused them some hard work.

When they did arrive at the store, Mr. Cross was as enthusiastic about it as Nick and Bud were. Mrs. Smith invited Mr. Cross to stay the night, but he said he must get back, although he could stay to dinner. After dinner was over and Mr. Cross had left, they all started taking inventory. By twelve that night it was finished, so the next morning the two proud partners were in possession of their own business.

When the door was unlocked and they were inside, Bud grabbed Nick by the hand.

"Well, Nick, this is the day we've been waiting for a long time," he said, "and right now I'm thanking you, because you're the one who made all this come true. If you hadn't been just the right guy that you are, I never would have stuck it out like I did, nor would I ever have met Marge. I've a lot to thank you for — and, right now, I'm doing it."

"Forget it, Bud, but here's one thing I want to talk to you about. My father used to say that partnerships were a good thing to steer clear of. I don't believe that, but, anyway, I want this understood. If you ever see me do anything that you don't understand, or that even might look suspicious to you, you come right to me and ask what the deal was. Of course I will do the same. In that way, there should be no misunderstandings. And another thing — any deal you make, whether it's right or wrong, I'll back you up and I'll expect you to do the same by me., Okay?"

"Yes, sir, you bet," agreed Bud. "We got along for eight years, so I'm not worrying about the future. Say, did you hear Mrs. Smith mention we get mail here three times a week?"

"Yeah, I knew that. My gosh, I'd better write the *Denver Post* and let them know where to send the paper. This is mail day."

Old Doc carried the mail. It was twenty-five miles to the Agency and, except in winter, when the snow was very deep, the round trip was made in a day. He was generally back by four o'clock in the afternoon.

Mrs. Smith told Nick that Old Doc was a fine, honest Navajo, a real Medicine Man and in great demand. When he was out on a case or when the weather was too rough, his grandson, a boy of twelve, took over the duties of mail carrier. This would likely have annoyed the Postal Department as a mail carrier is supposed to be of age, but, as Mrs. Smith said, "What they don't know won't hurt them." She said she didn't suppose there were many white men of sixty-eight who would care for a fifty-mile ride every other day, for three dollars a ride. But the old man always came back with a smile, bought a few groceries, and drank a bottle of pop before he rode the four miles back down the trail to where he lived.

She said that Old Doc was well-to-do and didn't need the job, but it made him feel important to be trusted with the government mail.

The inventory was figured that day, the six thousand paid to Mrs. Smith, and a note signed for the balance due. Bud helped Mrs. Smith and Ned pack the things she was to take, and a Navajo freighter was engaged to take them to town and bring back a load of flour, also the money for wool buying.

Old Doc's son had a buggy. On the day after the freighter left, he came to take Mrs. Smith and Ned to the Agency, where they could get an auto to take them on in to town.

"I sure do hate to leave here," Mrs. Smith said, when she was seated in the buggy. "Maybe when I get homesick, you'll let me come and stay a bit. I wish you boys the best of luck. You'll make money here; we did, and don't think this six thousand dollars is all the money I have."

"You've been awful good to us," Nick told her, "and any time you want to visit us, we'll sure be glad to have you."

*     *     *

Wool season came and went. Wool started at fifteen cents a pound, but by the time it was ready to be sent to town, it had advanced to eighteen cents, which assured the boys of a nice profit.

163

And then June rolled along and Bud was leaving to
be married.

"Still wish you could be best man," said Bud.

"I wish so too," Nick told him, "but no can do. Mr.
Berger will find you one."

"If I find a pretty girl I think you'd like, I'll have Marge
invite her to visit us," Bud said. "You should get married too."

"Okay, I'll look her over when she comes," laughed
Nick. "And, say, you take plenty of money with you; a
guy shouldn't get caught short, first time he's married
anyway. Flash your roll, spend it too. Make those friends
of Marge's think you're a monied man. And hurrah for
our side — we're finally going to have a cook!"

Bud was to ride his pony to the Agency and Old Doc
would bring it back. He knew Mr. Cross would bring
Marge and him home when the time came.

Nick felt a bit lonesome after Bud left. Of course Bud
had been away other times, but somehow, this was different. He wondered again if marriage would change Bud
any. Marge seemed a swell girl, but what if she became
dissatisfied. Oh well, ford the creek when you come to it.

On the eleventh of June, Mr. Cross drove up with the
newlyweds. Besides all the luggage there was a large quantity of groceries, meat, vegetables, and other provisions.

"Congratulations," grinned Nick, "and, Marge, I think
I have a big 'Kiss the Bride' coming."

"You certainly have, and a big hug too. Otherwise I
know Bud would be mad," she said, giving Nick a warm
hug and kiss.

"Don't forget, Bud, you've got to carry her into the
house, although maybe you're not able."

"If that's what a guy's supposed to do, I'll show you
how able I am." Bud grabbed the laughing Marge, swung
her over his shoulder, opened the screen door and carried
her clear out to the kitchen.

164

"This has a fishy look to me," laughed Marge, "planting me in the kitchen. Is this supposed to be my room?"

"I did say something about our having a cook after you arrived," admitted Nick.

"Let's see the rest of the house while I'm still free," she said, so they started on a tour of the other rooms. "Gee, this is just as nice as Bud said it was. I love it and aren't we lucky to have such a nice home?"

"You said it," agreed Bud. "Well, I guess I'd better bring the things in; then we'll have lunch. Mr. Cross will want to leave before long." Mr. Cross had not come in the house. He was strolling around outside.

"Shall I get lunch?" Nick asked.

"After that subtle hint of dumping me in the kitchen, I suppose I must get it," she answered. "You may have to show me where things are though."

"Bud, show her, help her too. She don't start working the minute she gets here, unless she wants to. Remember, Marge," he went on, "this worthless husband of yours is plenty able at any time to get a fairly decent meal."

"Yeah, and how about you?" Bud asked. "He's a good deal better cook than I am, Marge."

"Nice to know there are two cooks here, because I'm not so hot, but willing," said Marge.

"And here's an idea and a suggestion. Never, never, under any circumstances, get up and get breakfast for him. I'll go even further; if I were you, I'd never get up until he brought you some coffee. The thing to do is to get the upper hand right at the start."

"Who is this old married man passing out this good advice?" asked Marge. "Bud, consider the foregoing the rule in this house. Any other suggestions, Nick?"

"Now see what you've gone and done," said Bud. "Up in South Dakota, wives not only get breakfast but they build the fire to cook it on."

"This is some little distance from South Dakota, isn't

it, Marge?" answered Nick. "And speaking of fire, you see that Bud keeps the wood box and coal hods full. I've known him to step right over an empty coal hod, pretending he didn't see it."

"Oh, yeah," snorted Bud. "Well, dear, you can see you're going to lead a dog's life around here, but I'm agreeable to everything he's mentioned, so far, that is."

"I'm going to learn to speak Navajo," announced Marge.

"She's too old, don't you think, Nick?" said Bud, as he dodged a swing from Marge.

"Who's too old, don't you think?" demanded Marge. "I'm not too old, am I, Nick?"

"Just the right age to pick up a new language," agreed Nick. "With Bud and me helping, we'll have you surprising yourself by the end of a month."

The next morning when Nick went to the kitchen, he found Bud sitting at the built-in kitchen table with a large stack of his famous cracker and canned milk hot cakes.

"Marge wanted to get up and get our breakfast, but I told her nothing doing," he said. "I think it's a nice idea, but she said she never heard of such a thing. I told her just to lie there and think about what a nice husband she has."

"Just hate yourself, don't you?" said Nick.

"You know something?" said Bud, paying no attention to Nick's remark. "I'll bet we could make better hot cakes if we had real milk."

"Probably we could, but where would we get real milk?"

"Well," Bud answered, "I don't know about New Mexico, but up in South Dakota, they get it from cows."

"And would you care to be tied down twice a day milking a cow?" asked Nick.

"I believe it would be worth it," he answered.

"Okay, let's get one. But, remember, you're going to be the dairy maid. I'll learn to milk, of course, so any time you're away, I can take care of it. And here's something

166

I've been thinking about. Next spring let's put in a light plant, water pump, refrigerator, and bathroom."

"I've been wanting to suggest that," Bud said. "We'll be better fixed to do it then. We're going to be here a long time, so let's spend some money and have things comfortable."

Just then Marge came in.

"Ah, breakfast is being served. I'll have a stack of cakes. I just heard you say you were going to have things comfortable. Aren't you comfortable now?"

"We were first talking about a cow," answered Bud.

"How could a cow make you comfortable? I should think it would be the other way around. You would have to keep the cow comfortable, if you were thinking of milk, that is."

"You're too fast for us," laughed Nick. "The word 'comfortable' came up after the light plant and running water."

"Oh, I see," she said, "the lights and water come right after the cow. Must take a lot of water for a cow. I suppose you want the electric lights so you can see to milk her on dark winter mornings. I thought they used lanterns around cows, or else how come the Chicago fire?"

"Again I say, you're just too fast for us," Nick said, "and it looked like you were looking at me when you spoke of milking on dark winter mornings. Even with the brightest of electric lights, you'll never be able to see me milking a cow on any such mornings. Bud said he was sure, if we'd get you a cow, you'd be glad to milk it."

"And we haven't been married a week yet," she groaned. "Are we going to raise hogs too?"

"There's a good idea," exclaimed Bud. "Nick, I told you we'd get some good ideas from Marge."

"I knew we would too," agreed Nick, "but let's get the cow settled first. Neither Bud nor I know how to milk. Bud said he thought you knew how, but, if you don't, it wouldn't matter as he says you are quick to pick up things."

"I am too, watch." She grabbed up a hot cake and

slammed it at Bud, catching him on the top of the head as he ducked.

"Soak him with another," grinned Nick, "because now I can see he hasn't been telling me the truth. Try one of these plates on him, they're cheap but heavy."

"Now that I've got him subdued, are you really going to get a cow? Wouldn't that be grand? Thick cream. And I just know I can make butter."

"Yeah, we're going to get one," Bud said, "and I'll do the milking. When I was in South Dakota . . ."

"Sure, he saw someone milk a cow, Marge, so, of course, he can milk," interrupted Nick. "Well, I'm going to the store. I'll write to Moab; he can get one of his Mormon friends to get us a good cow. They can bring her as far as his place and he can send her over the mountain with a Navajo."

One late July afternoon during a terrific rain storm, one of the numerous Indians in the store looked out the window and remarked that there was lots of running water outside. Nick came around the counter and took a look. A stream of water, six or eight feet wide, which looked to be a foot deep, was flowing through the yard. Just then Marge screamed for Bud, saying the kitchen was flooded.

"Bring the Navajos with you and come on," yelled Nick, as he dashed for the house.

There was some two inches of water on the kitchen floor. Marge had piled rugs at the door bottom, but this didn't seem to be doing much good. "Why didn't you holler sooner?" Nick asked.

"I just discovered it," she answered. "What are we going to do?"

Nick ran to the front door. Bud was coming with the Navajos.

"Get them each a shovel," he cried. "Maybe we can turn the stream. It's sure flooding the kitchen."

But they couldn't turn the stream. If it hadn't suddenly

broken through under the foundation of Nick's bedroom, the kitchen would really have been flooded.

In a few minutes, a Navajo, who had gone to the other side of the house, came yelling that the water had broken out and was going to go into the well. The well was about twenty feet from the house, a dug well, eight feet in width and some fifteen feet deep. It was walled with rock and had a board and roofing paper top.

"Good Lord, don't let it get in the well," roared Bud, and, telling the Navajos to hurry, he started on the run. But the water had already broken through and he could hear it running in. "Get some rocks, boards or anything," he yelled. "We've got to get this stopped."

Some of the Navajos started digging to deepen the water course, while others brought rocks to Nick and Bud, who finally plugged the hole, but not until a lot of that dirty yellow water had poured in.

Flash floods like that one didn't last long, and by the time the hole was plugged, the water was slowing up.

"Sure has ruined our drinking water," Bud said. "I'll have a couple of these fellows start pumping. Two or three hours pumping may clear it out so it won't taste and smell too strong."

"Boy, we'll have to put a gang to work up above making a dike. We can't have this happen again," Nick said.

In the kitchen, Marge was furiously sweeping the water toward the open door. Her face was red and covered with sweat. "It didn't say anything about this in the marriage contract, Bud," she groaned, "and I can't make any headway against this dirty water. The door seems to be on a hill."

"You go sit on the table," ordered Bud, as he took the broom from her. "Tell those two women to come in here, Nick. You better go get a couple more brooms too." Then he sloshed over to Marge and, between kisses, told her not to worry. In an hour the women would have the water out and the floor scrubbed, so she'd never know it had happened.

The water from the well smelled somewhat for several days, but Marge boiled all the water they used to drink, although Bud claimed it wasn't necessary.

"Oh, yes, I know," laughed Marge, "you drank worse water than this in South Dakota!"

As they did not have another cloudburst that summer, they didn't know how the dike the Navajos had built would work, but it looked as if it would turn the water.

\* \* \*

September twentieth, they started buying lambs. This was something Nick knew very little about. Bud, however, did know sheep.

"Well, you can do the lamb buying," said Nick, "although I want to learn how to tell the different ages of sheep. We'll have to take our platform scales out and weigh one at a time, won't we?"

"Sure, and we'll have to set it some way so they'll weigh five pounds light, because you know as well as I do that they'll bring every lamb in stuffed to the gills. When we sell them, you know they've got to stay in a corral twelve hours without feed and water."

The mountain lambs were good, well improved stuff, the bulk of them weighing around sixty pounds, with an occasional one, eighty or even more. When one of these extra heavy ones was put on the scales, Bud always took a look at its teeth. The Navajos, who could tell a lamb from a yearling at a glance, would razz Bud. But, as plenty of them tried to slip in yearlings for lambs, Bud calmly continued his dental observations. Yearling wethers, while larger, were worth less than lambs.

When Bud came in at supper time after the first afternoon's buying, Marge took a good sniff, and said, "Good heavens, what stinks so? Is it you, Bud?"

"Not that I know of," he answered, "I don't smell anything."

"It's nothing, just the sheep smell," said Nick.

"Well, it certainly is something, and how he can stand it is funny to me," she said. "But I suppose I should be glad he isn't wrassling goats. One thing sure, he'll take a bath and change his clothes every night. I couldn't have our bed smelling like a sheep corral."

"Fussy dame, isn't she?" laughed Bud. "She'll get used to it."

"I won't get used to it because it isn't one of my favorite odors. Of course, if you'd rather sleep in the woodshed . . ."

"Oh, I'll clean up after supper," interrupted Bud. "Maybe it's worse than I think."

"You must be a light thinker, if it isn't," Marge told him. "Of course, Nick, I suppose I could stand this smelly husband of mine — if we had no water or soap, that is — because this is part of the business and you're going to make money out of it."

"Be firm, Marge," he said. "A daily bath may weaken him, but it won't really injure him any."

After supper while they were doing the dishes, Marge said, "Aren't there any good silversmiths around here, and, if so, aren't you boys missing a good thing by not putting them to work for you?"

"Sure there are silversmiths here," Nick answered. "They're always bringing rings and bracelets, but we can only use so many."

"If they make rings and bracelets, I should think they could make other things that are not so common. Something new and different. I'll bet Fred Harvey would take all you sent them."

"I told you this gal had ideas," said Bud, "and this might be a good one. Silver is cheap and we could have good heavy stuff with deep, clean designs. Copy some of the Navajos' old heavy things."

171

"I'm game to give it a trial," agreed Nick. "Marge can draw up some designs of whatever she thinks of. Probably the silversmiths won't get the idea right away, but they'll catch on."

The next day Nick ordered a hundred Mexican pesos. By the time they arrived, Marge had some designs ready, so, when a silversmith came in, the boys could show him what they wanted and give him enough silver to make whatever it was.

"The first one or two tries probably won't suit Marge," Bud said, "but what the hell, we'll keep them at it until they do get them right."

"Yeah, and we'll pay them for the work just the same, so they won't get discouraged," said Nick.

One day, while one of the best silversmiths was in the store, Marge brought over a small table bell. It was about five inches high with a figure of a man for the handle. She shook hands with Little Silversmith and handed him the bell. He looked it over, rang it, and asked if it was a present.

"Good Lord, no," exclaimed Marge, "my uncle brought me that from England. Ask him, Bud, if he can make one of an Indian with a robe around him for a handle, like this," and she showed him a sketch.

Little Silversmith shook his head. Too much work and maybe he couldn't get the silver so the bell would ring. But Marge went to work on him, through Bud, and he finally said he'd try one.

"This will take four pesos," Bud told him. "At fifty cents an ounce, your work would come to two dollars, but, if you can make these bells and make them very nice, we'll pay you double, four dollars."

This was something Little Silversmith could understand; he was going to get twice as much as the other silversmiths. He would try to make this bell very nice. In two days he was back with a perfect, sweet-toned bell.

"You see," exclaimed Marge, after Bud had called her over, "money talks."

"Yeah, and besides that, he's a top silversmith," Nick said.

"Well, let's go into mass production on these," said Marge. "They come a little high, but plenty of people will buy them. He can make them. We'll keep him at it and, when we have a couple of dozen, send them to Fred Harvey's Indian Department. I'll bet none will come back."

Marge was right. The Harvey people wanted to know if they had any more new items and, if so, to send them samples. This turned out to be the beginning of a long and prosperous business.

The lambs showed a nice profit when they were delivered. It had been a wonderful autumn. Snow came in early December, starting about noon; by evening, there was a good six inches. During the night it cleared, and in the morning it was twenty-two below.

"Sure white whiskers on that old Chic Sales seat out there this morning," growled Bud to Nick, "but I haven't heard Marge complain."

"This one back of the store was a bit frosty too," said Nick. "It's a damn shame, but you tell her things will be different before another winter rolls around, because, as soon as the ground thaws in the spring, we'll have plumbers at work out here."

The stoves kept the house warm, but it was different in the store. The big round-bellied stove kept the customers plenty warm, but back of the counters it was different — just a little too cool for comfort.

"You know what we ought to do?" said Nick one cold morning. "We ought to take this board facing off the front of the counters and put chicken wire on, like Moab fixed his."

"What's holding us?" said Bud. "We've got the wire. Let's go to it. I'm getting chilblains the way it is."

By noon they had the change made, and it was a great improvement.

It was cold through most of April, but the first day of May broke clear and warm. "You know what I think I'll do," announced Nick at the breakfast table. "Yesterday was warm and clear and it feels warm this morning. They won't start shearing for another week at least, so I'm going to ride up north and see if there's anything to this vanadium strike. Maybe I'm overlooking something and maybe I'd better stake us a few claims."

"Go ahead," urged Bud, "it'll do you good to get away for a few days."

The Navajos had told the boys that there had been quite a few white men going north. The Navajos thought maybe they had found gold. But Nick had found out that it was vanadium they had located. "I wouldn't know vanadium if I saw it," he admitted, "but I can stake us out some claims anyway, so I'll throw a couple of blankets and some grub on your pony and go take a look. It's only about fifty miles. Could make it today if I had to, but I'm going mostly for the ride, so I'm not hurrying."

He jogged leisurely along, stopped at noon to eat lunch, camped in the pines that night, and the next afternoon reached the rimrocks where the vanadium was supposed to be. He rode along the great wall for two or three miles without seeing anyone. Finally he saw smoke from a camp fire. As he drew nearer he saw a man sitting, with his back against a tree, a short distance from the smouldering fire. Further away he noticed a hobbled burro.

The man was small, rather dirty looking, and his face was covered with a short grey beard. "Hello," Nick greeted him.

"How de do," the man answered. "Where're you heading for?"

"Just riding around," Nick told him. "You look like a prospector."

174

"I am, but I'm sure wasting my time around here."

"Thought there was some talk of vanadium up here," Nick said.

"There is," he answered, "it's all along up there and I guess it always will be there."

"How's that?' 'Nick asked.

"How the hell would you ever get it out of this dang rough country? It would cost more than the stuff is worth," and he spat a long stream of tobacco juice at a stink bug that was crawling toward him.

"Well, I'd better be drifting," Nick said.

"If you're going to camp, you might as well camp here with me," the other said, giving the stink bug the other barrel, so to speak.

"Thanks, but I want to go further on today. See you on my way back." *She-oh-chea* (I'm a liar) he added under his breath.

I expect the old fellow knows what's he's talking about, thought Nick. What he said sounded darn reasonable to me, after seeing this country, so pretty soon I'll find me a nice clean place to camp for tonight, and tomorrow I'll head for the foothills and mosey along them on my way home. He saw a hogan some distance ahead, so rode over to it. After visiting with the mother and daughter awhile, he bought enough mutton for his supper and rode on. He could roast the meat on a stick and he still had enough crackers to go with it.

The wind came up during the night. Nick woke up early, as he was cold, to see a cloudy sky that had all the appearance of rain or snow. The Navajo woman, the afternoon before, had told him the Square Rock store was some six miles to the east. He decided to go there and get something for his lunch, also some canned fruit, cookies, and candy in case he could not make it home and had to stay the night with some Navajo family. Travelers were always welcome but the little present would make him doubly welcome and remembered, especially by the children. In an hour he was at Square Rock. A terribly lonesome and desolate place, Nick thought, no trees or anything green, just bare rocks. No ponies tied around, but that was due to the weather no doubt.

Nick tied his horse to the hitching rail, then walked over to the store and went in.

Nice and warm inside as the huge potbellied stove was certainly putting out heat. The store was well-stocked as Nick could see at a glance. The Trader rose from a comfortable-looking armchair and came over and greeted Nick, saying "My name is Pete Cooper." Nick told him his name was Nick Norton and where his Post was. He looked this rather large man over. He seemed to be about forty, red-headed, freckled face, nice blue eyes, a friendly appearing man. Nick liked him right away. Only thing different from most men was the large iron hook where his left hand should have been.

"Guess you are wondering about this iron hand. A cornered mountain lion and I had quite a tussle, he chawed my hand while I was sticking my hunting knife into him as fast and deep as I could. I won the fight, but he gave me an infected hand which an Army doctor had to cut off. You'd be surprised at all the things I can do with this old hay hook. Well, I have a coffee pot on the kitchen stove. Let's have some while we visit."

"Fine," agreed Nick, "it will really hit the spot on a day like this."

"Say, Norton," exclaimed Pete, "how about some nice wire-grilled shoulder of fat lamb and deep-fried dough puffs."

"Sounds mighty good," Nick replied.

"All right," and he let out a yell, "Ena, come here a minute." Presently a tall, slender Navajo woman came. A real nice-looking woman, who looked to be between thirty-five and forty. She stopped at Pete's side with her hand resting on his shoulder. Looks like she thinks quite highly of this Pete character, thought Nick.

Pete quickly told her what was wanted.

"She speaks some English but it embarrasses her as she knows it is not good," he explained.

"Your wife?" asked Nick politely.

"Well, Ena and I think we are man and wife but I suppose a good Christian missionary would not consider being married in the Navajo manner quite legal. Oh well, we'll battle that one out when they get on our trail."

"Anyhow, after seeing a Navajo wedding performed, I'll say you are married," agreed Nick, thinking here was a white man who seemed to have a happy marriage with his Indian wife. He wondered if he and Glacie might have been . . .

"You ever seen what the Navajos call the Painted Cave?" asked Pete.

"Never have, never heard of it either, is it near here?"

"Eight or ten miles, mostly east. Ena took me over once. Navajos don't talk much about it, as they have a shrine right near which is watched at all times by a nearby family consisting of a Navajo woman and a small daughter, light-skinned, who we think had a white father. The back wall of this large cave is absolutely covered with yellow handprints, must be a vanadium paint mixture the ancient ones knew about."

"Maybe that's the way they kept track of the tribe," suggested Nick.

"Maybe I shouldn't have said 'watched over by a family,' as really two do not make much of a family, do they?" Pete remarked.

"Well, here is our lunch." The men kept Ena busy for awhile deep-frying the squares of dough in the boiling fat.

"Now," said Nick, "that is positively the best meal I ever ate, and I do thank you two for a very pleasant stopover. It is not snowing too heavy yet, so I feel I should

177

get a-going. If it gets too tough later on, I can find a family where I can spend the night and then make it home tomorrow. Please come see us some time."

"We might just do that," Pete told him. "If you are ever up this way again, Ena will be proud to fix you another good Navajo meal, won't you Ena?"

"Yes," she shyly answered, as she shook hands with Nick.

After brushing the snow from his saddle, Nick mounted and headed south. His thoughts were too full of Glacie and "what might have been" to notice the weather, but by afternoon the snow was coming down much faster. He knew he could not make it home that day, so he began to look for a hogan. He should be nearing Whiskey Creek soon and if he followed it down he would soon find Navajo homes. At the creek he turned downstream and, before he had ridden far, he came to a well-traveled trail and followed it to a large log cabin. He dismounted and knocked on the door. Cora, a girl he knew, opened the door. Behind her he could see her sister.

"Come in, and what are you doing way over here and in a big snow?" she asked, as she shook his hand. Then she called, "Zelda, come here, Nick is here."

"This is nice," Cora said, "and just about in time for supper. Put your horse in the big shed. You'll find plenty of hay there."

"Thanks, Cora, I'll do that right away." He led his horse to the shed, where he removed the saddle, bridle, and blanket. As he rubbed the horse's back, shoulders, and neck with handfuls of hay, he thought of the two girls in the house. They had been to the Riverside school and found they liked the white folks' ways and food. When they came home they decided that they were not going to live in a log and dirt hogan, so induced their father and their three brothers to cut logs and build a three-room cabin.

No smoke hole in this roof, just a stovepipe from the cook stove, thought Nick, nice and warm too.

"Wash over there," said Cora, "then sit right down at the table."

"You girls live well," Nick remarked, after the girls had brought on a roast of lamb, boiled potatoes, large slices of yeast bread, and poured the coffee. "I wish more of the Navajos would build log houses and get stoves."

"They will, as fast as they are able to," Zelda told him, "and they will certainly live better then."

After supper they talked a long time, then a bed was fixed for Nick.

When he awoke in the morning the sun was shining, so after breakfast, he thanked the girls, saddled up, and started for home. He knew it would be a slow ride, as the snow was real deep in many places.

Bud saw Nick as he rode up about one in the afternoon.

"Oh, Marge," he yelled, "come a-running. The old prospector is back, or at least I think it's him. He's hiding behind quite a bit of brush. Pile off, podner, thar's sowbelly and beans awaiting you. Any gold up in them thar hills?"

"Have you really got some beans, Marge?" Nick asked. "They'll taste mighty good to a hungry man. And get this, Bud, no more prospecting. I've been!"

# CHAPTER 10

ON THE FIFTEENTH OF MAY, the plumbers came. The tubs, toilets, light plant, and water pump had already been hauled out by Indian freighters. Four strong-backed Navajos had been engaged to start digging ditches as soon as the plumbers showed them where they were to be dug. In ten days the job was done.

"Boy, oh boy," exclaimed Nick, "looks like we got everything now, eh, Marge? And, if it's agreeable to Bud, I think we should get us a nice new car next year."

"I'm for it," agreed Bud. "Mrs. Smith sure spoke the truth when she said we'd make money here. Navajos say there's going to be a fair crop of piñons this fall, which won't hurt us any."

"Make all we can while we can," said Marge. "Something might come up, you know, like, perhaps, more stores in the neighborhood."

"Yeah, if things go good for five years more, we'll do all right," Bud said.

"Well, nobody can cheat us out of our bathroom and

lights anyway," laughed Marge. "I was a pretty good sport not to squawk about that before. Now, don't you agree with me?"

"I certainly do," Nick answered.

Quite often, on Sunday, Bud would get another pony so he and Marge could ride together. One autumn afternoon, while riding along the edge of a small cliff, they noticed a Navajo grave. It had been shallowed out in the rocky soil and then covered with rocks. The pack rats had been working around it, loosening the dirt; and the rains had washed it away so Bud could look under the rocks and see the skeleton. Rings and bracelets still encircled the bony fingers and wrists, and, around the waist, was a large concho belt. The bead strings had rotted away, but, judging by the little heaps of coral and turquoise, there must have been quite a number of strands. Beside the skeleton was a fine old silver bridle and a smaller silver belt.

"Oh dear," exclaimed Marge, "it's a shame for all these lovely things to lie here in the dirt. Do you suppose the old gentleman would mind if I just took that small belt? He isn't wearing it."

"Well, I don't believe in bothering their burials, and never have," Bud said, "but I can't see any harm in taking this one belt when there is so much stuff in there. Gee, he must have been someone of importance."

Bud reached in, pulled it out, and put it in his pocket. Then he scraped and pushed dirt to cover the hole and placed rocks on the dirt. As they mounted their ponies and turned to go, they noticed a coyote sitting on a little knoll some fifty or so yards away. Bud was a little surprised to see one so close, and told Marge it was probably watching to see if they had taken anything. When the coyote saw that they were looking at him he began to howl.

"You know," Bud said, "the Navajos believe the spirit of old people often enters the body of a bear or coyote. Maybe that's the old man himself who's doing the howling."

"Don't be silly," Marge said, but, nevertheless, she kept looking back as they rode along.

They had ridden about half a mile when Marge whispered, "Bud, that coyote is following us."

"Sure is," agreed Bud, "probably lives over this way."

When Marge showed Nick the belt and told him where she got it, he said, "Well, I don't see any harm in that, except that I don't believe that I'd take anything out of a grave. I just have that kind of feeling about it."

The coyote must have followed them home, because, after dark, it sat out a little way from the kitchen and howled. After an hour or so, it began to get on Marge's nerves. "Bud, go out and chase that thing away. Maybe I don't want this belt after all. There's something queer about this coyote business, and I just believe I'll ride over in the morning and put the belt back."

"Good girl," said Nick, "now I'll go out and put a couple of quick shots around that coyote so he can go home."

The next day a Navajo freighter arrived, and, after the goods were carried into the wareroom, Bud got a hammer and set to work opening a huge box. This contained an assortment of blue and white enamelware they were badly in need of.

He was busy peeling the paper from coffee pots, pans, and washbasins when he came to a different shaped piece. He unwrapped it and found it to be a bed chamber. It wasn't the old-fashioned, heavy crockery thunder mug that reposed under beds in the good old days, but was really a very attractive piece.

Bud took it out to the store to show Nick. There were a couple of men and three women there. "What do you figure to do with these things?" he asked. "Educate the Navvies up to a higher standard of living? But, remember, they don't have beds."

Nick took it and right away the women began to *Oh* and *Ah* and wanted to see the new pot. The first woman to get her hands on it asked how much it cost — no matter what, she wanted it.

Nick got the invoice and found what they cost, then told her the price — a dollar fifty.

Fine, fine. She thought they would cost more, certainly lovely stew pots, nice with the handle on the side too.

Then the other women each wanted one, so Bud finished unpacking the box. "There is only one more. Two is all they sent," he said.

Both of the two potless women wanted the remaining one, so Nick had them draw straws for it. "Guess we'll have to order a dozen of these," said Nick. "Looks like a hot number. You can never tell what will strike their fancy."

On November nineteenth, in the middle of the afternoon, it began to snow. That was nothing to worry about because any time, after the first of November, snow could be expected, and, anyway, the warerooms were always filled with the winter supplies before then. The next morning there was a good foot of snow, and still coming.

"Begins to look like a snowstorm, doesn't it?" said Bud.

"Yeah, and also looks like we got a job of shoveling to do," answered Nick. "Guess it won't be so bad though, if it doesn't get to blowing."

But it did blow, and the snow began to drift. By night the fences around the Indians' fields were covered and there were huge drifts everywhere. The wind went down with the sun, but snow fell most of the night. The sun rose that morning on a white world. Trees, bushes, roofs were all white. The snow was a good two feet deep on the level.

"I guess the storm is over," Nick remarked, coming into the kitchen where Bud already had a fire going.

"Enough's a-plenty," Bud said. "How are the sheep going to get anything to eat now?"

"Got me," Nick answered, "and I almost wonder how you're going to get to the barn to milk."

"I was just going to ask you that," grinned Bud. "You

know, I hit my right hand an awful crack on the stove this morning, and I doubt if I can milk for a day or two."

"Oh, yeah, let's see that crippled hand."

"Don't show much, but it's terribly sore. You can't really see anything; it's hurt internally."

"Sure, sure," Nick said. "Well, I'll help you shovel through to the barn, and I imagine a half hour on a shovel handle will work all the soreness out of your hand."

"Of course it might, but I doubt it," he answered. "Say, Old Doc didn't get the mail last night, but then he couldn't make the trip in this snow."

Old Doc generally took the mail sack the night before, so he could leave from his place, saving him the extra ride from his house to the store and back.

"We may be without mail for a few days until this snow settles," predicted Nick. "That won't hurt us any."

No Indians came to the store that day, but two or three waded over the next. Nick asked Big Nose how the Navajos would keep the sheep alive.

"Many will die," he answered. "All of the old ones will. My family are all out cutting bushes and branches and dragging them in. We will try making a log drag and scrape a trail to the south slopes, under the trees where the snow is not quite so deep."

"The snow should melt some on the south slopes," Bud said.

"Yes," agreed Big Nose, "but more snow will come soon. It is always that way."

More Indian men came during the day. Most of them needed coffee and sugar and they wanted to talk about the big snow and find out how others were getting along.

Old Doc did not show up, but, on the fourth day after the storm, one of his husky sons came, riding a big American horse. He said someone had to break a trail through to the Agency, so tomorrow he would take the mail and maybe get back the next day.

On the third day at noon, he came in and threw the mail sack on the counter. Yes, it was a very hard ride. He did not reach the Agency until after dark. The snow was too deep on the trail, so he had to travel the side hills, and it was slow, rough going and his horse got very tired. But in three days he would go again, if they wanted him to.

Soon a few others used the new trail, and, in another week, Old Doc tried it, but for the rest of that winter it was a two-day trip.

One bright cold morning in early December, the boys were surprised to hear the roar of a low flying plane. Sometimes a plane flew over, but they were always high on account of the mountains. As they ran out of the store, Marge came out on the porch.

"What is it?" she asked.

"Come over here and you can see it," answered Bud.

A big two-motored plane was coming in from the south, and flying very low.

"Looks like they are going to land," said Nick, "but I don't see where they could."

"Maybe they are out of gas and have to," suggested Marge.

The plane came roaring over, not more than a hundred yards above the roofs. Someone waved, but they could not tell whether it was anyone they knew.

The plane circled and again came low over the store. passing over White Horse's alfalfa field back of the store. They circled again to gain altitude and then slowly disappeared in the south.

"Now, what the hell does all that funny business mean?" asked Bud.

"That's what I'd like to know too," Marge said. "They didn't even drop a note."

"Maybe they wanted to see if we were still alive," laughed Nick.

"That was an Army bomber. I could see the bomb bay

beneath," asserted Bud. "Well, here comes Bidoni to ask a lot of questions that we can't answer."

White Horse's *Bidoni* (son-in-law) had been *bidoni* several times before, so now the Navajos didn't specify whose son-in-law he was, simply called him Bidoni.

"Big *bish-na-ti-e* (iron that flies)," he said, as he came puffing up.

"Yes, a big one," Nick answered.

"What were all those things they dropped?' he asked.

"What things and where?" asked Nick.

"Right out here in the field," he answered.

"Wait until I get my overshoes on and we'll go take a look," said Bud.

When Bud and Bidoni came back, they each carried a sack on their shoulders.

"Cripes, but it's hard walking with a load in that damn snow," puffed Bud. "There's six of these bags out there, if that means anything to you."

"What on earth is in them?" exclaimed Marge.

"Well, I can tell you what was in one," Bud answered, "because one of them landed in the arroyo on the ice where the snow was thin, and busted all to pieces. It had bacon, beans, rice, dried prunes, raisins, and a twenty-four pound sack of flour in it before it exploded."

"Probably someone thinks we are hungry," laughed Marge.

"Well, we'll let Bidoni bring in the others. He needs exercise," Nick said. "Let's open these and see what's in them, maybe some wool-lined shoelaces for Marge."

"Same stuff," Bud said, after they had opened the two bags. "Somebody's going to eat a lot of prunes."

As Bidoni staggered in with the other sacks, they were opened. In the next to the last one they found a note from the Agent, Mr. Gompers, saying the food was to be distributed among the most needy Navajos.

"Well now, isn't that nice?" exclaimed Nick. "Here's

maybe thirty dollars worth of stuff, which probably cost them a couple of hundred more to fly in. There's at least fifteen families around here who are sure tightening their belts these days. Divide this among them and it might last three days. Big publicity stunt is all it is."

"Sure it is," agreed Bud, "and I suppose they're flying all around, dropping their little two bits worth. Costs money to fly airplanes. Why don't they send the Traders the money and let them dole out the food."

"Good Lord, no," Nick answered, "you don't suppose they'd trust a Trader to do anything like that, do you? Why, they just know he'd pocket the money, never dreaming that it's to the Trader's interest to keep his customers alive."

"Yeah, and already we've passed out quite a bit of grub that I doubt if we ever see a nickel for," growled Bud. "And I'll bet we're not the only ones either."

Every few days more snow fell, two or three inches maybe, although it didn't appear to increase the depth on the ground any, probably the old snow melted and settled a little during the sunny days. The nights had been cold too; one night it went to twenty-eight below. Of course this froze the squash and potatoes the Navajos had stored.

By the middle of January, the poorer families had pawned all their jewelry, and, as they had no other purchasing power, they were getting in serious shape. Of course, Nick or Bud would slip them some grub, because, as Nick said, you can't let little kids starve.

The Navajos suggested writing to the Agent and maybe "Washingtone" would do something to help them.

Nick agreed to try this, although he didn't think it would do much good, and, if it did, it would be the Fourth of July before any food would arrive. Old Doc had told him, however, that the Agent had started to send up a sled with a load of oil cake for the sheep, but, halfway up they were forced to turn around and go back.

In due time a letter came from the Agent saying that he had no funds for that purpose, but he was sending an investigator right up to get the facts of conditions in their section, after which he would file a report to Washington.

"What did I tell you?" growled Nick. "He'll file a report to Washington and then he's done his duty."

In a few days "Tight Pants" arrived. He was really a nice young chap and had more guts than most of them, or he would have turned back when the going got rough. He said he started on snowshoes, but, as he had never tried snowshoes before, after a couple of miles of earnest endeavor, he had thrown them away. Altogether, he made ten miles the first day and reached a little shack that was kept stocked with provisions and wood. This was used by the government men — usually as a loafing place. By leaving early in the morning from there, he had reached the store before dark. His name was Twill and he was new in the service so he hadn't begun to swell yet.

After breakfast, Nick said, "I'll try and get you an interpreter, but I don't know how soon that will be."

"Why don't you go with him, Bud?" said Marge.

"Sure, I'll go with him if he doesn't want to wait until someone shows up."

"I wouldn't want to bother you, and, besides, I'm allowed expenses for an interpreter," explained Twill.

"Or, in other words, you have orders to get a Navajo interpreter," said Nick.

"Well, yes, that's the way it is," he answered, "although I can't see what difference it makes."

At ten a boy came in who could speak enough English to get by, so Bud saddled his pony for Twill, and, as the boy had his own pony, they rode away.

The store was closed when Twill returned in the evening so he came to the kitchen. He said he never would have believed such a state of affairs existed in a civilized country. He didn't see how anyone could exist on the

188

scanty supplies he found in the five hogans he had visited.

"I took an inventory of all foodstuffs," he said, "and it didn't take long, either. Listen to this one: Mr. Moccasin's home — five half-frozen squash, thirty pounds of squashy potatoes (weight estimated), one-half sack of flour, part of a small can of baking powder, one-half sack of salt. That's every darned thing they had. I feel ashamed to sit down to this supper."

"I suppose if Mr. Twill wanted to be accurate, he could state that the flour, baking powder, and salt were a present from these two robbers," remarked Marge.

"Gompers wouldn't believe it if he did," Bud said.

"I don't think you like Mr. Gompers very well," Mr. Twill said.

"Oh, he's all right," answered Nick, "except he seems to try and make it as tough as he can for the Traders."

"In another hogan, all we found was a half sack of corn, which they parched before eating," went on Mr. Twill, "although the woman did say she was coming to the store today."

"We'll give her some coffee and sugar," Nick said, "but they ought to have plenty of meat; there's been a lot of old ewes died."

"Will they eat them?" asked Twill.

"They will and they are," Nick told him. "Must be plenty tough meat though."

The investigator went out again the following day, and, that night, he said he had seen enough. The next morning Bud saddled his pony for him to ride back on, as Twill felt he was all caught up on his walking for that winter. Bud thought, maybe, after he had sat in a saddle for eight hours or more, he would feel the same about riding. Old Doc would bring the pony back on his next trip.

A few days later the boys got a letter from Gompers saying, this being an emergency, they were to allow the needy Navajos ten dollars a month.

"Fair enough," remarked Nick, "that will keep them going all right. We'll get word out that they can get two dollars and fifty cents a week per family."

"Boy, will they come!" said Bud. "I guess there are around twenty families who need this help."

"One thing we want to be damn careful about, and that's to put down each article and the price. Also the date, the head of the family's name and have him thumbprint the bill; otherwise the government boys will suspect something. Oh yeah, and we'll make them in duplicate."

The first woman to benefit by this, thanked Bud heartily and profoundly. "Don't thank me," he told her, "thank the great White Father in 'Washingtone' for this royal largesse. And don't bust yourselves eating, because this has to last several days."

At the end of thirty days, Nick made out a statement, enclosed the original of each purchase, and sent them to the Agency.

On the next mail there was a letter from Gompers, wanting to know on whose authority this food had been issued; certainly he hadn't issued any such order. The only order he had issued was for ten dollars a month as per his letter of such and such a date.

Nick went and got the letter and read it again.

"Well, Bud, guess we're hooked," he said. "I guess this letter does say ten dollars a month for all the needy Indians. But, hell, I wouldn't have insulted them by even telling them of such a silly amount."

"Ten dollars to be distributed among some twenty or twenty-five families," snorted Bud. "Well, anyway, write the old boy a nice letter explaining things to him. He knows, from Twill's report, how hardpressed the Indians are."

"Soft-soap him and he might do something," grinned Nick. "How about letting Marge write the letter; she'll do a better job than either of us."

"Sure she will," agreed Bud. "We'll give her the dope tonight and we'll send it tomorrow."

Nothing was heard for a couple of weeks, and then a letter with a check came.

"What do you know?" exclaimed Nick. "We got our money."

"Hot damn, let's see what he says," said Bud.

"Well, he sent Marge's letter with Twill's report to Washington. He says we can continue as we're doing until the first of April."

A few mornings later, Old Black Sheep's wife came to the store, saying her husband was very sick. "What's the matter with him?" Bud asked.

She said he couldn't urinate and was in great pain.

"Well, now, Bud, what do we do in a case of this kind?" asked Nick.

"We can fix him all right," Bud answered. "Up in South Dakota I saw them dose a horse that was in the same fix with spirits of nitre, and there's a little bottle of it over in the house — if Marge hasn't thrown it out. I'll go see."

In a moment he came back. "Here it is, except I don't know how much to tell her to give him. As I remember they gave the horse quite a slug of it." Then he spoke to the woman. "Here's some medicine. Give him a teaspoonful. Then, in a little while if it hasn't worked, give him another. I guess that's about right."

"You're the doctor, Bud, and I hope it don't kill him."

"I don't think it will," he answered.

But she was back in an hour, saying the medicine was no good.

"What we need is a catheter," Bud said.

"What's that?" asked Nick.

"A kind of long, slender rubber tube. I saw one once in South Dakota. But we haven't any."

"Where do you suppose his waterworks is plugged up?" Nick asked.

"I don't know, but I imagine it would be his bladder. Probably the outlet of his bladder is plugged."

"My gosh, we ought to find something that would do. We can't let the old man die! How long would it have to be to reach his bladder?"

"How would I know? I know where the bladder is in a cow or a hog, but I've never helped butcher a Navajo. I'll go look through the house and see if I can find anything."

Nick looked around the store, then went into the office. There he saw an old sewing machine belt hanging on the wall. A Navajo woman had left it, so when someone went to town they could get one like it.

He went to the door and called to Bud, "How about this?"

"Say, that might do. Looks a little big, but it's round and sure worn nice and smooth. You want to go over and try it?"

"Not by a darn sight. You're the doctor, Bud."

"Okay, I'll try anything once," said Bud. "Guess I'll walk over. I can be there by the time I'd get the pony out and saddled. Oh yes, I'd better take a jar of vaseline."

"Well, success to you, Doc. He's a good old fellow and I sure hope you can fix him up."

In less than an hour, Bud came swaggering in and threw the sewing machine belt on the counter.

"Well, amigo," he grinned, "that water system is working perfect again. I'm some plumber. We'd better keep this belt just in case."

"You know, Bud, I just had a hunch you'd be able to do that job all right."

"Yeah," Bud answered, "and it didn't hurt him much except when I poked it through into his bladder or I suppose it did, because that hurt a little and he yelped, '*Cuddy-cuddy!*' (that's enough). So I pulled it back out and the water followed it, and, what I mean, it about flooded the hogan. The old man just lay there and groaned in a happy manner, just like a horse does when you've ridden him too far without stopping. And the old lady was just as pleased as if it had been her. Maybe I better go wash my hands."

"Next time, you could borrow Marge's rubber gloves, like good surgeons use," said Nick, with a big grin.

"Oh yeah, well, don't get any ideas in your head that I'm hankering to be an M.D.; although, when the road is closed, I don't mind doing what I can. I've got to tell Marge about this!"

A short time after Bud came back to the store, Baboon's wife came in. "Oh, oh," said Bud, "here's trouble."

"I guess," agreed Nick, "but *Etsitty Yazzi* (Little Silversmith) promised to be here by noon, and he can battle it out with her. After all, he's her nephew."

A couple of weeks before, Nick had borrowed an extra-fine old bracelet from her, to have a duplicate made. At first, she wouldn't loan it, afraid it might get lost. But, finally, for a dollar and with the understanding that her nephew was to do the work, she consented.

So when Etsitty Yazzi came in, Nick showed him the bracelet — which he recognized — and told him to make six exactly like it, but not to boil it up and whiten it.

Five or six days later he came back, pulled a dirty rag from his pocket, carefully untied it, and laid down seven shining bracelets on the counter.

"Oh," said Nick, "you made seven bracelets. Where is the old one I gave you?"

Etsitty Yazzi spread the bracelets into a row, and, after carefully studying them for a moment, picked one up and handed it to Nick.

"But wasn't there something said about not whitening the old bracelet?" asked Nick.

"That's right," he smilingly agreed, "but it was so old and dirty looking that I thought it best to clean it."

"Your aunt will be very mad at you now," said Nick.

"Oh no, I think she will be glad to have it bright and clean."

But he was wrong. She came in the next day and asked if her bracelet was there.

Nick went and got the seven bracelets. Marge had been looking them over, so now the old one was mixed with the others. Baboon's wife picked up two or three of them and remarked that her nephew was a fine silversmith. He certainly had made them just like hers, but where was her bracelet?

"It's here and I think I can tell which it is," Nick told her.

"None of them are mine, don't you think I know my own bracelet?" she petulantly exclaimed.

"Here it is," said Nick.

"You're a liar," she fairly spat the words at him. "You know mine was a fine old bracelet. You're trying to cheat me and steal my bracelet and sell it for fifteen or twenty dollars." She swept the bunch of them off the counter onto the floor.

"Your nephew cleaned your bracelet for you," Nick said, as he gathered them up.

"You're a liar," she again told him, "and you give me my bracelet or I will go and tell the Agent."

"Guess I'd better saddle up and go get Etsitty Yazzi to come over," said Bud. "Let him battle it out with her. You're getting nowhere."

Nick set out a bottle of pop and some cookies, which the old woman accepted, muttering, "liar," "cheat," and "thief" all the while.

She went after Etsitty roughshod when he came. He finally convinced her that the bracelet was hers, but she'd like to see them try to borrow any more of her jewelry!

It was along in August when, one day about noon, a couple of Navajo policemen came in with a letter from Gompers.

"Well," said Nick, after he had opened and read it, "I

guess the typhus must be spreading. Here, read this," and he handed Bud the letter.

It said that the government was stationing policemen at all trails crossing the mountain with strict orders to see that no one crossed from either way. These two policemen were each allowed to buy two dollars and fifty cents worth of food and horse feed each day. This was in addition to their regular salary. The policemen thought this was pretty soft, but, if the Agent wanted them to lie around up there and eat and sleep, it was all right with them. The ponies could eat grass, so the total allowance was spent for food and they lived high, besides being able to entertain visitors at meal time.

The third day after they were at their station, Nick and Bud were a bit surprised when a couple of silversmiths from across the mountain came into the store and laid their completed work on the counter.

"How did you fellows get by the policemen — or were they asleep?" asked Nick.

"One was awake," the silversmiths answered, "and, when we told him you were in a great hurry for these things, he said, 'All right, take them right down and bring me back a bottle of pop.'"

"I'll be darned," Nick exclaimed to Bud. "That's one kind of a way to guard a mountain pass."

"Of course, we can use the silver, but, if there's any chance of getting the typhus along with it, I'm for doing without the silver," stated Bud. "But, as long as they are here, we'll take it in as usual and give them more to do."

The next day Jim Scott, one of the policemen, came down to load up with grub.

"Didn't the Agent tell you no one was to cross that pass?" asked Nick, in an angry tone.

"Sure, sure, we know all about that and it makes the Navajos very mad too," smiled Jim Scott, showing his big white teeth.

"If you know all about it, why did you let two silver-smiths come across yesterday?"

"Oh, the silversmiths?" and Jim showed much surprise. "But they had silver things that you were in a hurry for. They said you would be very mad if they didn't give it to you."

"But the Agent told you no one was to cross on that trail," Nick reminded him.

"Then you don't want your silver?" Jim asked.

"We want it, but you must do as the Agent says, so you will have to tell them they can't bring any more."

"Maybe they will run off somewhere and sell it to some-one else," suggested Jim. "Some silversmiths do that. But, all right, we'll chase them back."

A week went by and no Navajo passed the guards. And then, early one afternoon, Bud looked out the open door and announced, "Here comes Black Moustache."

Three of the silversmiths, who worked for the boys, lived across the mountain. Two of them had been to the store since the guards had been posted. And now, here was the third silversmith — Black Moustache.

"Let's not say anything to him regarding his passing the guards," suggested Nick. "I'd like to get that dope from Jim Scott."

"Okay," agreed Bud, "he'll be down tomorrow most likely."

Black Moustache only mentioned that his cousin was camped in the pass and that he had eaten with him. This had delayed him so he would have to hurry, or he would not get home before dark.

In the middle of the morning on the next day, Jim Scott came smiling into the store. The boys had agreed not to mention Black Moustache, but wait and see what Hosteen Scott would have to say.

He laughed and talked and wondered how long his soft job would last, while he made his usual purchase of canned

196

meat, peaches, pears, apricots, watermelon, and candy. Lots of candy — cookies, too. He always came to the post to do the shopping, leaving his partner to guard the trail. But he did bring the extra pony to pack the heavy load back to camp.

He had everything sacked and, as it looked like he was ready to go, Nick decided to find out why he let another silversmith pass.

"Did you see any silversmiths yesterday?" he asked.

"You mean those two who work for you?"

"No," answered Nick, "we have another silversmith who lives beyond the pass and I thought he might have his work done by now. His name is Black Moustache."

"Oh yes, my cousin," exclaimed Jim Scott. "He came to visit with me yesterday and he ate a big meal because he hasn't hardly anything to eat at home. Does he work for you?"

"Yes, he works for us, and you can be sure he has plenty to eat today, since you let him bring his silver here and get all he needed."

"Did my cousin have silver work with him? It must have been tied to the saddle so I didn't see it." Jim Scott smiled broadly and looked over at Bud to see how he was taking it.

"But why did you let him come this way?" Bud asked.

"Did my cousin come this way? I thought he was going home." He seemed greatly surprised.

"But you have eyes and you know where he lives," said Bud.

"But I didn't see which way my cousin went. After eating and talking and smoking, I was thirsty, so I walked down to the spring for a drink and when I came back my cousin was gone."

"You can't beat that," said Nick to Bud. "But the other policeman must have seen him leave. Why didn't he stop him?"

"He wasn't there, he was away hunting rabbits," answered Jim.

"Just what I thought," said Bud.

"I guess I'll have to write to the Agent and tell him to send two good policemen up here," Nick told him.

"No, no, don't do that," exclaimed the frightened Jim. "No one else will ever get by us. My cousin is a bad man and I won't feed him again."

"Well, if you let one more Navajo by, I'll sure tell the Agent," Nick sternly stated.

"Will it be all right if I bring the silver work down and get the silversmiths more work and some groceries?" asked Jim.

"Say, that's an idea, Nick," exclaimed Bud. "Why couldn't he do that?"

"Sure, no harm in that, and it will keep the smiths working and fed. All right, Jim, you find out what groceries they need, and you come get them. Bring one of their ponies along to pack the stuff back on."

But this plan did not go into effect, because the typhus scare ended and the policemen were ordered back to the Agency.

# CHAPTER 11

BLACK SHEEP, THE OLD MAN Bud had cured with the sewing machine belt, had two grown sons, both of whom lived not far from the old man's place. The boys had English names, although only one had been to school. He was the younger brother and his name was Fred. Willie was the other boy.

Now, as Willie came into the store, both Nick and Bud noticed that he was limping much worse than usual.

"He should go see a doctor about that hip," Bud remarked.

"Must be three months he's been limping around," agreed Nick, "and it's certainly getting no better."

Speaking in Navajo, Bud said, "Why don't you go to a doctor?"

"My father has sent for a Medicine Man. He will be here in three days."

Marge stepped into the store, "Is Willie getting worse?" she asked.

"Sure is," Bud answered. "He should go to a good doctor,

but he won't. He's going to have a big ceremony, and you know how that will be. The excitement and admiration of the crowd with him being the central figure, the chanting, the body painting and the sand paintings every day, and the ceremonious quaffing of vile concoctions — he'll claim he's well, whether he's helped any or not. If a really sick Navajo can last through a Nine-Day Ceremony, I'll say from there on out he'll live."

"Back up there, *Se-kis* (my friend), you know a good Medicine Man makes some remarkable cures," Marge said. "How about that sore you had on your arm that the government doctor didn't help any, even after three tries? Didn't Old Doc cure that sore with just two applications of the green alfalfa-looking stuff?" Marge waited to see what Bud had to say to this.

"Sure, and Old Doc knew at once the kind of sore it was, while the white doctor didn't. Oh sure, if a Medicine Man knows what it is he's trying to cure, he'll come close all right."

After the big ceremony, Willie claimed he was much better and would soon be all right. But it didn't work out that way, for, as anyone could see, he was in pain and he limped worse than ever.

Then, one afternoon, some days later, Willie's father and Fred drove up, got out of the wagon and came into the store.

"Where have you been?" Nick asked.

"We took Willie to the Agency and then on into town," Fred answered.

"In the wagon?" asked Bud. "Why didn't you ask to be taken in our car?"

"My father wanted to go in the wagon, but the Agency doctor took us to town in his car," Fred told them.

"Let's go out and see Willie," suggested Nick.

He was lying on some hay with a quilt over it. He surely looked feverish and sick.

"The Agency doctor examined his hip and said it was tubercular," said Fred. "Then the doctor said we would go to town, so we did. There a surgeon examined it and put the X-Ray on it, and he said it was just as the Agency doctor thought. Then he put a cast on Willie's leg and said he would have to wear it a long time, but maybe he can't because it hurts him very much."

"He'd better keep it on, even if it does hurt," Nick said. "Maybe in a day or two it will stop hurting. Go get him some pop, Bud."

"Wonder if he will leave the cast on," said Bud, after the wagon had been driven away.

"Hard to tell, but it must be a tough thing to wear."

Bright and early the next morning Willie's father was at the store. "Does Willie feel better this morning?" Nick asked.

"My son is not so sick and hot since the white rock has been taken off his leg," Black Sheep said.

"You took it off?" exclaimed Bud.

"He could not bear the pain, so, in the night, I took the axe and broke it off," Black Sheep told them.

"What will you do now?" asked Nick.

"I have sent for Star Gazer. He will tell us if my son can be made well. If so, Star Gazer will let us know which Medicine Man to send for to make the cure. I will need money, much money, maybe two hundred dollars," and he looked inquiringly at the boys.

The family owned lots of sheep and their lambs would bring much more than the amount he was asking for.

"What do you say to that, Bud?" asked Nick.

"Okay with me, except we haven't that much cash here."

"Well, I'll go to town and get it, unless you want to go," Nick said.

"No, you go ahead, Nick, you haven't been for a long time." Then Bud spoke to Black Sheep, "We'll get you the money."

At ten, Nick went over to the house, bathed, shaved, and put on his good clothes. "Guess I'll eat a lunch before I go," he told Marge.

"My, you look handsome," she said. "I can't understand why some girl doesn't grab you off. What do you do, bite and kick?"

He wore a pair of tannish-colored checked riding breeches with tan laced boots. His Pendleton shirt was colorful, but not gaudy. The Stetson hat was a light cream color with a medium crown and a two-and-a-half-inch brim. Altogether it was a nice outfit, and, Marge was right, he did look handsome.

"I fight them off," he said in answer to her question.

"Well, I wish you would find a nice girl, and I mean a NICE girl, because you deserve the best. Don't you think you would be happier with a good wife? Doesn't it look like Bud and I are happy? Do you know, week after next, we will have been married seven years?"

"Bud is a lucky stiff," Nick said with a grin. "But what's the matter? Are you lonesome enough to want another woman around here to fight with?"

"No, I'm not lonesome. You find the right girl and there'll be no fighting."

"Well, I'm going to stay in town tonight so, as you seem to have your heart set on me marrying, I'll try and pick me up a girl tonight."

"Oh, no, you don't," laughed Marge. "You've got to know a girl quite a while before you can be sure she's the one for you."

"Oh, yeah, well Bud sure did know you a long time, didn't he?"

"Well, that was different, as you can see. But anyway, Nick, don't you dare ever ask any girl to marry you until I have sized her up."

"That's a promise," he assured her. "Homely girls are the best bet, aren't they?"

"Sure, sure," she agreed, "and a swell looking fellow should do his best to land a homely girl."

He picked up his hat. "So long, Marge. I'll try and bring a girl out tomorrow and let you look at her teeth and count the rings in her neck, before I pop the question."

"What is it you are going to town for?" she asked.

"Money, my dear, money," and he blew her a kiss as he passed on into the hall.

The road was dry and dusty and the Buick hummed along, slowing down only when it had to turn out into the sagebrush to avoid the high centers left in the road where the rains had washed it and no car could hope to pass over. A couple of miles beyond the big dammed-up lake, Nick noticed a car in the distance. As he drew nearer he saw it was stopped, and, in a few moments more, he saw why it was stopped.

Well, the darn fool, thought Nick, couldn't he see that a car couldn't possibly clear that washed-out center. Must have hit it hard too, because his front wheels are six inches off the ground.

He pulled up beside the car and stopped. A fleshy young man with a strikingly pretty girl were the occupants.

"Howdy," said Nick pleasantly, "looks like you're riding kind of high."

"They should have signs up to warn people on these roads," growled the driver. "Who are you and do you think you can get us off of here?"

"Norton is my name, and it will take a lot of work to get you off of there. I'm supposed to get to town before the bank closes. Are you crippled in any way?"

"No, I'm not crippled," the fellow answered, in none too sweet a tone.

"I didn't know, I just supposed you'd be out jacking up the back end and getting dirt shoveled in the tracks so you could back out. Mind if I ask who you folks are?"

"My name is Stutz. I'm chief clerk at the Agency," he

hesitated, as if deciding whether to introduce the girl. When it seemed he would not, she spoke up and said, "I'm Miss Sherman and work in the office there too."

"I'm glad to meet you," and Nick meant that in the singular. He certainly did not care for this Stutz fellow. For one thing, his eyes were too close together. The girl now stepped out of the car so Nick had his first good look at her. That look showed him she was the most attractive girl he had ever seen. He was positive of this at once. While she was in the car he had thought her hair and eyes were black, but now he saw he had been mistaken. The eyes were brown, deep brown and large and well-spaced. Her hair was a rich dark brown which the sun shot through with little glints of reddish gold. Her nose was of medium size and it crinkled upward when she smiled, and then Nick noticed the faint trace of a dimple in each cheek. Her complexion was not pink and white like Marge's, but more of an ivory shade with a faint blush of red on either cheek. She seemed some three inches shorter than Nick, slender but not skinny, a straight, well-formed, healthy body.

Stutz was out by now and came around to where they stood.

"Of course you have a jack," stated Nick, "but you'll need a shovel. Have you got one?"

"No, and if I did have, my hands wouldn't stand shoveling," he answered.

They are pretty soft and white, Nick thought, in disgust. "Well, you can take my shovel," he said. "There'll be Navajos along, I suppose, and you can put them to work. Shall I take Miss Sherman back to the Agency?"

"No, certainly not, she started out with me, so she might as well finish up with me."

Nick looked at Miss Sherman. She flashed him a smile and said, "I'll stay and keep Mr. Stutz company, but thank you."

204

"I've just thought of something," announced Nick, "so perhaps I'd better get your car back on all four wheels."

If this soft-handed Stutz had been alone, Nick would have let him sit there. A man who wouldn't try to help himself got no sympathy from Nick. But a girl or a woman could not be left sitting, on the chance that a Navajo would come along to help. So he set to work, jacking up the wheels and shoveling dirt under them. Then he cut down the road center in back of the car, building up the washed-out tracks, and, after an hour and a half of hard work, he got in the car and backed it out.

"How much do I owe you?" asked Stutz.

Nick's face turned red with anger and Miss Sherman look distressed. "Well, I'll tell you something, Buddy, *men* (he emphasized the word) out here don't charge for helping folks when they're in trouble." Now he knew he didn't like this fellow. "Are you going further up the valley?"

"We've got some things to leave at the shack by the lake," Stutz answered.

"Well, there are no more high centers that far, but plenty beyond," Nick told him. With a glance at Miss Sherman, he added, "I'll be going now."

When he reached the Agency he pulled up in front of Bill Dewey's store and went in. He was well-acquainted with the Deweys, as they often spent a Sunday at Blue Rock. Bill was big and blond and Nick liked him immensely.

"Hi, Nick," was his greeting, as he put out his hand, "how's everything up in the good country?"

"Just fine," Nick answered, "how are Nan and the baby?"

"All to the good, come on in and see them," and he led Nick into the living room.

Nan was a cute little natural blonde — although she did not seem so little when she was away from big Bill. Her eyes were large and blue, she had a pretty nose and mouth, and she was peppy and lively. Next to Marge, she was Nick's ideal of a wonderful wife.

After visiting a while, Nick said, "Who's this fellow, Stutz, who can't soil his hands with a shovel handle?" He went on to tell them all about it.

"Well, as for me, I'd a let him set there," growled Bill.

"I probably would too, except for the girl," agreed Nick, "and say, who is this Miss Sherman?"

"Virginia Sherman," said Nan, "all I know is that she works in the office, and is a sweet, pretty girl that we think the world of."

"I'll say she is," Nick said, "but can't she draw a higher card than that Stutz?"

"Maybe it's the violin playing," grinned Bill. "That baby can certainly play a fiddle."

"You can see Stutz is crazy about her, although I can't see as she's so hot about him," Nan said. "There aren't many young fellows around here anyway. Also, probably, he could make it rather unpleasant for her in the office if she didn't treat him halfway civil."

"Well, I've seen some pretty nice girls marry queer birds," Bill said. "Look what Nan took, for instance."

"Yeah, and I've been sorry ever since," Nan looked fiercely at her big husband.

"Why didn't you bring Marge and Bud along — or didn't you know there was a dance tonight?" asked Bill.

"I'm on my way to town," Nick answered, "and I'm not much of a dancer anyway."

"Well, you'd better stay," Nan said. "You can go to town any time. You know we have a spare room."

"Yeah, and I'd like to see you cut in on this fiddle player. Nice for Virginia to meet a he-man too."

"Will she be there?" asked Nick.

"Oh, oh, put another bone in the soup kettle, Nan, we're going to have company for supper. Run that old wreck around in back, Nick."

206

"Well, doggone you, I *will* stay," Nick exclaimed, "and, I don't mind declaring that I'd like to get acquainted with Miss Sherman."

Soon after eight Nan, Bill, and Nick strolled up to the Assembly Room where dances were held. A piano, violin, and guitar made the music. Some twelve or fifteen couples were dancing.

"Stutz and one of the teachers take turns at the violin," Nan remarked.

Nick knew some of the dancers. He saw the agent, Mr. Gompers, dancing with a red-headed teacher. Then he spied Miss Sherman. She was dancing with Twill, the fellow who had investigated the Navajo food supply. The music stopped just when Miss Sherman and Twill were close to where the three friends stood.

Twill and Nick shook hands as Nan said, "Virginia, I want you to meet and dance with a very nice young man, Nick Norton."

"In a way, I have met him. I introduced myself to him." She smiled enough so the dimples peeked out while the little wrinkles twinkled up her nose and disappeared in the corners of her eyes.

Nick heard himself ask her if he could have the next dance and her answer that he could. And then, Stutz appeared. They all spoke to him, but he scarcely acknowledged them before he said, "This is our dance, I believe, Virginia. Remember?"

"Oh dear, I thought you were going to play three pieces as you always do," she said, flushing. "I guess, Mr. Norton, you'll have to wait, if you care to, for the next one."

"Not if it's a two-step," Stutz said. "We always dance the first two-step of the evening together," and with that, he waltzed Virginia away.

"Say, what the hell is this, anyway," growled Bill. "Somebody ought to skin their knuckles on that fat lunk."

"None of that stuff, Bill, and don't be spilling ideas right out loud, or Mama will take you right home, and then how can you flirt and play jokes with the pretty girls? Ha, ha!"

The idea of calling a bunch of old maids and married women, pretty girls, seemed to strike Bill as funny. He haw-hawed in a very loud manner, but the third haw was changed into an explosive grunt, as Nan sank her elbow into his ribs.

"None of that funny stuff, amigo," warned Nan.

"You hadn't ought to jab a man like that when he isn't set for it," Bill told her. "You might bust something —hic — loose. See, you've given me the — hic — hiccups."

"You cut that out, Bill Dewey, everyone here is looking at us!"

"You can't just — hic — say to cut out the hiccups," said Bill, "but if I'm em — hic — barrassing you, I'll go outside."

"Get going then," snapped Nan. "I suppose they all think you've been drinking."

Bill hiccupped his way to the door and disappeared.

"He's really a loud hiccupper, isn't he?" remarked Nick. "But then, he's a big man."

"And a big fool," laughed Nan. "I can't tell for sure, but I'd bet money that he has no more hiccups than you or I. He's never come up here yet that he hasn't pulled something. One time he cut the suspenders on a big fat government man from Washington, who got so warm he foolishly took his coat off. Then he put a piece of limburger cheese in the pocket of a high-up Forestry Service man, and another time he brought a two-foot bull snake in his pocket and slipped it down between two teachers who were sitting on the couch. He claims they broke the sitting leap record. So you see, Nick, I did quite a favor by venturing out tonight with him."

"Don't they ever catch him?" laughed Nick.

"Oh no, he's too slick and innocent looking, the big goof. Here he comes."

208

"It took thirteen swallows of water to stop them," he announced with a big grin.

"That will be all the funny business for tonight, Bill Dewey," Nan sternly told him. "We'll admit those were natural sounding hiccups, although louder, much louder, than a good set of common unforced ones."

"Oh, oh," said Bill, as the music started again, "it *is* a two-step, isn't it?"

"Then maybe I can get the next dance with Miss Sherman," remarked Nick. "Come on, Nan, I know the two-step, too."

When the music ceased, Stutz led Miss Sherman to the opposite side of the room from where Nan and Nick were. As Nick started across the room, he saw short, fat Mr. Gompers step up to her. She must have told him the next dance was taken for Nick heard him say, "Perhaps the next one then." Then, as Nick joined them, "Oh, hello, Norton, how are you?"

"Fine, thank you, sir," answered Nick, as Mr. Gompers moved away.

"I'll warn you, Miss Sherman, I'm not much of a dancer." As the music started, he put his arm about her and said to himself, "You lucky dog, you'd better kick yourself. You must be dreaming."

After they had danced once around the room, she said, "Why, I think you are a good dancer."

"Oh, I may not step on your toes or trip you," laughed Nick, "but I'm certainly out of practice."

Small talk followed and then Nick said, "Why don't you come up to our place some Sunday with Nan and Bill?"

"I'd love to," she answered. "I have heard that it is a lovely part of the country."

"It sure is," he replied, "and you'll like my partner and his wife, Marge. She's a swell girl and she'll love you." Who wouldn't, he almost added. "Let's make it a date then, a week from tomorrow. I'll tell Nan and Bill."

"I'll be thinking about it all the week," she said.

Encouraged by her answer, Nick asked for the next dance.

"Mr. Gompers has the next, and then Alvin — Mr. Stutz — but after that . . ."

"Mr. Stutz sure rates, doesn't he?"

"Well, he's very nice to me and he helped me a lot when I first came and was green at the job," she answered.

The music stopped. "Okay, don't forget the third dance is mine," Nick said as he escorted her to where Mr. Gompers was walking to meet them; then he joined Nan and Bill.

"Some kid, eh, Nick?" remarked Bill. "You must of had a good look at her. See any flaws?"

"She's perfect is all I can say," he answered. "And say, can you and Nan bring her up next Sunday, not tomorrow, a week from tomorrow?"

"We can, can't we, Nan?"

"Sure," she answered. "Looks to me like Nick is trying to second-place Stutz."

"I sure am, if I can," answered Nick.

"I'm dancing this one with Nan," announced Bill, "you can have her for the next."

Stutz was back playing when it came time for Nick's dance with Miss Sherman. As the music started, Nick suddenly got an idea. "You look hot and tired," he told her. "Why can't we dance around to the door and then slip out and cool off?"

"I'd like that."

Nick took a quick look at Stutz, but his back was to them.

"Oh, it's lovely out tonight, isn't it, Mr. Norton?"

"Sure is, and don't you think, as long as we seem likely to be friends, that you might as well call me Nick? And, with your permission, I'll call you Virginia."

"You have it, Nick, and I think that's much nicer."

They strolled the full length of the tree-lined street.

Then they turned and slowly came back. A hundred yards from the hall, they saw a figure hurrying toward them. It was shadowy dark under the trees, so the man was quite close before he was recognized.

"Oh, hello, Stutz," said Nick, not too surprised.

"Virginia, you should know better than to be out here with this fellow," he hotly pumped out. "What do you know about him, anyway? You must have heard the reputation these Traders have."

"Just what is their reputation, mine in particular?" Nick asked.

"I'm not talking to you," Stutz fairly spat it out, as he turned his back on Nick.

"But I'm talking to you," insisted Nick, as he grabbed Stutz by the shoulder and spun him around.

"You keep your dirty hands off me, you lousy squawman," Stutz snarled.

"That does it, fat boy!" Nick swung hard with his open palm. Stutz stumbled, tripped, and sat heavily down.

"I'll get you for this," he whimpered, "you dirty son . . ."

"That'll do, Stutz," said Nick, as he held up his open palm threateningly, "there's a lady here, so, unless you want the other side of your face slapped, you'll talk nice or not at all."

Then Stutz surprised them by suddenly jumping up and walking rapidly away in the opposite direction from the dance hall.

"I'm sure sorry that had to happen," Nick said, "but there's a limit to what fellow can take."

"I'm sorry too," admitted Virginia, "but I certainly don't blame you."

"Well, let's forget it and have another dance," Nick suggested, "before all the musicians go home."

The first thing Nick did when they were inside was to locate Mr. Gompers and attract his attention.

"Mr. Gompers," he said, "something unpleasant just

happened outside. Your chief clerk insulted me and called me names I do not take from anyone, so I slapped his face."

"Well, I'll be frank with you, Norton, and say that I do not like that kind of business here, under my jurisdiction. We don't mind the Traders attending our little gatherings if they don't cause trouble. Right or wrong, you have caused trouble, so I feel that it is best if I ask you not to come again."

"Shall I go now?" Nick asked.

"May look better if you wait," Gompers answered.

The dance was over at twelve and Nan, Bill, and Nick walked home with Virginia. After they had bid her good-night and were strolling along, Nick told them about Stutz.

"You *slapped* him down, did you?" mused Bill. "Well, I doubt if I could have kept my hand *open* if I was dealing with that baby."

"I didn't want to hurt him or bruise him up," explained Nick, "he's just about like a half-grown kid. Agent thinks I'd better not come to any more of his dances."

"If he ever catches up with Bill — and he will — there will be two of you sitting on the outside looking in," said Nan.

"I only occasionally brighten up the dull routine of their dances, which should be appreciated, not condemned," stated Bill.

"Yes, if you don't play games that are too rough for middle-aged people," Nan said, as she swung along between the boys, a hand on each arm. "Seems like I heard something to the effect that the second sitter to leave the snake-infested sofa strained her back."

"Couldn't be," snorted Bill, "although I will admit there's still some life in some of those old gals."

They all slept late the next morning, and it was noon before Nick left. He took a room at the Harvey House, sat around the lobby all afternoon, went to a picture show at night, and then to bed.

As soon as the bank opened, he got what money he needed, made some purchases, and arrived home about one o'clock. He went into the store first. "I was delayed a little, Bud, but I knew it wouldn't make any difference. What's new?"

"Well, Star Gazer came yesterday," began Bud. "He came to the store first and I guessed who he was right away. He's a fine looking man, probably around sixty, six-foot tall, broad shoulders, straight and with a good full chest. Wears his hair long and has plenty of fine old beads. I set him out a bottle of pop and some cookies, and asked him when the star gazing would take place. He said tomorrow night if it's clear. He was tired and needed a good night's sleep. I asked him if he cared if we all came over and he said that would be fine. I'd like to see him perform, wouldn't you?"

"I sure would," agreed Nick. "Well, I've got quite a load of fresh vegetables, fruit, and stuff, so I'll take them in the house."

"Hi, Marge," grinned Nick, as he set a big box on the table. Then he surprised her by grabbing her and planting a big kiss on her cheek.

"Well, heavenly days, are you drunk, crazy or just glad to be home?" she exclaimed. "First time you've kissed me since the day Bud and I came to the Post."

"First time I've been this happy," he told her. "Wait until I get Bud over — there's no one in the store — and I'll tell you all about it."

After Nick had finished his story, Marge laughed, "I've always told Bud that some day the right girl for you would show up."

"Well, by damn," exclaimed Bud, "now I've got a whole week to wait to see this wonderful creature. She's not as pretty as Marge, I'll bet."

"Boloney," said Marge, "and you, who haven't seen her yet."

"She's no prettier," Nick loyally said, "she has a different kind of beauty."

"Thank you, boys, and I do appreciate the way you stick up for me."

"I'm just as pleased as anyone that you've found your girl," Bud said, "but how do you know she'll have you?"

"Well, if she won't, she's the loser," Marge stated emphatically. "Take your time, don't rush her," she added. "Girls don't like to be rushed off their feet."

"Says you," laughed Nick, "and you promising to marry this prune after knowing him three days."

"That was different, wasn't it, Marge? You could tell at a glance the kind of straight-forward young man I was — and am."

"Oh, yeah," jeered Nick. "Well, we're going to have a top-notch Medicine Man around here this week to help us pass the time; still, I don't mind saying, it will be a long week for me."

The next night about nine o'clock, the three got into the car and went over to Black Sheep's place. There were about twenty Navajos gathered there, as a few neighbors had dropped in. Old Lady Black Sheep and Willie's wife were roasting mutton over an outside grill; and, as fast as pieces were done, someone would step over and help himself. Black Sheep came over and shook hands, then said, "Go get some meat."

"Yes, we will," Nick told him. "Come on, Marge, you can eat a piece; it will taste good, and they expect us to."

They saw Star Gazer sitting a little way from the hogan. On a bearskin in front of him were some little bags and other objects. He was steadily chanting in a deep, low tone.

Marge said, "Kind of weird place, these quiet shadowy forms moving around in the firelight, and that continuous chant humming in your ears."

"It sure is," agreed Bud. "I want you to meet Star Gazer when he finishes. He is one fine old Navajo."

They visited in low tones with various friends who came up, Nick or Bud interpreting, when it got too deep for Marge. About ten-thirty the chanting ceased and Star Gazer gathered up his medicine things. He went to the fire and took a cup of coffee, but did not eat. Then he strolled over to where the Americans sat. Nick and Bud got up and shook hands with him.

"This is my wife," Bud told him, and Marge put out her hand.

"Yes, a good woman," Star Gazer said, holding her hand.

"I like her smiling face and am glad she is here." He looked up at the star-studded sky a moment. "It is time to start," he said, and moved on to the hogan.

"Isn't he a fine man?" whispered Marge. "Gee, I'm on his side; I'll believe he can do whatever it is he's trying to do."

"He sure radiates confidence," agreed Nick. "Well, come on, let's go in."

The hogan was clean and new. It had been put up when they had the first ceremony. Willie lay on a blanket in the center. He had been bathed, his hair was smooth and shiny from the soapweed shampoo, and he was dressed in clean clothes and wore a bright new silk handkerchief around his head.

After everyone was seated in a circle around the hogan wall, Star Gazer came in. He made a short talk. Then he politely waited until Bud had translated it to Marge as follows:

"He said when he goes out to consult the stars that everyone in here must remain absolutely quiet and motionless. If anyone moves it will spoil everything, so, Old Fusserbudget, get yourself as comfortable as you can. Notice children are barred."

Then Star Gazer took pollen from a little buckskin bag, and as he sprinkled it on Willie's hip, he chanted for a moment in a low voice. Finished with this, he said, "Keep quiet" — pushed the door blanket aside and was gone.

Possibly five minutes had passed, when those inside were surprised to see the sick man's brother, Fred, move as he pulled his blanket higher up on his shoulders. Seconds later the door blanket was jerked aside and Star Gazer angrily strode over in front of Fred.

"Are you a little itching child that you cannot sit still for a short time? If you cannot, then you had better go home and go to sleep."

Fred promised that he would not move again. He told the boys next day that he had moved on purpose as he did not believe Star Gazer would know, and he still couldn't see how he did know. Fred had evidently been to school too many years.

Star Gazer repeated the little chant over Willie, and again went out. No one moved this time. In about twenty minutes, he suddenly appeared at the door. He beckoned to Willie's father, who got up and went out. After a short wait, Star Gazer came again to the hogan and told the people to come. After everyone was out, except Willie, Black Sheep went in.

"He's going to tell his son now," Nick heard a Navajo murmur.

"Won't he tell us what he found out?" Marge asked in a whisper.

"I should think so, but I don't know," Nick answered. "This is all new to me too."

Star Gazer suddenly appeared out of the shadows and stood before Marge. Then he spoke in his low voice.

"Oh, what does he say?" Marge exclaimed.

"Well," proudly answered Bud, "he has given you a name — *Asun de-clo-e* (Laughing or Smiling Woman). Also he says the stars have told him that Willie can be cured."

"*Nezhun, nezhun, se-kis* (Fine, fine, my friend)," and she grabbed his hand. "And tell him, Bud, that it is

216

a good name and I shall always try to live up to it."

"Well, that last part is pretty hard to put into Navajo, but I'll do my best."

After which he asked Star Gazer if he would make the cure. He said, "yes," although he would have another Medicine Man to assist. This man would be sent for in the morning.

"If you think he was slipping around, peeking in cracks to see if anyone moved, you're just plain loco," stated Marge, after Star Gazer had moved on.

"Who in hell said he was?" demanded Bud, grinning fondly at her.

"Well, you might have thought it," she answered. "Anyhow I can tell you that man doesn't go around peeking in cracks. But how he could tell Fred moved is more than I know."

"Same here," admitted Nick. "Well, let's go home, it's getting late."

Fred left early the next morning to get the other Medicine Man.

Star Gazer came over about eleven, and, when Marge found he was there, she invited him over to have dinner with them. He enjoyed that very much and was very appreciative and polite, licking his knife thoroughly each time before taking more butter and loudly smacking his mouth with each spoonful of food. He couldn't do much with a fork. After numerous smacks, Bud suddenly started doing the same, maybe even louder. Marge glared at him and made threatening faces, but Bud only smiled right back and added an extra smack. Star Gazer missed all this and serenely ate and smacked.

When they were ready for dessert, Marge said, "Bud, take a couple of these plates out and help bring in the pie."

"You do it, Nick, if you feel like it. I just thought of something I want to ask Star Gazer," he answered, slipping Nick a big wink.

"Sure," Nick said as he got up and started helping clear the table.

Bud could faintly hear heavy threats being made by Marge, but he paid little heed to that. When she brought his piece of pie, she managed to hook his ear rather neatly with her elbow. "Smacking good cream pie!" announced Bud, looking innocently at Marge, as he called Star Gazer's smack and raised him two.

"You'll think so, you louse," she muttered.

Star Gazer, after waiting a bit, decided the meal was over, so he arose, thanked Smiling Woman heartily, and, as he had no hat to pick up — his having been on his head during the meal — he walked out.

"Just a word ere you depart, Husband, dear." Marge laid a firm hand on Bud's arm. When the other two were out, she suddenly began clawing both sides of his chest, below the armpits — tickling, the one thing Little Strong Man couldn't take. By now he was backed in a corner where he slid to the floor, Marge right on top of him with fingers furiously working.

"Now, let's hear some more of the funny smacking. Insult my guest and embarrass me, will you? Couldn't let the old fellow enjoy his meal in his own way, could you?" and she dug in her very hardest.

Bud broke away and got the table between them. "He did enjoy his dinner — and so did I," he laughed. "That's an old Navajo custom that's fast dying out, but some of us older fellows have not forgotten how to show our appreciation of fine food."

"It's catching," Marge admitted. "You almost had me doing it. Come around and give me a big hug and I'll forgive you, because I do like you fairly well."

The other Medicine Man, one who knew about the sleep-producing mountain herb, came with his medicines that night. The next morning Black Sheep came to the store to borrow a sharp knife. Bud's big pocket knife was always

218

razor-sharp, but, anyway, he gave it a few strokes on an oil stone, before handing it over.

"Pretty soon they will fix my son's leg," Black Sheep said.

"Gee, I'd like to see that," said Bud.

"Okay, Doc, you go right ahead, I'm not so keen on this cutting stuff," Nick told him.

"All right, see you later," and Bud followed Black Sheep out of the store.

At the hogan, Black Sheep gave the knife to Star Gazer, who, after running his thumb along the biggest blade, nodded approvingly.

The other Medicine Man, who was short and fat and round, was named *De-zho-le* (plump, roly-poly). He sat, softly chanting and shaking a small pebble-loaded gourd. At a word from Star Gazer, he arose and, from a pottery bowl, gave Willie a big drink of a good smelling dark liquid. When he sat down again and resumed his chant, Star Gazer joined in. Before long Willie's eyes began to droop and soon after he seemed to sleep.

A not-too-clean wash basin, half full of water, and a little pile of rags and cloth, that did look clean, stood next to Willie.

De-zho-le, still softly chanting, rolled Willie on his side. Then he made a small test cut, to see how Willie took it, but Willie was out, so De-zho-le went to work. It wasn't far to the bone and it didn't bleed as much as Bud expected, although he couldn't see as well as he would have liked, as members of the family had the front row.

De-zho-le scraped and jabbed the bone quite a bit, after which he poured medicine in. They seemed to be getting a lot of pus out of it, and Bud decided that was good. When De-zho-le was satisfied, he put cloth over the wound, and, on this, he piled some wet, green herb, then bandaged it. A right good job too, thought Bud.

De-zho-le assured them all that Willie would be all right

now. He was right about that too. In a month Willie was as good as ever.

The next morning after Marge had joined them at the breakfast table, Nick said, "Bud, why don't you and Marge go to town today and get some nice things for our Sunday dinner?"

"Oh, oh," grinned Bud, "looks like the boy wants to throw the dog a bit. Sure, we'll go."

"And I've been thinking it might be a good idea to trade in the old car and get a new one."

"Well, well, well," exclaimed Marge, "shall I get me a formal and Bud a tuxedo for the occasion? And I know how long you've been thinking about a new car — since last Sunday."

"Nick is right, we do need a new car," agreed Bud, "and, Kiddo, don't think we can't pay for one either."

"Maybe you'd better buy an airplane, they cost more," said Marge. "Perhaps Miss Sherman would prefer a plane."

"We won't consult her yet awhile," grinned Nick, "so Marge, you get the car you want, and, if you don't find it in town, go on over to Albuquerque. Just so you get home by Saturday."

Late Friday afternoon, they drove up in a large deep-blue colored 1925 Buick. Nick and three Navajos went out to admire it.

"This ought to win her," grinned Bud.

"Yaas, we rawther fancy it's rawther chic," chimed in Marge.

"That's what I call an automobile," agreed Nick. "How does she run?"

"Takes practically everything in high gear," boasted Bud.

"We had a nice time too," added Marge, "saw a good picture show."

"Got a load of good things in the trunk — and, say, this bus has a real trunk," said Bud. "We stopped to show it to Nan and Bill. They're sure coming Sunday."

It was before ten on Sunday morning when Marge suddenly exclaimed, "Here they come!"

The three rushed to the front hall door and out onto the porch. Nick ran ahead and opened the car doors. He shook hands with the two girls as they stepped out.

"Come right in," he invited, then introduced Marge and Bud to Virginia.

"Why don't you fix your road?" asked Bill. "Detouring those high centers is a little rugged."

"Good for you," Bud answered, "shake up your lazy old liver."

The girls walked on out to the kitchen. As soon as they were out of earshot, Bud exclaimed, "Hot damn, for once you didn't tell any lie. That gal has really got looks and maybe that blue shirt and slacks don't show her off nobly!"

As Nick beamed, Bud went on, "That hair! Those eyes! I wonder what nationality she is."

"White and Navajo, I suppose. That's what someone said," Bill answered.

"Must be mostly white," Bud said. "Anyway, that's the skin one loves to touch."

"Hey, Guy, isn't that your wife out in the kitchen?" Bill asked.

"You bet my wife it is; I'm just looking at her through Nick's eyes." He gave Nick a playful nudge. "Let's go see what the girls are doing."

"Well," Marge said, "what shall we do, eat here or go up the mountain aways?"

"Oh, you girls decide that," Bud answered.

"Let's have Miss Sherman . . . oh, rats! I'm going to call you Virginia, do you mind?"

"Me too," chirped up Bud.

"That's what I want you to call me," Virginia answered with a smile.

"Good," said Marge. "Now, Virginia, where would you like to eat?"

"If you really want me to say, why not eat here and then go up the mountain afterward."

"Smart girl," smiled Nan, "she knows we have big black ants as well as red ones."

They talked and laughed and picked at olives and pickles. Finally, Marge, in order to get a word with Nick alone, called him to the pantry where she whispered breathlessly, "Nick, she's darling and I love her already and we'll never fight, and I can see why you're crazy about her."

The dinner was marvelous and, when Marge brought the dessert from the refrigerator, she said, "I hope you like this pie, it's my boys' favorite." It was a large, deep chocolate pie covered with an inch of whipped cream.

"If I could cook like you, Bill would soon weigh three hundred pounds," Nan said.

"It's delicious," Virginia said. "We don't get anything like this down at the Mess."

"Nice to own a cow, isn't it, Bud?" said Nick.

"There are winter mornings when I positively hate that cow," Bud said, "and then, along comes one of these pies, and I love her — and Marge too," he added.

"Thank you, Little Man," laughed Marge, "you can see what he loves me for. Well, let's go, we can drive up the mountain road about three miles."

"We'll all go in our car," Bill said. "Save getting yours scratched."

"It's not a very good road, is it?" asked Virginia, as they bumped along.

"It isn't meant for cars, but by dodging rocks and high centers, it's passable," Nick said.

"Sure pretty country though," Bill remarked, as he turned off the road and stopped. He took a couple of old Navajo rugs from the car and spread them on the ground to sit on.

"Take Virginia over and show her the spring, Nick, and bring me back some violets," ordered Nan.

222

"Okay, if she'd like to," he answered.

"I would," Virginia said. "Is it far?"

"Three or four hundred yards," Nick told her.

When they were away from the others, he asked, "How's Stutz these days?"

"Oh, he's fine. He apologized for his bad behavior, but Mr. Gompers gave me a little talk."

"About me, I suppose."

"Well, yes. He thinks Traders are a rather wild bunch and he would rather I didn't get too friendly with any of them. I told him that the two I knew — you and Bill — seemed very nice."

"Thank you," he smiled. "I will admit there are some rough and tough traders. The majority though are good straight business men."

"Of course they are," she agreed. "Oh, is that the spring over there?"

The spring was in a shady little glen. The ground flattened out below, and here, in the soggy soil, were hundreds of violet plants, many still in bloom.

"Oh, aren't they fragrant?" exclaimed Virginia, and, before Nick could warn her of the boggy soil, one foot was in over the shoe top. She jerked back, lost her balance and landed in Nick's ready arms. Before he really knew what he was doing, he had lowered his head and kissed the smiling, upturned mouth. She blushed a rosy red, and Nick felt his own face turn hot.

"I'm sorry," he said, "but the temptation was too great."

"I'm sorry too," she said, "I didn't want that to happen. My foot is wet and look at my shoe!" She seemed eager to change the subject.

"Take it off and I'll clean it up," Nick said, "then we'll go around on the other side to get the violets."

With a stick and grass, he went to work cleaning up the shoe.

While he was doing this, Virginia watched him. After

a time, she said, "You can drive me home, tonight, Nick; then I'll tell you a lot of things about me, and, after I do, I'm not so sure you will want to kiss me."

# CHAPTER 12

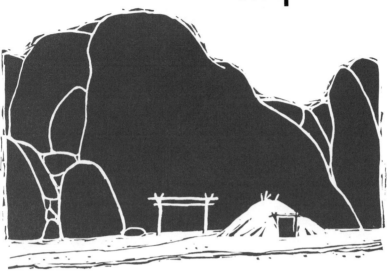

VIRGINIA PRESENTED MARGE with the bouquet of violets she had gathered and Nick handed his to Nan. They sat and talked until the shadows lengthened and Bill said, "Maybe we'd better get down out of here before dark. Besides, I could eat a pork sandwich and maybe a pound or two of that delicious macaroni."

"All right, let's go," agreed Marge. "The day has slipped by so fast, it's hard to realize it's almost night."

"I don't think I ever spent such a lovely day," said Virginia, wistfully.

When they were back home again, Marge persuaded Bud to make some lemonade, and after a big meal, they sat on the porch. At nine, Nan thought they'd better be starting down the valley for home.

"I'm going to drive Virginia down. Got to get some mileage on our new car," Nick told them.

"Sure, sure," laughed Bill, "got to get that car broke in."

"Well, we do, don't we, Bud?" Nick asked.

"Sure do, and I'm glad you thought of it, although I

can't see how you ever happened to. Could it be — but no, of course not!" He looked at Virginia, who blushed prettily.

"Come up again, when you can," urged Marge, "and bring Virginia, of course. You will come again, Virginia, won't you?"

"I love it up here," she answered. "It's been the nicest day of my life, and I thank you all for a wonderful time."

Nick drove the new car up just then. "Leave the back door unlocked," he said. "I may be a little late, because I shouldn't drive this new car very fast."

"We'll skip along then," Nan said. "Pearl will think we are lost." Pearl was the Navajo maid who took care of the baby when Nan was away.

Virginia got into the car beside Nick. After waving goodbye to the others, they rode along in silence until they reached the main road. Then Nick took a deep breath and said, "Now, what is all this terrible stuff you're going to tell me that you mistakenly think is going to change my feeling toward you? But anyway, before you do, I'm going to ask you if you could learn to like me enough to marry me?"

"Already, Nick, I like you too well," she answered. "But you wouldn't want to marry a Navajo, would you?"

"If the Navajo were you, I would. Is that all that's troubling you?"

"That isn't all," she said. "I have no idea who my father was. I think he and my mother were never married."

The car came to a stop. Nick was silent for a moment as he gazed at her. Then he took her in his arms and passionately kissed her mouth, her eyes, her hair.

"I don't give a darn, darling, if you were hatched in an incubator. I know what I want, and, maybe I'm not so pure, and maybe I haven't always been so virtuous. You'll have to dig up better excuses than those."

"And suppose my mother should want to come visit us? I'm not ashamed of her, and maybe you wouldn't be, but

226

how about your friends? She dresses in the Navajo custom; she'd be called a squaw, you know."

"Is your mother old?" he asked.

"She doesn't know her exact age, but she is close to forty, I think. She has worked hard and she has a cough that I don't like. I haven't seen her since last summer. I had this position offered me as soon as school was out, so, in order to get it, I could not go home. Before long I'm going to see her."

"Where does she live?" Nick asked.

"Up beyond the Twin Buttes. She has a little valley with a good spring all to herself, because there are Cliff Dwellers' homes in it, and most Navajos would not live there."

"Why, I know where that is," exclaimed Nick, "and I heard all about you and your mother. If the weather had been good when I was near there, I would have gone to see your place and then I might have known you sooner. Do you remember the old woman who used to come see your mother? I stayed at her hogan one cold, stormy night."

"Yes, I remember her. She was about the only one who called on us. Mother used to send the grandson for groceries at times. He was a nice boy and I liked him."

"The old grandmother had a great eye for beauty too. Did you know that? She told me you were a pretty little girl, and she suspected you were a stolen white child."

Virginia's silvery laugh rang out. "So, that's what she thought. Well, I'm afraid she is mistaken. Maybe it would be better if she was right."

"Right or wrong, I love you." He kissed and hugged her again.

"I think I love you, too, Nick, but all the time I know it is not right. What would Marge and Bud think if you brought me home as your wife? It wouldn't work and you know it."

"Marge and Bud are just the people you need never worry about," Nick told her, "but let's talk about us.

There's so much . . . do you realize I don't even know how old you are!"

"I was eighteen the second of July — two days before the Fourth — that's how my mother knows my birthday."

"Great snakes, I'm twice as old as you are! Did you know that? Maybe I'm too old for you."

She laughed. "Never! But since you are a mature, sensible man, you'll realize that we'd better be going. After all, I do have to work for a living."

"Just say the word and you won't," said Nick, as he drew her close, "and you will marry me, won't you, dear?"

"Oh, Nick, I can't say yes. I must think this over. You will too and you can talk to Marge and Bud, Bill and Nan too. I don't care. Tell them just what I have told you. I could get a transfer to some other Agency, which, perhaps, would be best. Then you would soon forget me."

"Don't you ever dare do that," Nick said fiercely. "I know what Marge and Bud will say, and the only transfer will be up to our house. And don't you ever say that I will forget you, because I never will."

"Nick, we must be going. They lock the dormitory door at eleven."

"I'll come down next Sunday," he said. "Is that all right with you?"

"Yes," she nodded.

"We'll make it before eleven," he said, as he started the car. "Probably Stutz will be waiting at the garden gate."

"I doubt it. He went to town this morning," she answered, as she snuggled up close to him. "This has been such a happy day. I'll always remember it as the most wonderful one in my life. And you must always remember, too, my big Nick, and feel happy that you could give a poor, nameless girl such happiness."

"Don't you worry, sweetheart, old Nick isn't through giving you happiness. He's going to kidnap you if there's no other way."

228

"I'm so well-fed and comfortable that I think I'm going to sleep. Do you mind?"

"Not if you kiss me goodnight first," he answered.

She slept, or so it seemed to Nick, until the car came to a stop in front of the dormitory. "We mustn't linger out here," she said as she glanced around.

"Till next Sunday, then," Nick told her as he fondly kissed her.

She ran across the walk and up the steps, and Nick turned the car and headed for home.

It was midnight when he swung the Buick quietly up by the side of the house. He went to the back door and let himself in. No need of waking anyone, he thought. But Marge was either awake, or a light sleeper, because, as he turned on the kitchen light, she appeared at the door in her bathrobe. Seconds later, a tousled Bud showed behind her. "Couldn't wait until morning to get the lowdown," she said.

"Yeah," put in Bud, "what's the good word, Nick?"

"I'm not sure there is any. Maybe I'm not going to get her so easy."

"Sure, but who's going to keep you from getting her, Stutz, or has she a husband?"

"No, she hasn't any husband, father either, or none that she knows of," answered Nick. "But let me tell you what the situation is," and he told them everything as Virginia had told it to him.

Marge sat silent after he had finished. Bud, who looked like he wanted to burst right out, evidently decided to hold everything until he heard what Marge had to say.

"Well, that's the last thing I ever would have thought of," she said. "The poor kid, I'm sure sorry for her."

"Is that all you've got to say, Marge?" asked Nick, surprised.

"What do you want me to say? You know . . ."

"Well, I'll tell you what I've got to say," interrupted

Bud, "if you can get her, grab her. I'm an awful good judge of girls — else how did I pick Marge — and, if Virginia isn't one swell girl, regardless of who her folks were, or are, then I'm a hog caller. We're nothing but Indian Traders — what could be lower — so who are we to get snotty and choosy?"

"I agree with the first part of your remark, Bud, and what you've told us, Nick, hasn't affected me one bit."

"Yeah, and another thing," said Bud, "how do you know that the old woman wasn't right? Maybe Virginia is a white girl that the woman she calls her mother, picked up somewhere. Such things have happened."

"You ought to go up there and talk to her mother, Nick," Marge said. "She probably will tell you the truth when she finds you're going to marry Virginia."

"Yes, I could do that. Maybe I should. I can get within seven or eight miles of her place in the car. Then I could borrow a pony for the rest of the trip. But I'd better wait until after Sunday. You may have to work on Virginia, Marge, before she'll see things in the right light."

"My gracious, it's one o'clock," exclaimed Marge, "we'd better go to bed. You'll sleep better, Nick, knowing Bud's and my sentiments."

"Sure will, and no man ever had better pals than you two. Goodnight, Bud." Then he put his arm around Marge and kissed her.

"Good gracious," beamed Marge, "twice in two weeks. Ain't love grand! Sweet dreams, Nick."

Two days later, as Nick was looking over the silver-smiths' account book, Bud remarked, "Things are pretty quiet this afternoon, so guess I'll go shine up the car. It's sure dusty."

"Fair enough," said Nick, absentmindedly.

Soon after that, a well-dressed Navajo strolled in. Nick looked at him for a moment. "Smiley," he said with a big grin.

"Chischilly," said Smiley, his natural smile spreading all over his face as he advanced and heartily shook hands with Nick.

"Where do you come from? You look like a rich man."

"I live way over there." He pointed to the east. "I'm not a poor man anymore. I have a fine wife, big and strong, not like the pretty slim one you liked so well," and he laughed heartily.

Nick laughed too, though now that time seemed part of another world.

"This wife has a lot of sheep too," he went on, "and goats and ponies. Yes, I'm a very lucky man."

"Did you know I lived here?" asked Nick.

"Oh, yes, I heard you did."

"Where are you going?"

"I'm going two or three days ride to the north to visit my wife's uncle," he answered.

Nick set out a supply of cookies and a bottle of pop, which Smiley started right to work on. "I am also going to stop and see *our* first wife." He smiled very broadly. "I hear she lives in a canyon among the bones of the old people. Did you know that? What's the matter? You are shaking."

My God! Glacie, it can't be, thought Nick — and I *am* shaking and I *am* sick. If what this fellow says is true, Virginia's mother is Glacie. That couldn't be, but, yet what about those little nose wrinkles they both have. On Virginia they had seemed vaguely familiar, but he hadn't given it a thought. To Smiley, he said, "The hot weather sometimes makes me feel sick. I am all right now. No, I did not know where she lived. Are you sure about this, and is it near the Two Buttes?"

"Yes, I am sure, and it is near the Two Buttes." He took a drink of the pop. "I am surprised," he went on, "and have you never seen your daughter?"

"What?" yelled Nick.

"Didn't you know there was a baby girl long ago? It wasn't my baby, because they say she is white."

Nick tried to control himself. He was cold and clammy now, and his stomach was churning. Maybe he was going to vomit.

"You still look sick," stated Smiley.

"Yes," Nick muttered. Then he turned and slowly went and got Smiley another bottle of pop. Smiley munched the cookies and downed half of the second bottle of pop. Nick tried to think but found it difficult; his brain was numbed by this shocking news.

Passionately in love with his own daughter. God Almighty, could this be possible? He felt like smashing the smiling face before him, but, no, he should thank him for happening along in time to prevent a terrible disaster. Nick shuddered when he thought of what might have happened.

Smiley had finished now and Nick pulled himself together enough to speak. "You are sure, then, that the girl is my daughter?"

"Of course she is," Smiley announced very positively. "Who else's would she be?"

"I must see her sometime," said Nick, hoping Smiley would now go. But this was his intention, and, after assuring Nick that he would stop on his way back, he left.

I don't believe it, said Nick to himself. Something would have warned me she was my own flesh and blood. Still, I don't know. I never saw her until a few days ago. He got a paper and pencil and checked the bygone years. Virginia was eighteen the second of July. Eighteen years. Yes, that was right, and, then, when had he left the sawmill — September or October — and he had been with Glacie the night before he left.

I suppose Smiley is right, he thought, everything checks out too close. But what will I do? Can we suddenly change and love each other as father and daughter? Oh, God, I don't know! He buried his face in his arms.

232

Bud came in, and, seeing Nick, ran around the counter and put his arm around his shoulders. "Good Lord, Nick, what's the matter? Are you sick?"

"The old bear trap has caught me just above the ears, Bud," he answered.

"Well, lock the door and let's go over to the house where Marge is."

"What's the matter, Nick, you don't look just right?" she said.

"I've had quite a shock," he answered, "the sins of the father, you know."

"What father?" asked Bud.

"Me."

"You mean you're a father?" asked Marge, very much surprised.

"I guess there's no doubt about it," he answered. "All through the years you've known me, you've probably thought I was a fairly decent sort of a guy; don't say a word until I tell you a story," and he told them the whole thing from the beginning to Smiley's disagreeable news of a few moments ago.

"Oh, I'm so sorry, Nick, I don't know what to say. I guess because there *is* nothing to say. I suppose what you said about the sins of the father about covers the situation."

"No sin about it," snorted Bud, "you take a horny young Buck from the East . . ."

"Bud," sternly interrupted Marge.

"Well, maybe I did put it a bit crudely. What I mean is . . ."

"That will do," Marge told him, "we know what you mean, and it doesn't mean a thing now. I still feel there's a mistake somewhere along the line. You say Virginia doesn't know who her father is?"

"That's what she told me," Nick gloomily admitted.

"Probably doesn't then," agreed Marge. "Well, I'll say what I think you should do. Go up north and talk to this old flame of yours. When she finds you have to know, one way or the other, she'll have to tell you."

"I hadn't thought of that," said Nick, brightening a little. "Of course she'll tell me. I'll start in the morning."

There was no sleep for Nick that night, so, at the first faint sign of light, he was up. He made and drank a couple of cups of coffee, got the car and drove away. It was not a good road he followed, but, with careful, watchful driving, it could be used. By one o'clock, he decided he had about reached the end of the trail, as far as the Buick was concerned. He looked for a hogan and saw one about a half mile to the left. He cut off across the sagebrush and, after a slow bumpy ride, made it.

A woman and a little girl of nine or ten came to the hogan door. Nick talked with them a moment and then said he wanted to borrow a pony.

"Where do you want to go?" the woman asked.

"I want to ride on up the valley. I will be back before sundown," he told her.

"Maybe you will run away with the pony," she said.

"Then you will have a nice, new automobile," he laughingly replied.

"Go catch a pony, the black one," she said to the girl.

"I'll help her," Nick said.

They caught and brought the pony to the hogan. The woman brought out a bridle and saddle blanket, then the saddle, which she tossed outside the door.

"Throw his saddle out," jokingly said Nick.

The woman laughed, "This is not my man's saddle. I have a good man, so I don't think I will ever have to throw his saddle out."

"I'm glad of that," Nick told her. Just before he left, he said, "I'll pay you when I come back."

"*Ah-cohn* (all right)," she answered.

An hour and a half later, he was at the entrance to the valley he sought. As he rode up, he wondered how he would greet Glacie, how she would look, and whether she would be glad to see him. A Navajo woman would change greatly in eighteen years. He was nervous and ill at ease. Now he could see the hogan. It looked strangely quiet around the place. No smoke either. Should, at least, be a barking dog. He knew there was no one there before he dismounted and went to the door. The hogan was empty, clean too, and looked as if it had been thoroughly swept recently.

"She's gone and taken everything with her," he exclaimed aloud. He looked around. The blanket loom poles still stood near the hogan. Then he noticed a large pile of ashes. He saw the end of a batten stick and a weaving comb that had not burned. So she's through with weaving, he thought. He walked around, looking here and there. Then he saw a well-worn trail leading up to a large cave. He followed it up until he stood on the sandy cave floor.

It was as Pete had said: the back wall was covered with red and yellow hand prints. Big and little and all in pairs. Some seemed to be partly scratched out; maybe as the people died the prints were scratched out. He noticed queer looking sand piles at the back of the cave. He went over to look. There were neat little hogans, corrals and lakes with little bushes for trees around the edges. Tears came to Nick's eyes. Here was where his little daughter had played; her little hands had built these and Glacie had probably seen to it that they had not been disturbed. Small moccasin tracks were still visible in the sand. The poor lonesome kid! He straightened up a couple of the little corral posts that some pack rat had knocked over.

He walked slowly down the trail to the pony, mounted, and slowly rode away from the Valley of the Old Ones.

Now he knew he should have told the woman where he was going. She knew Glacie had left and maybe knew where she had gone. But, anyway, he would have gone to see the place where Glacie had lived so long.

The woman, with the little girl beside her, sat at the loom weaving as Nick rode up.

"You were not gone long," she remarked.

"The woman I went to see was not home," and he told her where he had been.

"Oh no, she has been gone a month, maybe a month and a half," she answered.

"Where has she gone?"

"Some say she went to the Hopi people. Maybe she was lonesome for that Hopi man," and she laughed heartily.

"You really think that is where she went?" he asked.

"The people around here all say that," she answered.

"Here's money for the ride." He handed the little girl a silver dollar and gave her a gentle pat on the head. "I must go now."

Nick had to go back within fifteen miles of home, but, instead of continuing on that familiar road, he turned west. He was going to the Hopi village. He did not hurry, because he knew it would be very late at night before he could get there, and he could do nothing up there at night.

It was almost dark as he drove down into old Tom Keam's Canyon, so he decided to camp. There were always three blankets, canned meat, crackers, a canteen of water, and a small coffee pot in the trunk of the car. He did not feel like eating, so only made coffee. Then he lay down under the stars and fell into an exhausted sleep.

He was up at daybreak, made coffee, ate a little, and was on his way. The sand made slow going, but, before nine he was at the base of the Mesa. The road up looked terribly steep, so he left the car and walked up. There were plenty of women and small children in sight, but very few men. The men, he supposed, were down at the fields. He knew that most all Hopi children attended school, so, when a girl of fourteen or so came out of a house near him, he asked her if she knew a Hopi man who had a Navajo wife.

236

"Yes, I know one, but he isn't here," she said.

"Is the wife here? She's the one I want to see."

"I'll take you to where she lives," the girl said.

When they reached the house and went in where the woman was, Nick at once saw she was not the one he was looking for. But, anyway, he began to talk with her. After visiting a bit he asked her if she was the only Navajo woman in the village.

"Yes," she answered, "although there was another, but she died about twenty days ago."

Nick began to feel weak again, but he spoke to the girl. He asked her to tell him about this woman who had died. When she finished, Nick knew it was Glacie.

"What caused her death?" he asked.

"She coughed all the time and one night something broke inside her and the blood came out of her mouth and she died," the girl answered.

"Yes, I saw a man die like that once. Was she living with her Hopi husband then?" he asked.

"Oh, yes, and he was very kind to her. He liked her very much."

"Where is she buried?" Nick asked.

The girl said, "Come," and led him to the east side of the Mesa. "Down there," she said, "among those big rocks."

"Thank you, and here's a dollar for you for candy. I'm going now," and he walked back to the car.

"Too late," he muttered. "Now I'll never know for sure. Maybe it won't be quite so tough for Virginia. Girls can readjust themselves better than men. Well, I've got to get to the Agency and tell her; and, if the car missed the road and went into a canyon, it wouldn't be too bad. No, that's a coward's game, and I hope I'm not a coward."

He didn't stop to eat, so reached the Agency about three o'clock and drove right to the office. Stutz looked up and glared at him. Gompers seemed surprised when Nick strode in and up to the desk. He did not see Virginia.

"How do you do, Mr. Gompers," he said, "where's Virginia?"

"Miss Sherman is away," he answered.

"Where?" Nick asked.

"That, I am not at liberty to tell."

"You mean you won't tell?"

"I mean just what I said," he answered.

"If you knew the circumstances, I'm sure you would tell," persisted Nick.

"I'll be frank with you, Norton. It is Miss Sherman's express wish that no one know where she is."

"Well, then, thank you sir," and he turned and started out. He passed Stutz's desk, without a glance in his direction. He was a couple of strides past when Stutz grabbed up an ancient stone hammerhead, used as a paperweight; and, with all his strength, threw it at Nick. If it had struck Nick's head squarely, it might have killed him. As it was, it struck a glancing blow above the ear. Nick dropped and lay still. Sometime later, when Nick came to, he saw three old maids putting cold cloths on his head and fussing over him. Gompers was there too, but Stutz was not to be seen.

Nick sat up, knocking over a basin of water as he did so. He asked what had happened and they told him. He was surprised that his head did not ache too much, and, except for the very sore spot over his left ear, he was about all right.

"So the fiddler got up nerve enough to heave a rock," Nick said. "Where is he now?"

"Must be close to town by now," Gompers told him. "He'll probably slip back at night to get his belongings and then leave."

"If I can, I'll wait up for him," said Nick grimly. "I'm sorry to cause so much commotion."

"Don't mention it," Gompers said. "I don't think we want that kind of a person around here anyway."

Nick went down to see Nan and Bill. He said nothing about Stutz, but asked about Virginia.

"Well, now," began Bill, "if there was anything going on around here that I wanted to know about, I'd first hunt me up a Navajo policeman, Jim Scott. If there's anything happens around here — night or day — that grinning buck doesn't know about, it ain't worth knowing. Just go find him and make him talk."

"Thanks, Bill, and I know right where he is. I saw him as I came down. Goodby for now, see you later," and he hurried out.

Jim Scott was sitting in the shade over by the old barracks. Nick greeted him and asked him what he was guarding now.

"Nothing, nothing," he grinned, "but I had a hard trip this morning, so now have to rest."

"Where did you go this morning?" Nick asked.

"Oh, nowhere," Jim lied with his best grin. "I was only talking."

"Maybe," said Nick, looking shrewdly at him. "Anyhow, I want to know where Miss Sherman is."

"Ask the Agent," suggested Jim.

"No time," Nick said. "I've got to see her just as soon as I can. Maybe you took her on this hard trip."

"Chischilly, I did take her on a hard trip, but the Agent told me not to say where I went, so I can't."

Nick felt he couldn't waste any more time, so he said, "You'd better tell me pronto, or I'll go get the Agent to tell me and, while I'm there, I'll tell him what a no-good policeman and guard you are. Remember the silversmiths you let go by you?"

"No, Chischilly, you mustn't do that," he exclaimed. "You won't tell anyone if I tell you?"

"Of course not," Nick answered.

"This is a very nice easy job I have," Jim grinned, "so I will tell you where I took the pretty white girl who speaks Navajo. I took her as near the little valley of the old people as that automobile could go, which was very near, so, if anyone followed my tracks, they would not have far to walk."

"And then what?" demanded Nick.

"Then she got out with her little bag and thanked me and told me to go back and come again tomorrow night, and so I will."

"And so you won't, Amigo, because I'm going to get her and I'm leaving right now," and he got up and went to his car.

If I drive fast, thought Nick, I can be up there a couple of hours before sundown. And what did Jim say about following his tracks? Oh yes, follow them and one would get very near the valley. Leave it to a Navajo to find a trail to where he wants to go.

He forgot about the Buick being new, and, whenever there was a decent stretch of road, the Buick did its best. When he came to where he had turned off the previous morning, he saw car tracks ahead. He followed them a few hundred yards until they turned to the right. It was rough going, but the tracks were plain and he had no difficulty following them.

About a half mile from the entrance to the valley, an arroyo blocked all passage. The tracks circled and Nick got out and started on a fast walk forward. He came to the deserted hogan. There was no one there. He went to the trail that led up to the cave. There were small tracks and he followed.

He found her sitting by the toy, sand-built hogan, corrals, and lakes. She had two large dolls in her lap, one a Hopi Katchina man and the other a beautifully made Navajo woman doll.

"Oh Nick, what does it mean?" she exclaimed. "My mother is gone." She did not seem surprised that he was there.

"Virginia, darling, what are you doing here?" He went to her and kissed her as a man would kiss his daughter.

"I came to see my mother, but she is not here. Where can she be?"

"My dear little girl, you will have to prepare yourself for very bad news."

"Is she ill? An accident . . ."

He shook his head.

"You mean she's . . . dead?" Tears came to her eyes.

He put his arms around her shoulders and patted her hand. "She died suddenly some twenty days ago. She evidently felt she had not long to live, so she left here and went to her husband in the Hopi village."

Nick had no idea how grief affected girls. He wondered if she would wail loudly as the Indian women did. He wanted to kiss the tears away, but perhaps, that was not the proper thing for a father to do. He wouldn't tell her that he was her father now, as she'd had shock enough for one day. He thought, "Some day a man will come along and marry her and take her away, and what will I do then?"

She sobbed softly for some minutes, then wiped her eyes and blew her nose. "Crying does no good, does it, Nick? I am glad that I did not see her dead," her voice broke. "I want to remember her as I last saw her, smiling bravely, as she waved goodbye when I was leaving for school. And I don't care what she did in the past or how she got me, she was still the best mother a girl ever had."

"I'm sure of that," agreed Nick.

"And my father — I always called the Hopi man, father — was very kind to me."

Nick winced, but he said, "What was he like?"

"He was short, and a little fat, very good-natured and laughed and joked a lot. He tended to the sheep. My mother said I was not to be a sheepherder. Of course, as there were no other sheep here, they did not have to be watched all the time. He never let mother carry water or chop wood as most Navajo women do. He was wonderfully good to her."

"I wonder why she threw his saddle out?" Nick spoke in Navajo, using the old Navajo phrase.

"I don't know — unless on my account. She may have thought now I was grown, that he would try and get me. You know, Indian men are like that. You see, while Mother learned a lot of Hopi, she could not understand half that he said. I speak it like a Hopi. I was only about four when he came. Of course, he spoke Navajo well. He told Mother he was going to teach me Hopi, so he would only speak to me in his language. That must have been the way to teach me, because, in a year or so, I knew Hopi."

"Yes, that would be the way to learn," agreed Nick. "If you didn't herd the sheep, what did you do all day?"

"Mostly I played right here in this cave," she answered. "My children are all here asleep. I'll show you," and she moved to the back of the cave and dug in the clean, dry sand. She scooped out a foot or so of sand until she came to several small woven blankets. Under these were fifteen beautiful little dolls — eight boy and seven girl dolls, nestling in white carded wool. The boy dolls were wood, finely carved and wonderfully painted. The girls were cloth, stuffed with wool, and were dressed exactly like little Navajo girls. "My father made the boys and mother made the others. Father said the extra boy was to be an Antelope or Snake Priest when he grew up, but I'm afraid he'll never grow up. The mother and father dolls sleep here while I'm away," and she showed him a larger wool-lined bed. "And right there," she pointed a couple of feet to the right, "is a real sleeping baby, and it's wrapped in a rabbit skin blanket. I know, because years ago I dug right into it. Been there hundreds of years, I suppose. I didn't tell mother, she might not have liked it, and perhaps she wouldn't have let me play here any more. But

242

I told my father and he laughed and said, 'That just makes your family larger.' "

Tears came to her eyes again and she was quiet. Nick was sure she was thinking that now her family was very small, indeed. Gently he urged her to tell him more.

"There used to be lots of rattlesnakes around here and mother worried for fear I'd be bitten, but my father told me not to be afraid of them, and to call him when I saw one. So, when I came on one, I'd yell, '*kliesh, kliesh*' (snake, snake), and he'd come with a short, forked stick, press the snake's head down, and then pick it up and carry it out of our valley and turn it loose. Sometimes he'd let me hold one and stroke it the way he did, and it would straighten out and forget it was mad. Mother would scream and call father the worst Navajo names, but he'd just laugh and tell her the snakes liked me."

"I wouldn't blame them," Nick said. "Did your mother come up here much?"

"Yes, but not as often as father. She spent much of her time weaving. And, of course, she taught me to card and spin wool, and weave, too. I made these little doll blankets, but I'm afraid I'm not a very good weaver. I wonder what became of mother's sheep?"

"That's right," Nick said. "I'd forgotten about that. Well, we can ask that woman down below; she'll know. Perhaps your mother took them over to the Hopi country."

"I really hope my father has them. I would like that. I'm sure I do not want them. We can ask the old grand-mother who used to visit us. She liked us, and I liked *Noh-ti*, the grandson, and remember bringing him up here to see my children, although he wasn't much interested in them. I remember the grandmother was always questioning mother about me. She just couldn't understand why I was so fair-skinned."

Nick looked away. He could not meet her gaze, but she seemed not to notice.

"Father used to question mother and kid her about me and one night she got very mad and told him off. This night I had gone to bed as usual and, I suppose, they thought I was asleep. They were talking about the white people. How they were always after money, land too, and were trying to push the Indians back and wondered why they all had to come to the Indians' country. And I remember mother said, 'Well, we have lots of nice things to eat that our parents didn't have, and, anyway, some of the white people are very nice."

" 'One of them must have been very nice, because he got you a very nice little girl,' father said, and he laughed.

"Mother got very mad then. 'You nasty old *Kies-on-e* (Hopi); her father was not a white man. Neither was he a fat, squat little old toad like you. He was a big, strong, pale-faced Mexican, so now maybe you will keep your big mouth shut about my daughter being a white girl.' "

Nick gave a start and almost yelled at Virginia, but checked himself in time. Better go slow, maybe Glacie only said that to put an end to the Hopi's questioning.

"Do you think your father really was a Mexican? You remember you told me you did not know who your father was."

"Neither do I," she answered slowly, "except that he was a Mexican. When I was about fifteen mother told me all about it, except she couldn't tell me his name because she didn't know it. All she knew was that he was called *Naki-Tso* (Big Mexican) and later on she heard he had been killed in a fight or something."

Across the valley of the old people, the sun was slowly sinking, throwing its level rays into the cave where the man and girl sat close together among the brightly colored dolls. A feeling of deep peace and contentment settled over Nick. He drew Virginia to him and kissed her as a man should kiss the girl he loves.

"You will marry me, won't you? And don't worry about

244

my friends. The people who matter most to me, already love you."

"You are still sure you want me?" she asked, as she snuggled close to him.

"I'm sure now, and I'll be just as sure when I'm a grey-headed old man," he answered.

"Perhaps I had better then, because now I am truly an orphan," and she put her lips up to his.

Later, he said, "We'll be married at our house. Would Sunday do? And you know what? We'll ask Mr. Gompers if he'll come up and give you away. I guess he's not such a bad old fellow after all."

"He's been very good to me," Virginia said.

"And the way I feel now, I could even forgive Stutz — after I gave him one good punch in the nose — and let bygones be bygones."

The sun had gone down. "We'd better go," he said reluctantly. "Are you going to take your little children?"

"No, I'll put them back to bed." As she placed the little Hopi dolls down on their clean wool bed, she talked to them in a low cooing voice.

"What are you saying?" Nick asked. "Isn't that Hopi?"

"Oh yes," she smiled, "they only understand Hopi. I'm telling them to be good little boys and mother will come back before long to see them."

To the little girl dolls, she spoke in Navajo, murmuring each one's Navajo name as she laid them away.

As Nick watched her move about among her "children," giving and receiving comfort, he felt a sudden surge of gratitude toward Glacie. She had provided him with love twice — the first time, when he was just a boy, a stranger in a new country, and now this beautiful girl, part of her flesh, a love to warm him for the rest of his life.

Virginia had come to the last of her charges. She was smoothing the sand on the grave of the little baby in the rabbit skin robe. "I talk to this little fellow in English," she said, "because I do not know what his language was, and maybe he can understand English as well as any."

Nick waited as she took one last fond look around the darkening cave — at the little hogans, corrals, and brush-fringed lake. Then taking her hand in his, they started down the age-old trail of the Ancient Ones.